CHAPS

Visit us at www.boldstrokesbooks.com

What Reviewers Say About *Edge of Darkness*

"[*Edge of Darkness*]...wins points for its well-rounded and developed main character and its breezy, light writing style, making it a fun read...The plotline has its share of twists, turns and revelations...I look forward to reading more from Jove Belle."—*Our Chart*

"*Edge of Darkness* is a very well written book. It has sympathetic characters, an exciting story, hot sex, and a wonderful cliff hanger ending. This is a book that makes the reader forget everything but turning the next page."—*Just About Write*

By the Author

Edge of Darkness

Split the Aces

Chaps

CHAPS

by
Jove Belle

2009

ISBN 10: 1-60282-127-5
ISBN 13: 978-1-60282-127-9

This Trade Paperback Original Is Published By
Bold Strokes Books, Inc.
P.O. Box 249
Valley Falls, NY 12185

First Edition: December 2009

CREDITS
EDITORS: SHELLEY THRASHER AND STACIA SEAMAN
PRODUCTION DESIGN: STACIA SEAMAN
COVER DESIGN BY SHERI (GRAPHICARTIST2020@HOTMAIL.COM)

Acknowledgments

My aunt Mabel taught me many things, including the value of adventure, of facing life without fear or malice, and to never travel farther from your family than your love could reach. Even when she was thousands of miles away, she kept us all herded close to her heart, making the connection thrive where it would have otherwise faded away.

The same week we (by we, I mean me and my most excellent editor, Shelley Thrasher, who is an absolute gem and deserves to be worshipped regularly) tied a bow on *Chaps* and sent it off to copy edits, my aunt suffered a massive stroke from which she did not recover. It is my sincere hope that no matter where the next evolution takes her, she will always be in reach of my love.

She was an indomitable woman and I miss her terribly.

Mabel Campbell (October 27, 1926–July 30, 2009)

Dedication

For Tara, whose compass appears to be broken,
yet she manages to keep me on course.

CHAPTER ONE

C ome on," Penny led Eden to the corner, "you need a yoga mat."

A slender, fair-haired man pulled two mats from a low shelf and handed one to Penny. "So glad you could join us again, Penny."

Penny—Eden Metcalf's best friend and sometime lover— giggled. Eden stared, forcing her face to remain neutral.

The instructor's fingers lingered on the soft flesh of Penny's inner wrist, a far too personal caress. Eden cleared her throat.

"And you brought a friend." He extended a mat toward Eden, his grip too close to the end of it for Eden's comfort. He left Eden very little room to grasp the mat without brushing her fingers against his. The touch of strange men made her uncomfortable at best. Homicidal at worst. That this man had such obvious intentions for Penny pushed Eden closer to an extreme reaction.

Bamboo mats, rolled tight and edged with pastel fabrics, poked out of the open tops of cartons that lined the wall next to him. While the yoga lovers around her stretched out to greet the day, Eden pictured all the little mats rolled up tight and bundled around brick after brick of Luther Wade's finest-grade cocaine, packed for shipment into the United States. The absurdity of the moment assaulted Eden. She was jealous of the would-be, if not current, male lover of her first lover, and surrounded by the byproduct of her life-taking source of income. All in an environment that assured peace and serenity.

Laughter bubbled inside Eden, pushing past her lips before she could contain it. She laughed hard enough to draw the scornful attention of the instructor, the proffered mat dangling loosely in his hand.

Penny shushed her with a glare that said, "What the hell's the matter with you?" Rather than explain, Eden simply wiped the tears from her eyes, waved to the pale, Jesus-haired instructor, and stepped outside to wait.

Yoga, Eden knew from the moment Penny dragged her through the doors, was the bastard child of some worm-worshipping cult whose practitioners strove to bend, twist, and stretch themselves into boneless, flaccid creatures. The Egyptians, with their idol worship of cats, were more Eden's style. They knew what they were doing when they exalted the always fickle, often deadly, feline.

She was halfway through her second fragrant clove cigarette, the smoke wafting dangerously close to the swinging door of the fitness club, before Penny stormed out.

"Seriously, E, can't you just fucking relax for ten fucking minutes?" She plucked the brown-papered Djarum from Eden's fingers and took a long drag. Finally she smiled. "Tell me what was so funny."

Eden jerked her head toward the car and didn't answer until they were tucked safely inside, air-conditioning on high. "The mats."

Understanding flickered across Penny's face. "Shit. I never thought about that before." After a pause, Penny's demeanor shifted back to irritated. "Still, it wasn't *that* funny." Penny backed out of the parking space and headed toward the street.

"No, it wasn't." Eden considered, not for the first time, telling Penny her plan. Hell, Penny was in danger either way. Maybe it would be better for her to have something to give up when Luther questioned her. Then again, if she knew nothing, she wouldn't get killed out of some misguided sense of loyalty. "Are you working today?" Eden asked instead.

"I've got a couple of meetings scheduled, but nothing big."

Penny took the familiar route to Luther's place. Neither of them needed to discuss their destination. Eden started every workday sequestered in a private meeting with her boss. They discussed strategy, how to increase market share, and, as it was Eden's specialty, how to protect current assets.

"What about you?"

"Luther asked me to conduct an audit on one of the independents," Eden said. Just as with any legitimate business, drug trafficking had layers of operators, and sometimes an evaluation of performance was warranted. Eden laughingly called these situations Come to Luther meetings, similar to a Come to Jesus, except Luther didn't preach a message of love and forgiveness. And his disciples carried guns.

Through hard work and ruthless execution, Luther held the keys to the West Coast. The men covering a large portion of San Francisco had gotten sloppy with their financial manipulation of their books. Their profit margin had dropped about seven percent— enough to grab Luther's attention. When Eden reviewed the accounts, she concluded they'd been skimming for much longer than Luther suspected, essentially since the inception of their business agreement. If she played the situation right, he would never know the exact amount. And she intended to use that possibility to her advantage.

"Need any company?" Penny broke into Eden's thoughts as she pulled to a stop.

She shook her head, her mouth set in what she hoped looked like a casual smile. "Not this time."

Penny stopped Eden before she could climb out of the car and squeezed her hand. "Be safe, E. I worry about you."

Eden simply kissed Penny on the cheek and answered with her typical James Dean cool. "Don't worry, doll. I can take care of myself." She wanted to pull Penny against her and hold her long enough to remember the curves of her body. It'd been too long since she'd explored her lush contours. If everything went according to plan, she wouldn't get another chance.

But that kind of display would be enough to warn Luther—who

watched from the top step of the small brick house that served as his operational base—that something wasn't right. The paranoid, merciless man was difficult enough to keep in line. No reason to fuel his suspicions.

Eden closed the car door and walked away from Penny, her heart aching with every step. She turned to give Penny one last smile as Luther guided her into the house, one arm around her shoulders, his mouth set in a firm, hard line. Death and confidence colored the air around him, and she was his instrument of execution.

❖

Framed photos covered the wall behind Luther's desk. Rows and rows of eight by tens in precise lines like soldiers at attention. Or headstones. Luther's fallen warriors all.

Eden scanned the wall, Luther's grim memorial, a warning to those who dared defy him. Lucinda—young, brash, and eager to make a name for herself. She'd expanded her territory at record speed, but neglected to pay Luther his due. She'd died with a plea for mercy on her lips and a bullet from Eden's gun tearing through her skull. Carmine—ruthless and greedy, but not very smart. One too many enemies and he disappeared from service. Luther claimed to have no knowledge of his whereabouts. Eden believed him because she hadn't killed Carmine, so she knew Carmine didn't die under orders from Luther. But he would have soon enough.

And Gabriel. Above Luther's head and a little to the left, watching over Luther like a golden angel. Luther—white-out-of-a-box teeth bared in a grotesque smile—with his arm draped casually over Gabriel's shoulder. He'd died slowly, painfully, and by degrees. And Eden had watched, powerless, unable to save him from the siren song of Luther's fine wares. He'd drowned in a hazy promise of heroin heaven, too deep to be saved. A bullet from Eden's gun took his life as well. She hadn't pulled the trigger, but she hadn't been fast enough to stop it either.

How long, Eden wondered, until Luther added her picture to the wall? Would she get a position of honor over his other shoulder, poised to advise him from the grave? That would be her eternity, her penance for all her wrongdoings, forever sentenced to sit next to Gabriel and stare down at Luther's head all laid out in row after row of perfect brown-black braids. She'd always loved his hair. When she first joined his crew it added order to her otherwise chaotic world.

The question reinforced her decision to leave. Perhaps she wasn't too late to reclaim her life and live the right way, without blood and drugs coloring every breath. She wanted to be normal. If only she knew exactly what it meant to be normal. Hopefully she'd recognize it when she saw it and be smart enough to not run away.

"They're stealing *my* goddamned money, Eden." Luther gnawed the uncut end of a hand-rolled Cuban cigar.

Eden waited, silent. Luther needed an audience at this point, not a discussion.

"I want their heads." Spittle gathered on his lips. "Their fucking heads. No mercy. None." Luther issued his edicts, like lines from a script, in monotone. He didn't scream or rant. He simply spat out orders, knowing Eden would take care of the details.

She'd debated bringing him an actual head one time. But the work involved—it wasn't easy to sever the spinal column— combined with the mess, made the decision for her. Luther's heads were figurative, holding court on the wall behind him, their obituaries, small and easily forgotten, tucked in the corner of the frames. Newsprint left to age and curl in memory of lives cut short.

"No more college students." Luther set his hand, curled into a fist, on the desk for emphasis.

That fist, hard and oppressive, had guided Eden through years of unforgivable violence. She had spilled so much blood she was certain it soaked clean through her till no part of her soul was untouched. With each bullet she sold off another bit of her humanity, leaving it in tattered shreds. She knew if she didn't act now, she'd never find her way out from the dark shadow he cast on her world. She had no choice but to run, to pray he wouldn't find her, at least not before she found herself. She longed to reclaim her tainted innocence, even if she was unsure it was even possible.

But first she had one more job to do. More bullets to deliver in the name of Luther Wade.

Eden had cautioned Luther when he brought them on board five years ago. They didn't fit in his world, but he'd overridden her protests. A bunch of frat guys, all business and accounting majors—who wouldn't want to recruit that group? And Eden had agreed in theory. If Luther was the head of an investment banking firm, they would have been good choices. But for a drug-trafficking network? Too soft. They didn't understand the rules or, worse yet, the consequences for breaking those rules.

"I'll resolve this today." She left the meaning of "resolve" open-ended.

"Do you know how much yet?"

"I have a rough estimate. Let me be sure before I commit." Eden knew the exact number.

Luther would never accept that answer from another in his employ, but from Eden it was enough. He trusted her with his life. More importantly, he trusted her with his money.

"I leave this in your hands, Eden. You're the only one. All those other bastards? They'd fuck their own mother for a dime."

Eden's mother was long gone, so fucking her for a dime or otherwise was out of the question. Eden would, however, gladly fuck Luther for four point seven million and her freedom.

❖

Litter blew across the parking lot in front of the off-campus housing unit meant for UC San Francisco students. Eden scanned the dull tan exterior and counted the floors, mentally calculating the location of her business meeting. She drew her long overcoat tight around her, as much to hide her Glock 9mm as to protect against the cutting mid-May wind.

Eden climbed four floors, scanning for security cameras as she went. Odds were against them. The main entrance was open and unsecured, an oversight that would no doubt be corrected shortly after she left.

Apartment 409. Eden knocked, her supple leather gloves muffling the sound. Bare wood showed through the worn brown paint, and the metal number nine hung upside down by one nail.

The door swung inward and the sweet odor of recently enjoyed marijuana greeted Eden.

"I told you somebody was here." A small-framed man wearing a JESUS LOVES YOU T-shirt reported to the others inside rather than greeting Eden. His skin showed through in patches of the threadbare material. He left the door open and returned to his seat on the sofa.

Eden stepped inside and closed the door with a soft click. She scanned the apartment. "Terry, we have a meeting scheduled."

"I know, man." The shaggy-haired boy in charge was only a year or two younger than Eden, but he still lived and looked the part of a starving student, not a conspicuously wealthy, heavy-hitting drug dealer. "We were waiting for you."

Terry stood at the tall counter separating the kitchen from the living room, his thick-rimmed-glasses-wearing girlfriend clinging to his side. The only source of light was the flicker of the television set.

"We were supposed to meet alone." Eden hung her overcoat on a hook on the back of the door.

Terry looked her over, the lascivious inspection of a man who feels invincible. "We were supposed to meet tomorrow."

Eden ignored him. "Alone, Terry."

"These"—Terry indicated Jesus Loves You and another man seated next to him—"are my business partners, Mark and John. And this," he gave his girlfriend a long, tonsil-inspecting kiss, "is my girlfriend."

Eden stared hard at the girl. "She should leave now."

Terry scoffed, his arm in a proprietary circle around her waist. "You don't want to leave, do you, babe?"

The girl's eyes drooped and she shook her head in a barely controlled circle.

"So, what did you need?" Terry's voice, the defiant set of his jaw, irritated Eden.

"Luther sends his thanks, but it's time for you to return his money." Eden kept her voice low, monotone.

Terry's eyes widened and his nostrils flared momentarily. "What are you talking about?"

Early on in her career, Eden would have opted for some grand theatrical show at this point. Perhaps kick a chair, throw the bong across the room—they made a satisfying noise when they shattered—or even push over the television. As much as she enjoyed those little displays of temper, she'd quickly learned that they accomplished very little and left her with a bigger mess to clean up in the end.

"You're skimming." Eden spoke slowly and overenunciated each syllable. "Luther knows it. And right now you're making things worse."

"What? No way." Terry explained, "It's just a mistake. Really. I'll fix it right away." The tremor in his voice was barely detectable.

Eden smiled—the magnanimous smile of the person holding all the cards and who might be persuaded to be generous—and spun a no. 2 pencil on the kitchen counter.

"Terry, this would go better if"—Eden jutted her hip out, pulling her jacket open slightly so the well-used black pistol grip poked out above her belt—"you told me the truth. I hate asking the same question twice."

Guys like Terry were a pain in the ass to do business with. They all thought they were smarter than she was. Worse, they relied on that college-tested frat-boy charm, thinking if they poured it on thick enough they could get out of anything.

"Listen, man, it's not like that."

Eden hated being called "man." She cocked her arm back, her hand curled into a fist, and punched Terry in the mouth. Not hard, just a quick little jab to get him to stop talking and pay attention. The rustling of Terry's suddenly concerned business partners stopped instantly when she pulled her gun from her waistband and pointed it at the trembling girlfriend. "Tell your boys to settle down."

Terry spat blood onto the unidentifiably colored carpet that had seen one too many wild parties. "Back off, guys."

Eden didn't have to look to know that the two, Mark and John, had halted their motion. A quick glance confirmed that they were sitting tensely on the edge of the couch, ready to pounce as boys wanting to be men often were. Eden held out her hand to the girlfriend. "What's your name?"

The girl looked suspiciously at Eden's hand, like she held a stick of dynamite, the fuse lit and ready to explode. Still, she placed her hand softly in Eden's. "Annie."

This was the moment of truth. Eden watched as realization seeped in for Terry. For the first time in his life he might not be able to talk his way out of something. A little extra insurance going forward could be the difference between Eden controlling the tempo of the meeting or not. She tugged lightly on Annie's hand, pulling her in close. She hated to do it, to use her. If it were up to Eden, Terry's girlfriend wouldn't be in the room at all.

Now, with Eden's arm around her waist, the gun tucked casually at her side, Annie looked like she wished she'd left when Eden offered her the chance. Eden brushed her lips against Annie's ear and said, "You're going to be okay. Just relax and we'll all get through this together." It was a lie, but Annie softened against her, relieved for the moment.

"Let's start over. How much do you have and where are you keeping it?" Eden knew how much, so that question was a good litmus test of Terry's honesty. She could figure out where, but it would be easier with his help.

"I don't know how much. It's like I've been telling you, it's all a big mistake." Terry tried to grin but ended up with a sharp-lined grimace. Blood trickled from the split in his lip.

Eden waited, her patience taxed. Terry shuffled from foot to foot at her silent regard, but didn't change his story. With Annie pulled close, her back to Eden's front, arms loose around her waist, Eden threaded the silencer onto the barrel of her nine. It threw off the trajectory of a bullet and Eden hated to use it, but given the close proximity of Terry's neighbors, she didn't have a choice. Annie's shoulders shook, a high-pitched sob squeaked between her lips. Eden blocked the sound out, focused only on Terry now, the landscape of his face.

"Whoa, man, back up. That mafia scare tactic doesn't change anything. I still don't know the answer."

He looked right at her, his eyes wild with desperation, but still he lied. Eden knew the total and she wasn't a business major. It was just a question of simple math. Terry skimmed a half percent the first two months, then stepped up to a full percent. Two months later, another half. Up and up he'd climbed, growing more confident and less careful as he went. He'd been right to be cocky at first. No low-life drug dealer would notice a lousy half percent. They simply didn't check that close. They didn't have to. Everyone knew the consequences of that kind of action. Everyone, it seemed, but Terry.

Terry's voice droned, blending with Annie's barely audible keening. Eden switched the gun to her left hand and pulled Annie tight against her with her right. She looked at Terry one more time, a pause in movement, his last chance to stay the flow of blood. He didn't miss a beat in his constant stream of bullshit. Eden blinked slowly, regretting that it came to this. The silencer would absorb most of the noise, but she didn't want Annie to hear what was coming next. "Cover your ears," she cautioned Annie as she angled slightly and shot the boy on the right side of the couch. Mark, she thought. The bullet made a neat round hole in his forehead, his face a mask of confused surprise as he slumped backward, red soaking the plaid cushion behind him.

John stared for a full beat, then leapt up. "What the hell, Ter? You said this would be a piece of cake. Easy, you said. Look at Mark. I think he's dead, man. I think he's dead."

Eden watched him come undone, the reality of the situation slamming through the room, before focusing again on Terry. "Now, let me ask again. How much and where is it?"

Terry's face was frozen in a wide-mouthed "Oh," eyes blinking rapidly. Shock. Eden wanted to shake the answer out of him. She didn't have time for him to go into vapor lock.

"Terry! Focus!"

"I'll tell you." John was twitching, his skin shining with sweat. "It was exactly four million, seven hundred and ninety-two thousand dollars."

"John!" Terry regained his voice. "Shut up!"

Eden switched the gun back to her right hand and pointed it at Terry, holding him in place, and addressed John. "Do you know where it is?"

John nodded eagerly. "Yes, yes."

"No, John, don't tell—"

Eden didn't warn Annie before she pulled the trigger this time. It was a bit premature, since she didn't know for sure if John was being honest, but Terry had pushed too far. And worst-case scenario, John didn't know where the money was and she spent some time searching. Not the end of the world.

Terry collapsed on the floor, his hand clutched to his chest, blood seeping between his fingers. "Ah, fuck," he gurgled.

The second bullet entered his right temple, silencing any further protests.

Eden motioned to John. "Show me."

"It's in here." John slid the top off the low ottoman that he and Mark had been resting their feet on. Stacks and stacks of neatly bundled twenties and fifties lay inside. "It's all here. It was an experiment. You know, pull one over on the big, bad drug lord. Like something out of a movie. You can count it." He shifted side to side, all the while gnawing the skin on the sides of his fingers.

Eden let John ramble, let his words fade into the background. She needed to decide what to do with the trembling Annie in her arms. Leaving a live witness was suicide, but the thought of killing Annie just because her boyfriend was an idiot left a foul taste in Eden's mouth. That she didn't want to kill Annie gave Eden pause. A year ago she would have pulled the trigger without a second thought. Maybe this was the quiet beginning of her transformation to normal.

Perhaps Annie could be useful in another way? She noted the similarities between herself and Annie. They were the same height, same approximate weight, same hair and eye color. Annie was a few years younger, but that was workable. She didn't want to kill her, but she couldn't leave her here. Luther would investigate and she'd be dead as soon as she answered his questions. The moment Annie stepped through the door that morning, her fate had been decided. Death was a certainty. Now it was just a question of when and how. Eden's mind raced with the possibilities.

"Put the money in a bag," she directed.

John dumped his books out of a backpack and started stuffing bricks of green into it. The money filled two book bags to overflowing, the zippers stretched and pulled taut. John smiled, nervous and hopeful, the bags on the ground at his feet.

"Do you have any cleaning supplies?"

"Under the kitchen sink." John pointed toward the kitchen. "Are you going to kill me?"

Eden could taste his fear, his desperation for the word *no*. He didn't have the clarity of vision that Eden did. To leave him alive for Luther to discover, torture, and then discard would be an act of cruelty. "Yes."

John's eyes widened and the color drained from his face, a ghostly precursor to the death awaiting him. "Please, I won't tell anyone. I promi—"

One bullet, neatly placed in the center of John's forehead, silenced any further assurances. John had been the first to crack under her scrutiny. He could not be trusted to keep any secrets.

Annie stopped crying and stared, her eyes moving rhythmically from body to body. Eden needed to move quickly before Annie snapped completely. She sat Annie on a tall bar stool at the kitchen counter. "Stay here. Don't move, don't touch anything, okay?"

Annie barely nodded, her eyes glazed over.

Eden worked her way through the room, cleaning away all evidence that she and Annie had been there. Then she hiked the bags up onto her shoulders, left her gun on the kitchen counter, and led Annie out of the apartment.

CHAPTER TWO

The bank, which smelled of wood polish and mildew, was a prison for other people's money. Brandi Cornwell pictured stacks of cash sitting in vaults, bored and wishing for a glimpse of daylight. If it were 1908 instead of 2008, she'd just ride up on her horse, bandana covering her nose, six-shooters at the ready, and take what she needed. Hell, some people thought Idaho was still like that.

No. Brandi shook her head. She couldn't imagine any incarnation of herself—from this century or the last—taking what didn't belong to her.

"He'll see you now." The sunshine-faced receptionist smiled at her.

Last chance to just run away. Brandi braced herself for a reminder of why she was glad high school was long over and pushed open the door.

Bobby Miller was just as handsome at thirty-three as he had been at seventeen. The confident I-can-throw-a-football-better-than-anyone-else swagger that made teenage girls drool had settled into a confident good ol' boy charm. Of course, it didn't hurt that he was worth more than anyone else in the county. Still, Brandi liked him better this way, especially since he no longer tried to get her naked every time they were alone for longer than three seconds. Now he tried to get her family's land from her instead. She'd been able to fend that off with relative success. But the odds were tipping in his favor and they both knew it.

"I hate this as much as you do, Brandi, but I just don't see another way." Bobby loosened his tie, slipping it free and tossing it in the bottom drawer of his desk. "Christ, I hate those things," he muttered.

Brandi looked over the figures. She didn't see a hidden solution there either. "Bobby, there has to be a better option. This would kill my mom."

Would it? Did Jaylynn care about Maple Hearth as much as Brandi wanted her to? Why did she turn a blind eye to her father's mishandling of the ranch's finances in the first place?

"There is one other option." Bobby circled the desk and closed the glass door separating his office from the hustle of bank activity. The word *President* was etched into the glass next to his name. "Off the record," he flipped the ledger in front of Brandi closed with one finger, "and off the books. I could loan you the money. Just you and me and a handshake."

Brandi could feel his eyes on her skin, crawling down the V created by the open collar of her shirt. Maybe she was wrong about him not trying to get her naked. Still, it took longer than three seconds. She smacked him in the belly.

"Don't make me call your wife, Bobby." Erica Miller née Lucas had been two grades behind Brandi in high school. Eternally cheerful and wilder than she looked, Erica was exactly Bobby's type.

He grinned like a rogue. "Don't tease me, Brandi. When it comes to you, she's extended an open invitation."

Really? That was news to Brandi. How many times would she have to take Erica—and Bobby—up on the invitation in order to protect her farm from foreclosure? She shuddered.

"No, thanks. As nice as Erica is, you're still part of the package and that just doesn't work for me."

Bobby sobered. "I don't have to be. I can sit quietly in the corner."

"And watch."

"Well, yes." His ears flared red. "She is my wife, after all."

Brandi searched his eyes and found hints of the desperate

groping boy who'd felt her up all those years ago. So much of her past hinged on Bobby Miller and now it appeared her future—the future of her home—was in his hands as well.

"I'll think about it, Bobby." She re-opened the ledger. "But let's talk about the numbers for now."

The red ink on the bank ledger made her stomach clench. Not as much as the thought of sex with Erica while Bobby looked on, but it still set her on edge. Good thing she only had coffee for breakfast. The monthly payment schedule on the loan her father took against Maple Hearth was tight, but manageable. The balloon payment due just before harvest? Impossible.

It'd been hanging over her head since her father's death. She'd learned about it in the weeks following his funeral and had been trying ever since to find a way to make the money work. She was almost out of time.

"A good harvest would just about cover the debt." There was a mile of difference between "just about" and actually doing it. Not to mention that it wouldn't leave any money to cover the other expenses, like food and heat between now and the next harvest. Then there was the small matter of paying the migrant workers. Without their hard work, the crops would die in the fields. She tugged her hands through her hair and blew out a sigh.

"If you can pay some of it, I could probably hide the rest from the board."

Bobby's obviously sincere wish to protect her from her father's bad judgment touched Brandi. Moments like this helped Brandi remember why she hadn't written Bobby and his overactive sex drive off her list of friends long ago.

"Maybe." She left the rest of that thought unsaid. The board members were more likely than not to find the unpaid debt and demand immediate payment. Then they would take her home. Brandi didn't blame them. It was all nothing but business. But still, it stung to know that people her mama went to church with would take her land without hesitation. Just proved her theory that God stayed outside the door when money was concerned. "But I can't ask you to do that."

"What other choice do you have, Brandi? Talk to Lieghtner now, before it's too late."

Daniel Lieghtner, center to Bobby's quarterback, was a trustworthy real-estate man. He worked hard, didn't cut corners, and bought and sold at fair prices. Odds were, if Brandi approached him with her problem, he would buy the acreage himself rather than put it on the open market. Or Bobby would buy it. Friends or not, they still seemed like vultures picking over her bones before she was dead.

"I'll think about it."

"You need to do more than think, Brandi. I know it sucks, but you can't ignore it anymore."

Brandi saw red. "Is that what you think, Bobby? That I've been ignoring it? That I haven't thought every day about how to meet the impossible obligations that my father created? That I don't know that my friend, the sheriff, will come to my home with my friend, the banker, someday very soon if I don't find a way to make all the red in my personal finances turn black?"

Bobby's face took on the desperation of a man the moment he realized he had stepped into a den of rattlers, and his jaw flexed and released. "Settle down. I didn't mean it like that and you know it."

"I said I'll think about it." She closed the file and stood. "And I will." It was a miserable option, but not one Brandi could close the door on for good. Losing a portion of Maple Hearth would be painful, but certainly better than losing it all.

Dull gray brick showed through the faded blue paint on the walls, and the hole in the kitchen linoleum was bigger than Eden remembered. The tattered edges gaped at her, run-down and broken, waiting to be put out of their misery like the rest of her childhood home.

Eden hated this place and every God-forsaken memory that came with it. She lit another cigarette, letting the sweet, spiced tobacco calm her nerves. The rush of nicotine and cloves didn't compel Eden to smoke. It was the ritual that challenged her resolve to quit pack after pack. The crinkle of the plastic-covered paper as she shook loose a brown-papered cigarette. The click-whoosh of her lighter when she spun the wheel. The crackle of dried tobacco when she touched the flame to the tip. The sweet smell that filled the room and coated her lips. The warm smoke as it rolled into her mouth and crept into her lungs, then out her nose like a dragon exhaling fire. These were the ingredients of an intoxicating balm that Eden chased happily.

"Can I have one of those?" Annie's voice quivered slightly.

"I thought you didn't like cloves."

"There are a lot of things about today I don't like."

Eden couldn't argue with that. There were a lot of things that she didn't like either. Sitting across from a living, breathing witness to her most recent multiple homicide was pretty high up on the list.

She placed a cigarette between Annie's lips and lit it.

"You could untie me." Annie struggled against the rope securing her wrists to the arms of the office chair. She kept one side of her mouth clamped around the cigarette, distorting her speech.

"You don't want me to."

The tip of Annie's cigarette flared as she inhaled. She closed her eyes and held her breath for a moment before exhaling. The true sign of a practiced pot smoker.

"It's not marijuana."

"I *know* that." The cigarette dropped out of her mouth.

Eden watched as the ember scorched a hole in the battered floor covering, then crushed it out. "No more for you. You'll burn the place down."

"Not if you'd fucking untie me so I could hold the damn thing." Annie sounded downright petulant, like she somehow forgot that Eden was holding a gun and had recently killed three men, including her boyfriend. All while Annie watched.

Eden pressed her fingers to her eyes and counted to ten. She was seriously losing it. She should kill Annie—should have killed her hours ago—and be done with it. She had too many things to get done before she left tonight.

The large, white-faced clock on the wall tormented her as another minute ticked by with a click. The clock was a souvenir from a night of misadventure at the local high school. She and Gabriel had broken in shortly after Eden dropped out. She didn't have anything against the school per se. Just a simple matter of too much rage and nowhere to aim it. Petty vandalism seemed like a good place to start.

"Who lives here?"

"Nobody." Not since Gabriel.

"It's a dump. I want to go home."

Christ. Was Eden so far out of control that Annie actually thought she would let her go?

Eden stood and pressed the muzzle of her gun into Annie's forehead. "There's no going home, Annie."

Annie stared up at her, her eyes wide, desperate, and unblinking. "I thought you weren't going to kill me."

"When did I say that?" Eden's hand began to shake. *Fuck.*

"You didn't. I just assumed—"

"Bad idea." Eden tried to squeeze the trigger. Her hand shook harder, the tip of the gun burrowing into Annie's skin. She pulled it back with a growl and began to pace. Lap after lap she circled the kitchen table. Why the hell had her mind and body chosen this moment, when she was so close to escape, to develop a conscience? Annie shouldn't have been in the apartment earlier. Wouldn't have been there if her boyfriend hadn't been such a selfish little boy. Regardless, Eden knew the consequences of leaving behind a witness.

Eden dropped into a chair opposite Annie and set her gun on the table. For the first time, the weight of the weapon was too much to heft. Would she miss the seemingly endless supply of perfect, untraceable nine millimeters available to her as Luther's right hand? She always left the smoking gun behind and picked up a new one for the next job. Today she'd broken the ritual and collected four new Glocks *before* her meeting. The future was unknown and she wanted to be well armed when she faced it. Four guns might have been overkill compared to the one she always carried, but to the killer in her, more was necessary. When she dropped the gun she'd used to kill Terry and his friends, she left behind the physical evidence linking her to the crime. The gun in her hand was clean and would remain so unless she used it to end Annie's life. Whether she wanted to acknowledge it or not, the act of leading Annie out of Terry's apartment showed Eden's decision to let her live. If she had been able to kill Annie, she would have done it before laying the 9mm on the kitchen counter.

Annie's eyes darted from Eden's face to the Glock and back again in a rapid-fire loop. Eden curled her hand over the cool gray metal, but left it resting on the dinged tabletop.

"Don't do anything foolish, Annie."

Annie slumped against her chair, tears streaking silently down her cheeks. "I don't want to die."

"Nobody does."

A train rumbled by, the tracks close enough that the apartment vibrated with the passing of life outside the window. As children, she and Gabriel had pressed their faces to the glass and guessed where the long freight trains were headed. She'd longed to jump on one and never come back, letting the grinding steel wheels carry her away. Anywhere would have been better. She knew it then, and she was faced with that reality again.

"Where would you go?" she asked, the words barely audible.

"Shit. Out of this room, for starters."

Annie's answer startled her. It too closely mirrored Eden's childhood dreams of escape.

"No, that's where you'd go *from*. But where would you go *to*?"

The steam whistle pierced through the conversation, bleeding out its indictment. Their conversation, it said, was irrelevant. Get on the train and ride. Let the engineer worry about the destination. Eden imagined herself running along side a flat car, arms and legs flexing as she grabbed the iron handle and pulled herself up. She'd lie in the middle of the car, arms and legs spread like she was making snow angels against the hard surface, and stare up at the night sky, counting the stars as they grew brighter with the recession of L.A.'s lights.

"I don't know. Maybe I'd go find my mom." Annie sniffed.

Eden didn't want to find her mom. She was the type of woman who wouldn't buy drinks in bars because they were too expensive. For the same price as two watered-down martinis, she could get a fifth of vodka from the liquor store. She had given Eden that lesson in economics as she'd shaken the last clinging drops from a bottle that had been full a few hours before.

"Where is she?"

"Utah, maybe? She married a Mormon and left me here with my dad."

"How long ago was that?"

Wrinkles creased Annie's forehead. "Twelve years ago. I was fourteen."

"And you haven't seen her since?"

"I talked to her a couple of times, but…" Annie shrugged.

Eden had never been to Utah. Couldn't imagine anyone choosing that state. Did they? Or did people chug along until destiny dumped them out where they belonged?

"How would you get there?"

"Hitchhike?"

"That's a good way to get killed."

Annie snorted. "So is getting high at my boyfriend's place." She stared hard at Eden.

"Did you love him?" The question slid out and Eden struggled in its wake.

"Not really. He was good in bed and he had great weed."

"No," Eden corrected her, "Luther had great weed. Terry had a death wish."

Annie didn't respond.

"He'll kill you for sure, you know?"

"Luther?"

Eden nodded.

"He's your boss?"

"Not anymore. Terry and company was my last job."

"Are you allowed to quit that kind of business?"

"No."

"So he'll kill you, too?"

Eden sighed and traced circles on the table. "Probably. If he catches me."

"Is that why you haven't killed me? Because you quit?"

She shook her head, miserable. "I don't know." The disconnected coldness that allowed Eden to execute Luther's enemies had bled from her like the spreading pool from Terry's fatal wound. She'd made her final kills in the name of money and could find no justification for taking Annie's life. "You don't deserve to die."

"Terry did?"

"Terry was stupid. He knew the rules and he broke them."

"And paid with his life." Annie's voice was soft.

"Yes."

They sat in silence, minutes ticked by.

"Where would you go?" Annie asked.

Eden bit back her reflexive, sarcastic answer of "I could tell you, but then I'd have to kill you." That kind of statement wasn't funny when the person making it had proven capable of murder. "I don't know."

"Do you have anyone?"

Penny. "My family is gone."

"You could come to Utah with me." Annie raised her eyes to meet Eden's gaze.

Maybe this was how it happened. How people ended up in unexpected places. Someone offered hope and the other person grabbed on with all their might.

Eden kept her expression bland.

"Did you say good-bye?" The underlying note of fear in Annie's voice disappeared completely.

"To who?" Eden asked.

"Whoever you're going to miss."

"There's only one person. And to tell her would be very dangerous."

"Maybe you can call when we get there."

Eden marveled at Annie's confidence. Nothing had changed physically. She was still tied to the chair. Eden still had a gun. But she spoke with resolve, the assumption that Eden would not let her down.

"Maybe." Eden shrugged as the whisper seeded itself into the back of her brain and began to unfurl. Once she was out of L.A., maybe she *could* call Penny. Buy a prepaid cell phone and explain why she'd run. Eden shook off the notion as foolish. Still, the hope of hearing Penny's voice again eased the ache in her chest. She rubbed her temples.

"So what's the plan?"

Eden circled the table and cut free the ropes binding Annie. She left the 9mm sitting on the table. A test or just blatantly stupid? Eden couldn't say. But would it really be so bad to die here, by the hands of a woman who had a right to spill her blood? And if she didn't pounce on the opportunity, Eden would know she could trust her.

Annie rubbed the grooves left on her wrists, but didn't move from the chair. "Well?"

"First, we have to get rid of my car."

"Get rid of?" Annie sounded disappointed.

"Luther owns it. I can't take it."

"Off a cliff?" Annie suggested.

"I was thinking the river."

"Hell, if you really want it to disappear, leave it on the street in this neighborhood."

It was currently parked against the curb in front of the building. Eden shook her head. "Nobody around here would dare touch that car. It belongs to a killer."

"Right. The river it is."

Annie stood and walked to the window. Eden watched her closely, her muscles coiled and ready to spring if Annie made a wrong move.

Annie dropped onto the couch with a light "oof" and stretched, head on the arm, feet almost touching the other end. "Don't worry. I'm not going to run."

"Why not?"

"Where would I go?"

"Good point." Eden nodded. "I also have some business I need to take care of before I leave town."

Annie's head bobbed with acceptance. "Does that business involve food? I'm starving."

Eden paused. How much should she tell Annie? Too late to turn back now. She either pulled the trigger, thus eliminating her worries, or exposed her vulnerabilities. Betrayal would mean nothing less than death for Eden, but that would be fitting punishment for her crimes. More importantly, if she hoped to ever be truly free from her life as Luther's executioner, she needed to find a way to trust.

"Okay, here's the plan." Eden rolled the dice and took a chance on hope.

❖

Moonlight crept through the grime-covered windows high on the warehouse wall, lighting Eden's way through the stacked boxes of merchandise. She flicked her lighter open then closed, open then closed, staring up at the giant towers of snow white addiction wrapped in the respectable veneer of legitimate business. To an unsuspecting passerby, and even to the city officials and inspectors paid to root out corruption, the crates looked like an endless supply of bamboo mats, the kind housewives across America stepped onto for their ritualistic Sun Salute and Downward Dog.

Who would be Luther's avenging angel when he realized she had betrayed him? Peter Fuentes, Eden's childhood friend and Luther's hired gun looking for a promotion? It wasn't an answer Eden planned to learn. If she hid her tracks well enough, the moment of truth would never come.

Be safe. Penny's words of caution echoed loud in Eden's head. So loud, she was sure the warning would bounce off the warehouse walls and alert the guards to her presence.

Footsteps sounded in the next row over, heavy and certain— Peter making his rounds with the confidence of a man who was accustomed to pounding his way through obstacles. Eden slipped silently behind a short stack of wooden crates labeled Housewares and waited. She considered letting him pass unmolested. After all, Peter had been her first fumbling kiss. A terribly botched attempt at mimicking the acrobatically inspired backseat antics of his older sister and her boyfriend, they'd come together in a borderline painful crush of lips and teeth, hidden behind a stack of old tires in Peter's backyard.

They'd been friends once upon a time, Eden reasoned as she raised her Glock 9mm silently to the level of Peter's heart. They shared history. She didn't want to kill him. Maybe she'd get lucky and Peter would turn the other direction and skip this part of the warehouse completely on his rounds. Once she'd finished what she needed to do here, she could warn him via an anonymous phone call. It was possible he would escape in time.

Eden shrugged off her poorly timed sentimentality as she listened to the sound of his progress, one foot after another. She'd been willing to walk away from Penny—*Penny*, her first everything—so allowing nostalgia over Peter to interfere at this level of the game would be stupid. He turned back toward the office and Eden lowered her gun. As long as he kept going, her childhood loyalties would be tested no further that day.

Her choice to betray Luther and run clung to her like thick tar—dark, acrid, and burning. She'd felt his relief when she looked him in the eye like a trusted friend and promised to take care of the situation in San Francisco. He'd clapped her on the back and pulled her into a big hug. "You're like a daughter to me, Eden. You know that."

A *daughter*.

Business came way above family for Luther—his own daughter tucked safely away from the dirt and danger of his profession.

And she'd driven away, false assurances fresh from her mouth, her ears still unwilling to believe she was lying so brazenly. If Luther found out…

No. He wouldn't. Eden shook her head, drawing her focus back to her surroundings. The authorities hadn't had time to find her car yet, but they would soon. Then Luther would believe she was dead. As long as she was careful, gave him no reason to believe otherwise, she would be safe. The laws of nature would limit his vendetta. Even Luther, with all his power, couldn't resurrect the dead, and he didn't waste time chasing ghosts.

So why was she creeping through his warehouse, coming within feet of discovery? Shutting down distribution at this location would be little more than an annoying speed bump on the drug-trafficking superhighway.

She could simply shoot Peter if he popped up in her path. God knew she was a better killer than he was. But she hoped to avoid that option. Gunfire, while it would eliminate the immediate threat, would draw attention. And Luther had an entire army he could send after her if he was interested enough.

Still, she couldn't simply get on her shiny black Ducati—a new purchase for her new life—and ride away. Not until she shut down the flow of drugs from the source. Destroying the warehouse wouldn't stop Luther. Hell, it wouldn't even slow him down for more than a couple of days. No matter what she did, it wouldn't be enough.

But at least she was doing something.

Logically, she knew nothing could erase the immorality of her past. The imprint of her years as an enforcer was indelible, etched in her memory with agonizing clarity. But when Gabriel died—smoke curling upward from the gun dangling loosely in his hand, tears not yet dried on his cheeks, and the ever-present glaze of black tar heroin in his eyes—Eden surrendered. With him went her only reason for searching Luther out. She no longer needed to protect and provide for a man-child incapable of looking out for himself. Gabriel's death showed Eden how poorly she'd performed in her role as unsolicited guardian. No matter how hard she fought or how loud she yelled and argued, she couldn't sway her brother from his path.

Eden slipped to the centermost spot of the warehouse. The dead faces from the day before—Terry, John, and Mark—faded into the black hole of her memory. Eventually, she knew that the register of names, her personal book of the dead, would rise up and demand her attention. For now, however, she had work to do. The middle of the building, farthest from the windows and accidental discovery, housed a large work area. Long tables were laid out with product for cutting and packaging, destined for street-level sales. The banker's scales lined the tables waiting to be loaded and evaluated. Stacked to the side, haphazard and forgotten, lay the broken-open crates.

Eden pulled the small bottle of lighter fluid from her jacket pocket. She didn't need much, just enough to give the flame purchase. Still, she emptied the contents of the bottle over the stack and tables, flipped open her lighter, and stepped past the point of no return. Rather than the instant, raging inferno like something out of big-budget Hollywood, the fire started slowly, flames licking their way lazily through the discarded wood. Black, thick smoke climbed toward the ceiling and Eden heard surprised shouts. After a pause, an alarm sounded.

It was time to go.

Eden ran for the exit, her gun at the ready, with smoke and heat chasing her through the aisles. She burst out the side door, no longer worried about discovery. The guards were in a full-on scramble, their voices rising in a confused melee. She turned and watched for a moment before she climbed aboard her motorcycle. Fire, she learned, spread quickly through warehouses with poorly maintained and malfunctioning sprinkler systems.

Amid the building roar of unchecked flames, Eden rode the throttle hard toward the open road. The unmistakable crack of gunfire sounded as she pointed the bike east to where Annie waited and away from her life.

CHAPTER THREE

Eden spun a sugar packet on the well-polished countertop and concentrated on looking lighthearted. "You sure you'll be okay here with your mom?"

"Sure. I mean she's crazy for Jesus and all that, but she's really nice, too." Annie chewed the inside of her lip. "You could stay, too, you know."

"I need to go." Eden glanced over her shoulder. Marsha, the crazy-for-Jesus mom herself, waved from the front seat of her minivan. The hopeful smile she'd adopted when Annie introduced herself still hadn't faded.

"Okay, but you know where to find me if you need anything."

"I do." Eden paid the waitress and headed toward the door. "But you're going to have your hands full."

Eden led the way to the parking lot, then stopped between their two vehicles. Annie's four-year-old twin brothers bounced in the backseat, while her eight-year-old brother played a video game and her twelve-year-old sister read a book.

Annie threw her arms around Eden's neck and squeezed. "You're going to be okay." Annie's declaration sounded suspiciously nurturing.

"Yeah, I'll be fine." Eden wasn't sure if it was true or not, but either way, she was confident that Utah wasn't the place for her. Cars sped by on the interstate—the constant drone of movement that marks every roadside diner in America—drawing Eden to the road. Still Annie clung to her.

"Thanks for helping me find my mom." Annie released Eden and wiped her eyes. "I couldn't have done it without you." The sweet, caring young woman held no resemblance to the barely there girl Eden had met at Terry's. Could Annie have evaded that whole phase of her life—dating a drug dealer and subsequently witnessing his execution—if she'd moved with her mother years ago?

The farther Eden traveled from Los Angeles, the more the weight lifted from her, leaving her unfettered and free to run. How much of that was linked to Annie and her easy forgiveness? Would the emotional burden return to Eden when Annie left her life?

Annie hugged her one last time, rose on her toes, and kissed Eden on the cheek. "Call Penny and check in. It'll be okay if you do."

"Maybe." Eden wasn't convinced, but the urge to follow Annie's suggestion was overwhelming. "Go on. Your mom is waiting." Eden nudged Annie toward the van.

Annie climbed in and waved as her mom pulled away. Eden watched her go, wondering if she was making the right decision. She sensed she was, but Eden wasn't used to listening to her instincts when the message was something other than *pull the trigger*.

Eden continued to stare, long after the van disappeared down the road. Finally, she climbed on her bike and pointed it toward the Utah-Idaho border.

❖

The brim of her Stetson provided Brandi with precious little shelter from the midmorning sun. She slapped the southern Idaho dust off her Levi's and turned a critical eye to the section of barbed wire in need of repair. It would have to wait.

She whistled loud and sharp, calling her horse, Ranger, away from his respite. He'd taken up quarter in a tiny patch of shade below a burned-out cottonwood. Lightning had blasted the tree last summer and it needed to come down before it got hit with a windstorm and fell of its own accord. That was another thing to add to her endless list of chores.

Ranger ambled up and nuzzled Brandi's shoulder as if to say, "You called me. Now what?"

Brandi raked her fingers over the long patch of white on Ranger's nose and gathered the reins. She'd come back later this afternoon with the right supplies and repair the fence. And if she had enough time, she'd cut down the tree and begin quartering it. The smoke damage made it bad firewood, but it'd been a long while since she and her mom had hosted a bonfire.

A bead of sweat trailed down the valley between her breasts as she lifted herself onto Ranger's back. It was only ten a.m. and the white fitted tank she wore was already sticky with perspiration. She clucked her tongue, letting Ranger know it was time to head home.

Brandi set an easy pace for Ranger. Days like this, she considered leaving the saddle at home and riding bareback. He would probably prefer it, but her mom was another story. On the few occasions when Brandi did venture out without a saddle, her mother worried and fretted the entire time Brandi was gone, convinced that she would fall off and break her head open without a pommel to hold on to. That would be quite a feat for someone who had been riding as long as she could walk, but still her mother worried. The need to placate her mom won out over comfort, so Brandi used a saddle.

They followed the fence line to the old, rarely traveled two-lane highway. As they neared the blacktop, Brandi spotted a would-be motorcycle rider about twenty feet down the road and headed her way. The woman pushed the presumably malfunctioning mechanical ride along the side of the road. Her helmet and jacket were strapped to the seat with a bungee cord. Sweat glistened and rolled down her shoulders and arms, and the exposed skin of her neck and shoulders above her black tank top shone red from the sun.

The black Ducati was equipped with soft-side saddlebags that bulged to bursting, clearly filled beyond capacity. The small tent and bedroll strapped to the backrest completed the picture. This rider was not out for an afternoon jaunt turned stranded neighbor in need of a ride home. There was no telling how far from home this woman was, and that added up to more than an inconvenient break from her afternoon chores to play rescue ranger. All of this translated into an unexpected guest at the ranch, and that inconvenience would last longer than the afternoon.

Brandi was simultaneously irritated and intrigued. She didn't have time to play hostess to a marooned traveler, but as far as distractions went, this one was definitely nice to look at.

Ranger rolled his head, a big, slow loop. It was horse language for "Can we go now?" Brandi ran her hand down his long neck, hugging him as she patted his chest. "I would never have to push you up a hill, would I, boy?" she whispered into his ear. He blew hot air out his nose and twisted his head to the side and back.

Brandi draped the reins over Ranger's neck and pulled her Stetson forward and off her head. Her short, spiky hair tended to stick out in every direction, sort of avant-garde dyke. The dyke in her craved spiky hair, but her hair craved creative independence. A wild outcrop of peaks and valleys was the result. Brandi pushed her hand through her sweat-drenched locks, slicking it down momentarily only to have it pop back up after a few seconds.

She held her hat in her hands as she spoke. It was the only polite thing to do. "Do you need some help?" It was a lame question, given the circumstance, but it seemed a good place to start.

The woman stopped her forward motion and lowered the Ducati's kickstand. She gave a rueful smile. "Don't suppose you have a parts store in your saddlebag, do you?"

"Nope." Brandi tried for apologetic, but was afraid the word came out more sarcastic than anything. She dropped her hat on her head, pushed it way back off her forehead, and swung out of the saddle. She landed with a dull thud a few feet from the woman and extended her hand. "I'm Brandi."

"Eden."

Some things shouldn't be done in this kind of heat, like shaking hands. The press of sticky, wet skin seemed too intimate for two people who were meeting for the first time. Brandi wanted to hold on and yank her hand away at the same time.

Brandi stuffed her right hand deep into the pocket of her worn jeans and grabbed Ranger's reins with her left hand, just to keep him from ambling home without her. He was well behaved, but the promise of shade and sweet oats was hard to resist. He shifted side to side, bored and ready to move on.

"So, you planning on pushing that all the way to the next town?" Brandi indicated the Ducati by raising her chin in the motorcycle's general direction. She forced herself to look Eden directly in the eyes, resisting the urge to linger on the supple black riding chaps clinging to her legs. They were a stark contrast to the soft brown pair that Brandi had worn during her rodeo phase. The image of Eden, clad only in her chaps and a matching black Stetson and straddling her motorcycle, flashed through Brandi's mind. She hoped the flush of fire that started in her belly and crept up her neck and face would be mistaken as effects of the hot sun. It'd been too long since she'd gotten naked with another woman. Apparently that affected her ability to see a stranger without turning into an ogling, lust-filled teenaged boy.

Eden laughed. Not the cloying, overly enthusiastic laughter Brandi was used to hearing from the women she met on the rare nights she ventured into town in search of company, but rather the tight, controlled laughter of a woman who found precious few opportunities to laugh. "I figured I'd just keep pushing till I happened across a house. Then I'd use the phone or something."

"Well, you're headed in the right direction. Next house is mine. Of course, it's about two miles from here."

"Two miles?" Eden grimaced as a bead of sweat rolled down her cheek. "That's a lot of pushing."

"There is an alternative." Brandi offered up her best smile, the one she used when trying to convert straight women to the dark side. It'd worked on more than one occasion. "You could leave the bike here and ride back with me. We'll grab some lunch and come back with my truck and pick it up."

Eden looked skeptical, her eyebrows furrowed together. "I don't know… Will it be safe here?"

Brandi thought about it before answering. She could count the number of vehicles that passed by here on any given day on one hand. Odds were it would be perfectly safe. And the thought of Eden's front pressed against her back as they rocked along on

Ranger's back made her mouth water and her belly tingle. Still, even on a deserted stretch of southern Idaho two-lane, unexpected things could happen.

Brandi sighed as the prospect of Eden riding with her evaporated into the heat waves rippling off the blacktop. "I can't promise that." She twirled her hat in her hands, reluctant to suggest the only other solution. No way around it. "Change of plans. You wait here and I'll come back with my truck."

"You'd do that? That'd be great." Relief and gratitude flooded Eden's face and overflowed from her eyes. The look was almost enough to make Brandi forget her disappointment over not sharing the ride. Almost.

Ranger nudged her shoulder, reminding her that she'd promised him shade, water, and a snack. Brandi patted Ranger's flank and smiled at Eden, a smile she infused with confidence and trust. She wanted Eden to know she would definitely return for her. "I'll be right back." Brandi set her hat on her head and swung up into the saddle. It was damn near impossible to keep from turning around to wink at Eden. She was always up for a good flirt. Somehow she managed to keep her ass in the saddle and her head pointed forward.

Brandi made it home, tended to Ranger, and collected her truck, sans trailer, in record time. There really wasn't anywhere to turn a truck and trailer where Eden was waiting, so the lack of maneuverability heavily outweighed the benefit of taking it. Thirty-four minutes after stopping the first time, she spotted Eden pushing her bike toward her on the opposite side of the road. Perhaps if she'd turned and winked when she was riding away, Eden would have trusted that she'd return. Nah. Somehow Brandi couldn't picture Eden filling the damsel-in-distress role. She waved as she passed, then flipped the truck around to pull up in front of Eden.

Eden had reached a section of road where giant cottonwood trees stretched across the pavement. Light and dark flickered over her skin as the breeze played through the treetops, making her sweat-slicked skin flash between gold and dark silver. Brandi gripped the door handle white-knuckle hard and gulped down the urge to chase the pattern with her tongue. She stifled the impulse and stepped out of the truck. Eden stopped and rested the motorcycle against her hip. She greeted Brandi with a slow smile that spread across her face like a sunrise over the horizon. It set Brandi's gut on fire, and the greeting she formulated in her brain crumbled like a dry riverbed. Evidence of moisture remained, but none could be found.

"You came back to rescue me." Eden pushed her hair out of her eyes. When Brandi rode away on Ranger, the chestnut mane had been braided. Now it flowed long and loose down her back, a lock or two falling in her eyes with the help of the breeze.

Brandi walked to the back of the truck, hands held stiffly at her side. She didn't trust them to stay put. Her fingertips itched to get lost in Eden's hair, to pull her close. Brandi's lips would fit perfectly against the curve of her neck. She licked her own lips and cleared her throat. Her brain was misfiring, but it hadn't crashed completely. She focused hard on what Eden had said and forced a response. "Of course I did. Couldn't leave you stranded."

"Maybe next time I can rescue you." Eden winked and Brandi forgot how to breathe.

The thought of rescuing Eden made her insides tingle and throb. The thought of Eden rescuing her turned them into full-on mush. She wanted to reply with something super sexy cool, but all her tongue would produce was, "Uh…" So much for Casanova. Brandi forced herself to think about other, decidedly *not* sexy things: puppies, broken fence line, cold lemonade, anything to keep her from getting slapped if Eden turned out to be a mind reader.

Brandi fell back on her one infallible guideline for living: When all else fails, do something productive. That motto kept the family ranch, Maple Hearth, alive and thriving. Her grandfather had hung the sign declaring the name of his family's homestead to the world in 1932. Now the burden of keeping the land out of the hands of the local banker fell to Brandi.

With her grandfather's lesson in mind, she sucked in air and lowered the tailgate. "Let's load 'er up." She grabbed the ramp out of the back and extended it to the ground. For this trip she'd brought their old Chevy. It was a hard-used ranch truck and looked the part, but it was a two-wheel drive that sat closer to the ground than her four-by-four. That made the angle of the ramp doable. Plus it had a longer bed, so there was no question about whether the motorcycle would fit.

She climbed into the truck bed to pull the bike into place and hold it steady while Eden pushed it up from the side. Cruisers like this one were not made to comfortably climb a ramp into the back of a truck. They were designed to hug the road and give the rider an 80 mile-an-hour, vibration-induced orgasm. After a little swearing and a lot of straining, they got the bike settled and the tie-downs in place.

Brandi hopped out and debated opening the passenger door for Eden. She didn't trust herself to be that close to her so she opted against it. The inside of the cab, even with the windows open, was sweltering when they climbed inside. "We could run the air if you want." Brandi hoped Eden would decline. She hated the false cold more than the dry heat.

"The breeze will be enough once we get moving."

And just like that the edge was off and Brandi was comfortable in the stretched-out cab with Eden. Lust was one thing—not always entirely manageable, but not life-altering. Little things like agreeing about the AC, that's what made life livable. Brandi pulled back onto the road and headed toward home.

Eden sat closer to the middle than necessary, not hugging the door like most would in a strange truck with an unknown person. Brandi glanced over at Eden, her hair flying in the wind. One strand—there was always one that insisted on doing its own thing—was stuck to her cheek, locked in place by the fine sheen of sweat covering Eden's body.

"Thank you." Eden's voice was louder than a whisper, but not by much. "For the ride." Her eyes held a hint of amusement and a whole smoldering dose of lust. She opened her mouth to say more, then stopped herself. She sucked her bottom lip between her teeth and released it slowly.

Brandi divided her attention between the deserted highway and the heat pulsing off Eden, the pull of her dark eyes, the beat of her heart echoing just below the skin at the base of her neck, her long, smooth fingers trailing through her wind-blown hair as she held it away from her face.

Brandi almost missed the turn into her driveway. Dammit. She pulled her eyes away from Eden and focused on the gravel road in front of her. They allowed their dogs to roam free on the property, and Brandi would never forgive herself if she hit one because she wasn't paying attention. The dogs were good at getting out of the way, but you never knew. And she needed a reprieve from the hot scrutiny of Eden's eyes. She felt like she was being dismantled from the inside, and it was unnerving yet soothing.

"We're here," she said softly, reluctant to break the silence threaded between them.

Cheyenne reached the truck before the other dogs. An energetic border collie, she bounced up and down. At the top of each jump, she poked her head inside the open driver's-side window to say hello to her mistress. Her yips of excitement sliced through the mood, leaving Brandi feeling open and exposed. She pulled her mental barriers back in place and wrapped herself up tight as she laughed at Cheyenne's antics. "Come on. We better head in."

Brandi held the screen door open and Eden passed through, again a little closer than necessary, but not close enough to touch. The radio was tuned to the local country station and turned up loud. Patsy Cline crooned her way around the room and Brandi lowered the volume.

"Hey!" Her mom's voice came from the back of the house. "I was listening to that."

"Ol' man Richter stopped me on the way home to complain about the noise. Took me three hours to get away from him so I could come turn it down," Brandi joked. Jacob Richter was their closest neighbor, four miles to the east and well out of Patsy's range.

"In that case, turn it back up. He needs a little more music in his life." Jaylynn Cornwell was a right looker in her day, or so she said. Brandi believed it because at sixty her mom could still turn heads and stop traffic. She bustled into the kitchen carrying a wicker basket full of wet bedding headed for the clothesline out back. She pulled up short when she saw Eden standing in her kitchen in her black leather biker boots, chaps, and vest. She straightened her hair reflexively, balanced the basket on her hip, held out her hand to Eden, and introduced herself without skipping a beat. "I'm Jaylynn Cornwell, Brandi's mama. She didn't tell me to expect company today or I would've had a glass of iced tea ready for you."

Eden shook the offered hand with a relieved smile. "Nice to meet you, Mrs. Cornwell. Don't be too hard on Brandi. I was a bit unexpected."

Jaylynn dropped the basket by the back door. "Call me Jaylynn, honey. Or just Jay. But none of that Mrs. Cornwell business. I'm just not that old yet."

"Mama, I'm going to give Eden the nickel tour. Be right back." She placed her hand in the small of Eden's back and guided her toward the living room.

Jaylynn, her head buried in the refrigerator, waved them on and said, "Good, that'll give me a chance to pull together a proper lunch."

They rounded the corner into the large living room and it was time for Brandi to remove her hand. She didn't. Her fingers had melted into place from the heat and the burn was making its way up her arm to her neck and shoulders. She stood quietly, the task of showing Eden around forgotten for the moment.

Eden shifted slightly, turning her face to Brandi. "Your mom seems nice."

Brandi snorted out a laugh, her hand falling naturally to her side. She ached to reconnect. "My mom is a lot of things. I don't know that I would count nice among 'em."

"Watch your mouth, young lady. You shouldn't count deaf among 'em either," Jaylynn scolded from the kitchen.

"Yes, Mama." Brandi rolled her eyes and snorted. Time to begin the tour. "Okay, this, as you can tell, is the living room." It stretched out in front of them, decorated with comfort in mind. Two large, overstuffed couches sat perpendicular to each other in the far corner, and two supple brown leather recliners rounded out the horseshoe configuration. They were angled together for comfortable conversation in front of the fireplace. Brandi spent many winter nights curled in the far sofa with a book surrounded by the down-home warmth only possible from a wood fire.

"No television?" Eden looked surprised by the omission.

Brandi forgot that other people expected it to be the focal point of any home. "No. We don't watch much, but we do have one in the family room." She nodded down the long hall. "Come on. I'll show you."

She pointed out the formal dining room as they passed. The house didn't have an open floor plan like the houses built nowadays. Brandi liked it better that way. It grounded her in the history of her family. Her grandfather had built the place from the foundation up, and that was something to be proud of.

The oversized arched entrance to the family room didn't have a door, unlike the entrance to the dining room. She stepped down into the sunken room and into the sunlight that the bank of greenhouse windows invited into the room. French doors led out onto a large back deck that was also connected to the kitchen on one side and the laundry room on the other. Oversized houseplants held court along the glass wall.

Brandi had majored in forestry at Colorado State. The financial struggles at Maple Hearth had spoiled her plans to go to work for the forestry service. In the six years since her return, the few plants she'd collected in college threatened to take over the entire room. To hear Jaylynn tell it, Brandi came back home and brought the forest with her.

In the corner sat a twenty-seven-inch television. It looked abandoned and forgotten with one small love seat pointed at it. "Look, a TV," Brandi said.

"Forget the TV. Look at that fern," Eden said appreciatively. The fern in question sat on the floor in a squat, round pot and stretched up to the top of the window. "What do you feed that thing?"

Brandi shrugged. "The usual, water and sunlight. And a little fertilizer once or twice a year. Nothing special." Brandi fidgeted. She loved her plants, but she didn't love talking about them. In her estimation, it took away the power of their relationship. And she couldn't exactly explain that they grew because she loved them.

She'd tried to say that once to a friend but it earned her a hearty belly laugh. Now she kept it to herself.

Eden fingered the delicate fern, a look of concentration on her face. She turned slightly to face Brandi. "You must love them very much."

Brandi reminded herself to breathe. "I do."

Eden nodded once and walked back across the room. She stopped in front of Brandi and held her gaze, then wrapped her hand around Brandi's, slow and easy, and squeezed. "Show me the rest of the house."

The remainder of the tour passed in a blur for Brandi because the memory of Eden's hand robbed her of her ability to focus on the mundane. The curve of Eden's mouth as she smiled, shy and confident at the same time; the flecks of gold in her eyes glinting in the light as she tucked a loose piece of hair behind her ear; the rise and fall of her chest beneath the leather vest; the occasional brush of her arm against Brandi's as they walked from room to room—all this chased every other thought from her head.

Brandi showed off her bedroom from the doorway, afraid to step inside. The bed was big and soft and inviting. The air between them crackled and popped, and the color around Eden screamed bold intentions. The rest of the house faded to muted sienna, not really the absence of color, but not defined enough to grab on to. Brandi tugged gently at her hand, leading them away from temptation. "Let me show you the guest room."

Sandwiched between Brandi's room and the office, it was the smallest of the bedrooms. It still provided the same amount of temptation. Funny how the size of the room didn't change anything between two people. Eden pulled Brandi over the threshold. She closed the door with a deliberate, slow sweep of her arm, her eyes locked on Brandi's. The soft click as the door slid home signaled her intentions with absolute clarity.

Eden stepped deeper into the room and faced Brandi. She released her hand and placed both hands lightly on Brandi's hips. She waited, her eyes asking permission to proceed. Brandi melted under her touch. A wave of molten lava coursed from Eden's hands through Brandi's belly in gentle, unstoppable waves. Brandi gasped, her lips parted, unable to speak, and Eden increased the pressure.

Brandi let Eden pull her close and guide her back at the same time. With the hard surface of the door at her back and the supple invitation of Eden molded to her front, Brandi struggled to stay grounded in the day. One more moment in those eyes and she'd be lost.

The kiss was soft, gentle, almost chaste. Just a brush of Eden's lips against hers. The room spun out of focus and Brandi's knees liquefied. She lowered her eyelids and surrendered to the exquisite, searing beauty of Eden's mouth opening to her. She weaved her fingers into Eden's hair, pulling her closer. She lingered there, the soft cinnamon of Eden's breath filling her senses.

White-hot spots danced behind Brandi's eyes and she pulled away, gasping for air. The distant sound of her mother singing along with the radio edged its way into the room. Brandi's eyes fell closed, a brief moment of surrender, and she forced them open. "Wow." Her hands tracked down Eden's abdomen.

Eden, lips slightly parted, slid her hands beneath the hem of Brandi's shirt. "Wow is right."

The buckle at the top of Eden's chaps stopped Brandi from moving her hands farther south. Chaps. Black leather motorcycle chaps. Reality slammed in on Brandi from all sides. Eden was here, now, but as soon as her bike was fixed, she'd be gone. This wasn't the back room of a lesbian bar. She hadn't been drinking and found herself in the desperate scramble to find a playmate for the night. She lived here. The only thing between her and her mother—who was singing off-key and loud in the next room—was a hollow-core door. No matter how hot Eden was, this was not a dalliance Brandi could pursue. She didn't bring her flings home with her.

Brandi grasped Eden's hands and pulled them away, her body stiff.

"Stop." The command was quiet but firm. No room for debate.

Eden stepped back, confusion and desire written across her face. The question was clear in her eyes.

"This will be your room during your stay." Brandi battled to keep her voice level, indifferent.

Eden reached out and looped one finger in the waist of Brandi's jeans. The brief contact was not nearly enough after the raging inferno that threatened to engulf them. "I don't understand."

It was a simple statement. Brandi wanted to explain. But she couldn't. She'd had anonymous sex before without the promise of happily-ever-after, but on those occasions she'd sneaked away before the sun came up. There was no sneaking away here. The emotional mess would be too big to clean up if she indulged this urge.

She turned her face away from Eden, her jaw twitching with tension. "I'm sure lunch is ready by now." She slipped out the door and headed to the kitchen, leaving Eden to follow along or not.

CHAPTER FOUR

That went well. Eden unbuckled her chaps and slid them off. She folded them casually over the back of the lone wooden chair in the room and settled her vest on a hanger before she followed Brandi at a distance, trying to determine where exactly she'd gone wrong. Brandi, with her deep, meaningful glances and lingering touch, had sent all the right signals. Of that much, Eden was certain. And those lips. Hot damn, the woman could kiss. Not since that first time with Penny had she felt so given over to the moment, lost in the sweetness of another woman's satin-smooth kiss.

The warm invitation of Brandi's home, her touch, her arms pulling her closer had been real. Then she'd pushed Eden away, her voice stamped iron hard in refusal. Eden shook her head. She'd tried for too much too fast and possibly destroyed the chance of anything happening in the future.

Future? What future? She'd be here long enough to fix her busted engine. No future in that. Then what was she hoping for with Brandi when she'd eased her against the wall? A quick fuck with Brandi's mom in the next room? Brandi wasn't that kind of girl. For that matter, neither was Eden. She wasn't opposed to physical comfort from a stranger, but she had no interest in being overheard, especially by her paramour's mother.

Lunch was spread out over the counter, far more than the three of them could eat. A heavy ceramic bowl overflowing with fluffy white rolls. Another full of dark yellow potato salad with paprika sprinkled over the top. A platter loaded with bacon, ham, and turkey. A plate piled high with lettuce, tomatoes, and long, thin pickle slices. A wooden cutting board with three loaves of unevenly sliced bread, the aroma teasing Eden from across the room. A casserole dish of baked macaroni, crusted over with cheese.

Brandi pushed her hand through the unruly spikes atop her head and wiped the back of her hand across her red, swollen lips as she stared at Eden.

"You should fix a plate now, while there's plenty."

Eden didn't want to eat anymore. She wanted to chase the haunted look from Brandi's eyes, but had no idea how. The only reliable method of communication she was skilled at involved a gun and bloodshed. She nodded, short and tight, and forced her feet to move, one in front of the other. As she picked a chipped white plate from the stack, the screen door leading to the backyard screeched open and a weathered man in a sweat-darkened John Deere ball cap stepped into the room.

"Still need to fix that spring," he muttered as he filed to the food, a line of similarly clad men falling in behind him.

Eden dropped a healthy scoop of macaroni on her plate, passed on the greens in favor of the homemade bread slathered in butter, and watched Brandi engage the workers.

"You say that every day, Rich, but it's still squeaking." She handed a plate to the next man in line. "Only turkey for you, Carlos. I promised Maria."

Carlos pushed his hat back on his head. "Can't believe that woman finds a way to nag me when she's not even here." He took three healthy slices of turkey, paused, then added a fourth. "Damn stuff just doesn't fill me up." He added three rolls and a scoop of potato salad.

Eden sat at the table and Jaylynn placed a tall glass of iced tea in front of her, condensation rolling down the curved side. Brandi stood by the back door, distributing glass after glass to the men as they filed out to sit at the long picnic table in the yard.

"I'm going to join the boys." Jaylynn took her plate and left Brandi and Eden alone in the kitchen.

Eden watched as Brandi carefully filled her plate, taking far longer than necessary for the routine task. She turned, half-full plate clutched in both hands, her glance shifting from the open chair near Eden to the wooden screen door. Finally she sat next to Eden, her face carefully guarded.

"I take it those men work here?" Eden tried to sound casual, to help Brandi relax.

Brandi shrugged. "Some of 'em."

"Some?" Eden took a bite of macaroni, the sharp flavor sparking her taste buds, inviting her to eat more.

"Six of them work at Maple Hearth."

"Six?" At least fifteen men sat laughing with Jaylynn in the backyard.

Brandi paused, her face thoughtful. "Yep, six."

"What about the rest?"

"Just as easy to fix a little extra." Brandi tore off a bit of roll and popped it in her mouth.

"Not where I come from." More than once she'd seen someone bigger and stronger yank the last bite of food from another's mouth. It was every man for himself in the concrete jungle of L.A.

Brandi stopped chewing. "Where's that?"

Eden took a long pull of tea, thinking about her answer as the cool liquid slid down her throat. "Los Angeles." She hadn't intended to tell the truth, but sitting at Brandi's table, eating her food, the taste of Brandi's mouth fresh on her lips, it seemed the only real option.

There was a long pause as Brandi resumed chewing. She finished her roll, then said, "Going back?"

"To L.A.? No." She was revealing too much.

"Where are you headed?"

The question came faster than Eden was prepared for, and she thought carefully before answering. "Everywhere."

"Oh." If Brandi didn't understand, she gave no indication. "How about you? Going anywhere?"

Brandi laughed, but the sound wasn't happy. "Hell, no. For better or worse, this ranch is my life."

"Is that a good thing?"

Eden searched Brandi's face. Brandi moved her hands to her lap.

"Most days." Brandi didn't elaborate and her eyes said the topic was closed. "Tell me about your favorite place."

Eden took a bite of bread and chewed carefully. She thought about Brandi's question, the not-so-subtle change of subject. As much as she wanted to know the story behind the days when the ranch wasn't enough, she mostly wanted to keep Brandi seated at the table. Her plate was well on its way to empty and she didn't know how long she could hold Brandi back from her chores. She brimmed with pent-up energy, her foot tap tap tapping against the floor.

"I don't know about favorite, but this one place has always stuck in my mind. In California, just north of the border. Immigration patrols all over the place, surprise raids at the drop of a hat." The dusty town had felt hollowed out, like someone sucked the soul out the windows at night while the citizens slept. "I'd been there less than a day and had already decided to head out. I couldn't stand seeing people rounded up like cattle and herded into those vans. It was awful. I stopped on my way out of town to fuel up and grab a bite, and this old Mexican woman—must've been eighty years old—asked if she could read my palm.

"My natural instinct was to say 'hell no.' I just don't buy into all that crap. But her eyes…" Eden shivered. The empty, yet knowing depths reached to her across the distance. "They still cut through me just thinking about them."

Brandi stared, forkful of potato salad suspended mid-air. "What did she say?"

"She said I was in the wrong place. And that I'd find my answers when I stopped riding and started walking."

Eden held Brandi's gaze, waiting for her to respond. Brandi's lips parted, but no words followed. Eden ducked her head and focused on her sandwich. She didn't look at Brandi for the rest of the meal.

As soon as they finished eating, Brandi cleaned up like the house was on fire.

"The local repair shops are listed." Brandi pointed to a battered phone book resting on a shelf below an old-fashioned wall phone. Eden flashed to the six Brady children battling over the one phone while Alice fixed applesauce in the background. Had Brandi had similar battles over this phone?

Brandi made it halfway out the door when Eden stopped her by placing her hand on her arm. "Do you have any brothers or sisters?"

"No." Brandi regarded Eden's hand, then lifted her gaze to meet Eden's.

Eden pushed the slow burn of Brandi's bare skin beneath her fingers to the back of her mind. Or at least she tried to, but the persistent heat radiated up her arm and through her body like an echo through a canyon. The weight of Brandi's stare, the silent question begging to be answered, froze them together. Eden swayed a breath closer to Brandi.

Slowly the sounds of life filtered back in. Jaylynn's light soprano singing an old Alison Krauss tune as she gathered the dishes from the long table out back. The buzz of the ceiling fan making lazy circles in the living room. The hum of the refrigerator in the corner. Cheyenne pressed her face against the screen door and a low whimper vibrated from her throat.

Brandi pulled her arm away and dropped her gaze. "I better get back to work. Mom will be here if you need anything." She slipped her Stetson on her head as she stepped out the door. "Come on, dog."

Eden watched her go, dust rustling at her feet, the tight curve of her jeans rocking, and Cheyenne bouncing at her side. What would it take to keep her from climbing on her horse? Something far beyond Eden's limited ability to offer, that was certain.

❖

Brandi cursed and clamped down tighter on the unforgiving wire. Even with the right tools, barbed wire was a pain in the ass. She should have taken Rich up on his offer to complete the repair when he stopped her as she tore out of the barn riding Ranger harder than any horse deserved in this heat. Pure stubbornness kept her from saying yes. Now she needed to finish the job.

Ranger swished his tale and snorted.

"Yeah, yeah. I know. That's what I get for pushing you so hard." She looked up from her work, sweat rolling down her face and neck. Her leather gloves were heavy and slick. "Just a little more."

She twisted the wire taut and snipped the loose end. Ranger rolled his eyes.

"Stop looking at me like that. I don't know why she's here."

For a horse, Ranger had a way of cutting to the heart of every matter.

"No, I don't know how long she'll stay." Brandi straightened, stretching the sore muscles in her low back. "Best not to get attached."

Ranger pawed the ground and pushed her shoulder with his nose.

"I agree, she'd probably look real good in Levi's and ropers." She tucked her tools into the saddlebags. "Probably look better out of them."

Brandi had long since stopped questioning the wisdom of carrying on a conversation with a horse. Anyone with half a brain knew that horses make the best therapists. She shuddered to think about how much money a psychologist would charge to listen like Ranger did.

She'd been working this section of fence—and talking through her thoughts with Ranger—for several hours. The sun's low position in the sky told her that suppertime had come and gone. She needed to get home. Her mama would have her hide for being so rude to their guest, but still she held back, tweaking the ends of wire long past completion.

"Can't put it off any longer." She swung onto Ranger's back and patted him on the neck. "Let's go."

She let Ranger set the pace, his steady feet picking their way across the field. His ears twitched.

"I don't know if she'll kiss me again." Brandi finally answered the question Ranger had been asking all afternoon. "Of course I want her to. But she can't. She'll be leaving soon."

Ranger blew air between his lips.

"No, I can't make her stay." Brandi scrunched up her face. "Why would I want to? I barely know her."

Why, indeed? Her reaction to Eden was a mystery. Brandi had experienced quick, fumbling encounters in dimly lit clubs, sure. But too much beer and the ache of too long since the last time had fueled those encounters. This was different. She wasn't sure if she liked it. Whatever *it* was.

The house grew larger on the horizon and Brandi halted her informal therapy session. She didn't need to explain to her mama, or Eden, God forbid, why she was talking to a horse.

The bed of Brandi's truck was empty, no motorcycle in sight. Brandi's heart raced. Had Eden left while she was off indulging her need for time and space?

She led Ranger into the barn and blew out a sigh of relief. Eden's Ducati was parked in a corner. The sleek black machine looked out of sync with the hay and farm equipment.

Ranger paused, sniffed the polished metal, and continued to his stall.

"Your mom said I could store it here." Eden stepped out of the shadows. "I hope that's okay?"

Brandi eased Ranger's bridle off and scratched his nose. She didn't look at Eden as she prepared his bag of oats.

"If that's what Mama said, then it's all right with me."

Eden edged closer, heat radiating off her. Brandi handed her a wire brush and ducked under Ranger's neck, escaping to the other side. "You can help me brush him."

She loosened the buckles, heaved the saddle off with a grunt, and dropped it on its stand. Eden whispered in Ranger's ear as she brushed his shoulder, his coat starting to shine under her care. Brandi picked up a second brush and started on the other side. Ranger sighed into his bag of oats.

"I never brushed a horse before." Eden's voice was soft.

"Really? You must be a natural." Brandi grinned over Ranger's back at Eden. It was hard to believe that Eden had never cared for any animal, let alone a horse. Ranger was enjoying her attention, which spoke volumes as far as Brandi was concerned.

Eden patted Ranger's neck.

Brandi inspected Ranger's hooves, clearing them of dirt and debris with a small file from her back pocket.

Eden's motions slowed as she watched Brandi. "You do this every time?"

"Once a day." Brandi rose, inches away from Eden. "Ranger's a good horse. He deserves it."

Eden stared at her mouth. "Now what?"

"Now," Brandi stepped away, "I let him rest." She removed the bag of oats and hung it on the wall. "Come on." She motioned Eden out of the stall and swung the gate shut. Time to get inside and see what her mama had planned for them for the rest of the night.

❖

"Do you plan to make a habit of missing supper?" Jaylynn tapped her foot, her hands fisted on her hips. The table was cleared, dishes done, all signs of the evening meal erased. Jaylynn's way of telling Brandi that she was on her own.

"No, ma'am."

Jaylynn wore navy blue slacks and a matching blazer. Tailored lines and pressed smooth. She looked mighty fine, much younger than her sixty years. Brandi noticed the matching flats and was surprised. Five years ago Jaylynn swore she'd never wear flats. She believed that if a lady couldn't wear a nice set of heels, no matter how low, she should just stay home. "It's karaoke night at the Elks. Sure you don't want to come along?"

The last thing Brandi wanted to do any night was hang out with a group of old straight people at the Elks lodge. She straightened Jaylynn's collar, then kissed her cheek. "No, you go have fun with your friends."

"Don't wait up for me." Jaylynn laughed and headed out the

door. She paused. "Since you're staying home, do you mind bringing the wash in?" She pointed at the stark white sheets billowing on the line.

"Of course not." Brandi forced herself to stand straight and not scuff the toe of her boot against the floor. Her mom seemed bent on treating her like a child. She didn't need a reminder about laundry. That, combined with her hormones raging at her over Eden, made her feel like a blushing twelve-year-old.

"And you," Jaylynn extended a finger toward Eden, "you be sure and tell me if she runs off and leaves you alone again."

"I will." Eden's smile was a little too self-satisfied for Brandi's taste.

The door closed behind Jaylynn with a heavy click.

Eden turned to Brandi. "I'll help."

Before Eden could make it to the door, Brandi redirected her down the long hall to the laundry room. "We need to get a basket first."

Eden walked close behind Brandi. Not close enough to touch, but close enough for Brandi to feel the heat stretched tight between them. She wanted to turn and take her in her arms, hold her close. She continued down the hall. When she crossed the threshold to the laundry room, Eden placed her hand on Brandi's shoulder and spun her around. Face to face, she took a step closer, her feet between Brandi's. Brandi gasped and pressed back against the dryer.

"Why are you running away from me?" Eden's breath was uneven, making the sentence come out in choppy sections.

Brandi wanted to kiss Eden. Hard on the mouth. Hard enough to take the question out of the air and force it back where it came from. She stared at Eden's lips. Soft, inviting, begging her to do just that. She gulped air and said, "I don't know what you're talking about."

"Yes, you do."

"Eden." Brandi adopted her most brittle, ice-princess tone. "If you don't want me to run, stop chasing me like a damn dog in heat. I picked you up on the side of the road and brought you to *my home*.

And what do I get for my efforts? This." She indicated Eden's body, still kissing-close to Brandi. "I'm amazed you haven't dry-humped my leg yet."

Eden recoiled as though she'd been slapped. The last bit, Brandi realized after the words left her mouth, was a little over the top. Still, it had the desired effect. Eden was no longer flush against her, testing her resolve. Brandi's body missed the contact immediately.

"I apologize." Eden's voice was emotionally blank, her face a void.

"No," Brandi said with a sigh. "I'm sorry. It's not like I wasn't flirting with you. It's not every day I come across a too-hot-for-reality woman stranded and in need of rescue. You scrambled my brain and good manners." She looked at the wall just over Eden's left shoulder. "I just can't have a one-night stand. Not here."

"I understand." Some of the warmth returned to Eden's eyes, but she was still reserved.

"Come on," she said gently. "We need to get the laundry in." With a wicker basket on one hip, she led Eden into the cool evening air.

The white sheets danced on a light breeze and the fading sunlight played across the surface in alternating bursts of fiery red and dark shadow. It was one of those beautiful, only-in-a-movie-does-it-look-this-good kind of moments. Brandi wanted to push Pause on the sunset, hold time there for just a little longer. But the sun was fading fast and a job needed to be done. She pressed forward, breaking the spell.

They fell into sync with one another, working in harmony. It was comfortable, like a pair of faded blue jeans—perfect fit and worn soft in all the right places.

"Tell me about your ranch. What do you do here?" Eden's voice was low and quiet.

This was an easy question. She could answer it without thinking about Eden's fleeting touch. "Everything. Mostly cattle. But we also have a small herd of horses and several acres in hay, wheat, barley, and oats." She pointed toward a metal barn in the distance. "That's where we keep the bulk of the farming equipment. We're thinking about adding a field of hops. They grow well around here and the market is always good." Brandi couldn't help it. Talking about Maple Hearth excited her. She talked a little faster and gestured a little more, forgetting the sheets.

Eden smiled and moved closer to Brandi, barely room for a breath between their shoulders. "What about that?" She pointed to a building just to the left of the barn. From the outside it looked like a small college dormitory.

"That's the bunkhouse."

"I thought those only existed in Steinbeck novels."

Brandi laughed. Before they built this one fifteen years ago, she'd thought the same thing.

"Tell me more." Eden slipped her arm around Brandi's waist.

"Everything we do depends on the season. In the spring we plant. And the calves are born. It gets crazy for a few weeks." Brandi started to get carried away sharing the details of her life with Eden. It would have been easy to fall deeper into the moment, to lose herself in a long, lingering kiss. But Brandi deserved better than to be a distraction sandwiched between the sheets in the fading sunlight. She needed a reality check and she needed it quick. Brandi stepped away from Eden and changed the subject. "Did you find your part?"

"I think so. It'll probably be special order. No telling how much time it will take to get here. Then wrench time after that." Eden's smile didn't make it to her eyes.

"Do you know how long parts usually take to arrive?"

"A week or two? Not really sure."

Two weeks—three if the part didn't arrive as scheduled. Brandi had to fight her body's reaction and keep Eden at bay for a seemingly short time. Lord have mercy.

"Let's finish the sheets."

"Right." Eden nodded. "What do you do with all these?"

Brandi inclined her head toward the bunkhouse. "Gotta put something on the beds in there." She plucked a clothespin and dropped it in the bucket. "What did you think? It's not like my mom and I need twelve sets of white sheets."

"I had no idea. Maybe your mom is into expressionist art and the next time these sheets appeared they'd be covered in paint and glitter."

Brandi arched her eyebrow. "I don't think so."

In no time at all they finished taking the sheets off the line, folding as they went. Brandi told Eden stories about life at Maple Hearth and listened to stories of Eden's life on the road. Odds of her surviving the next two weeks, until the end of July, grew dimmer as the evening wore on.

CHAPTER FIVE

S team rose off Brandi's cup as she made the short trip from the house to the barn. Didn't matter how hot the summer got, mornings in southern Idaho were cool, and Brandi needed brewed caffeine to get started. Gravel crunched under her boots and echoed in the crisp morning air.

She gulped her coffee and grimaced. Black and double strong. It was hard going down, but would launch her into the day quicker than the cream-and-sugared version she normally drank. A sad substitute for a good night's sleep, but it would have to do since she didn't get that last night.

"Eden?" She poked her head into the barn and waited. No response.

The Ducati lay in pieces, disassembled in a way that Brandi hoped made sense to Eden.

Ranger pawed the ground and snorted. She was taking too long with his morning oats.

Brandi stood on the bottom rail of the stall and scratched Ranger behind both ears, the coffee forgotten on the workbench. "Hold on, I'll let you out of there." She kissed the white splotch of hair on Ranger's nose and dropped to the ground. Today she was headed into town, a job that required her truck, not her horse.

Rather than returning to the house, as was her normal practice after setting Ranger to graze, Brandi followed her impulse and returned to the barn. She justified the wasted steps with the need to retrieve her morning coffee. Never mind the fact that she'd managed to remember her cup every other day she completed this routine task.

She stood just inside the door. The amber light of the sun rising in the east streamed around her, stretching her shadow across the floor, long and lean like a character from the DC comics of her childhood. She waited, listening for signs that Eden was nearby. Eden's voice, slightly muffled, barely reached her, strained and filtered through a layer of wood. Brandi followed it to the door separating the barn proper from the makeshift office area. Constructed by her father, the room had long since been forgotten and neglected.

Unlike Brandi, who laid the books out over every surface of the sturdy kitchen table, he'd preferred to do the books away from the scrutinizing watch of his family. Privacy was the key to his most famous financial failures, like the decision to plant all the fields with potatoes several seasons in a row, depleting the soil's nutrients and forcing Brandi to leave the majority of the fields fallow during her first season as manager of Maple Hearth. She'd only returned to growing them three years ago, opting to stick with nutrient-replenishing crops, like alfalfa, for longer than traditional wisdom recommended. She wasn't interested in following the *Farmer's Almanac*. She just wanted to return her land to a healthy, productive state.

Brandi stopped a few feet from the door. Any farther and she'd be past general curiosity and well into the land of eavesdropping. She held her breath and listened.

"I'm fine." Eden sounded uncertain.

Strange. Brandi wouldn't have pegged Eden for the type to talk to herself. Maybe that's why she sought out the secluded room.

"Really, Pen, I'm okay. I swear."

Okay, she wasn't talking to herself. She must have a cell phone because Brandi had canceled the service to the land line in the barn during the months following her father's death. It was a useless expense that she'd never seen a reason for.

"No!" Eden's voice cracked. "Do *not* tell Luther."

Brandi made a note. She had two names to connect to Eden's past. Pen and Luther.

"Please, Penny, I need to stay dead. You know that."

Dead? This was why her mama taught her not to stick her nose in where it didn't belong. She invariably learned something she didn't want to know. So far, however, she'd only added to her impossibly long list of questions about Eden. No answers appeared forthcoming.

"Forget I called. I didn't want you to worry, but…" Eden's voice faded.

Brandi swayed toward the door, unwilling to take the last few steps but wanting to hear the end of the sentence nonetheless.

Cheyenne's excited barks warned Brandi away from the door seconds before Cheyenne tore into the barn. Brandi stepped hastily away from the office, turned, and caught the bounding collie mid-jump.

"Who's my good girl?" Brandi balanced the squirming dog against her body and rubbed her fur briskly with one hand, digging her nails in to scratch the way Cheyenne liked. She heard the office door open.

"Good morning, Brandi." All traces of tension were gone from Eden's voice. The warm, seductive charm was back in full effect.

"Morning." Brandi released Cheyenne and faced Eden.

Eden stood, arms folded over her chest, shoulder against the door frame, her legs crossed at the ankle. She tilted her head to the side and a curious smile teased her lips. A bright white athletic top hugged her, formed tight to her skin, and loose, worn jeans, with a small hole below the fly on the right, rested low on her hips, threatening to slide to the floor with the slightest encouragement.

Black smudges of grease stood out in contrast against her perfect, tanning-bed skin on her wrist, reaching down the top of her hand. Also on her arm, just above the pronounced curve of her bicep. The muscle grew firmer, flexed tighter as Brandi followed its line up to the pulse of life at the base of Eden's neck. Another mark there, leading down into the V between Eden's breasts. Brandi watched the rise and fall of her chest. Eden's breathing became more rapid.

"Did you need something?"

Oh, yes. She definitely needed something. But the barn floor wasn't the place to take it.

Eden stepped toward her, pulling the office door shut. Her face was hungry, determined.

"Brandi?" Eden stopped inches away. She traced the line of Brandi's jaw with her fingers, feathering them slowly over her skin.

Brandi needed to regain control or she'd be naked and spread out on a bale of hay in record time. As sexy as that looked in the movies, Brandi knew from experience that it wasn't much fun.

She stilled Eden's fingers with her own, drawing her hand down to her side and holding it there. "Town. You want to go?" As much as she wanted complete sentences, she was happy with the stilted half-thoughts that squeaked their way out. "For parts?"

Eden grabbed a rag from the workbench, her long braid swaying across her back as she turned her body. "Sounds good. Let me get cleaned up first?"

"Right. I'll meet you inside." Brandi tripped over the smooth floor, caught her balance, and made her escape to the house, nervous laughter on her lips. A poor but safe substitute for the taste of Eden's tongue.

A forty-miles-per-hour breeze poured through the windows of the truck, ruffling Brandi's hair. Eden was grateful, not for the first time, that her mother, useless as she was, had taught her how to braid hair before dedicating her life solely to the repeated pursuit of the bottom of a bottle of rum. Or vodka. Or whiskey.

"See that tree over there?"

Brandi pointed to a tree that, to Eden, looked the same as every other tree they'd passed. Eden nodded. Even if she couldn't tell one tree from another, she still wanted to hear what Brandi had to say about it. Eden was all over the emotional map about Brandi.

First, Brandi flirted with her. If they'd been in a club in Los Angeles, Eden would have fucked her on the dance floor just to listen to her come to a heavy drumbeat.

Then, when Eden's interest was piqued, Brandi pushed her away only to apologize moments later. She'd never taken the time for the go-away, come-back tug-of-war that Brandi was playing with her. The same mixed signals from any other woman would have made Eden focus only on the go-away part of the message. There were too many other women to choose from for Eden to waste her energy waiting for one to decide if she wanted her. Then again, she'd never been stranded in Idaho with nothing better to do with her time. She'd reel Brandi in eventually. She had no doubt.

"I fell out of that tree when I was seven. Broke my arm." She pointed at a time-faded scar above her elbow. "Here. The bone came clean out. My mom heard me screaming all the way from home."

"Here?" Eden touched the slightly whiter patch gently. She didn't censor the sudden impulse to comfort Brandi, but went with the moment and lowered her head, kissing the scar. She lingered too long, her warm breath bringing bumps to the surface of Brandi's skin. "All better."

Brandi stared straight ahead, her face a mask of concentration.

"What else?" Eden prompted her. Kissing Brandi's arm was a foolish indulgence. She didn't want Brandi to close up because of it.

"Right there." Brandi indicated mile marker 52. "I got my first speeding ticket. Eighty-five in a fifty. Back then, we called that a thirty-seven-dollar light show."

Brandi smiled recklessly, the freckles across her nose and the gleam in her eyes making her look much less than the thirty or so years Eden guessed her to be.

"Thirty-seven?" Eden calculated in her head. Thirty-five miles over the speed limit in L.A. would cost over $500. Not that Eden ever exceeded the posted speed. She couldn't afford even the slightest infraction. Someone in her profession didn't want to draw avoidable police scrutiny.

"It would cost a lot more now." Brandi laughed. "Everything was cheaper then, including driving stupid."

"I've never gotten a speeding ticket."

"Never?" Brandi's voice was covered with disbelief.

"Nope." Eden considered elaborating, but it would have been foolish to share her past with Brandi.

"Down that road there." Brandi nodded to the right.

Eden didn't see a road, just a dirt path that didn't look wide enough for a car. "That's a road?"

"More a trail, really, but that's not the point." Brandi tapped out a rhythm on the steering wheel, the drumbeat of the song playing on the radio. The music was too quiet for Eden to make out. "It leads to a pond where all the local kids go to swim. That pond, that's where I had my first kiss."

"You'll have to show me some time."

"The pond or the kiss?"

The pond became irrelevant. Eden wanted that kiss. Now. Before Brandi changed her mind and told her to go away again.

She shrugged. "Both."

"Want to hear about it?"

Eden's heart thudded. Was Brandi offering to talk dirty to her? Crawling down the road—too slow for the drivers of the line of farm trucks behind them, but too fast for Eden, who wanted this comfortable time with Brandi to last forever—with the late-morning sun burning through the windshield, how far would Brandi yield? Eden was willing to find out.

"Yes."

"We drove out there, a big group of us. I went because Louise Taylor—L.T.—said she was going. She looked right at me and asked, 'Who else wants to come?' She mouthed the word *you* at the end of the sentence and winked. I nodded. Pretty sure my mouth dropped open, but I couldn't speak. Nobody else even noticed. My boyfriend, Bobby, was right next to me, but he was yelling across the parking lot to some other friends. That boy was always loud. Larger than life."

Eden conjured up an image of Brandi several years younger, unsure of what was happening, but knowing she wanted it. She cast herself as L.T., cocky and dangerously flirty. She would have stood close, her mouth next to Brandi's ear, and whispered, "You want to come with me, Brandi?" She would have played hell trying to get Brandi to forget about the sweaty teenage boy clinging to her hand. Eden clenched her fists and bit her lip. "Go on," she urged.

"So I went. I rode with Bobby and L.T. drove her own car."

Again Eden pictured Brandi sitting next to her boyfriend, focused on the taillights in front of her, wishing she was in the car with L.T. instead. Eden would have seduced Brandi into her car, found some excuse for them to ride together rather than apart. And she would have flirted all the way down the broken nothing of a goat trail Brandi had pointed out.

"Bobby laughed the whole way. He'd been trying to get past first base for months. That pond promised victory to him."

"Wait." Eden was confused. "I thought you said it was your first kiss? Doesn't first base involve kissing?"

"Oh, I'd kissed boys. Starting in second grade. But they didn't count. Not really."

"Okay." Eden stared at Brandi's ripe-strawberry lips. God, she wanted to take a bite. "Go on."

"Anyway, we get to the pond and everybody's yelling and running around. Pretty soon some kids are stripping down and going swimming."

"Did you?" The answer was irrelevant. In Eden's version of Brandi's teenage adventure, Brandi was gloriously naked and begging Eden to touch her.

"Oh, hell, no. No way I was getting naked in front of Bobby. He was already too hard to handle. That would have sent him over the edge. But L.T. did." Brandi's voice grew distant. "Bobby had me pressed up against a tree, his hands inside my shirt, around my waist, and his tongue most the way down my throat. And I was bored. I'd gone there to see L.T. and all I was seeing was the near end of my patience with Bobby.

"And then she stepped into view. Bobby moved on to kissing my neck. Convenient, really, because it gave me a better view of her. She smiled and said, 'I'm going swimming.' No one else was around at that point. Just me and her. And Bobby. And she pulled her shirt over her head. She wasn't wearing a bra." Brandi hesitated, the smile in her voice holding more memory than her words. "Her breasts were oh-my-God perfect. I swear I forgot to breathe. I held Bobby tight to my neck, terrified he'd shift positions and block my view."

Brandi laughed as she made the turn onto Highway 55.

"Then she unbuttoned her shorts. Levi's. Were 501's with the button fly popular in L.A.?" She glanced over at Eden.

"Not really." But Eden could understand the appeal. Buttons popping open were pretty high up on her list of sexy. "Finish your story."

"Right. She did this sort of shimmy-shake and her shorts slid down her body. I have no idea what happened to her shoes and socks. Or her panties. But there she was. Completely, wonderfully naked. She stood there watching me watching her, with Bobby working his hand down my pants."

Eden's stomach clenched, heat spreading with Brandi's words. She squirmed in her seat, not wanting to break Brandi's concentration and pull her out of the story.

"As soon as she dove into the water, I realized how far I'd let Bobby get. His hand was inside my underwear, his fingers dangerously close to sliding into me. He moaned in my ear, saying how wonderful I was, how beautiful. How wet I was and how hard I made him. And it felt really good, him pushing against me, needing me, his mouth on my skin, sucking and kissing, his fingers groping against me, touching the right parts in spite of his desperation. And I thought about letting him do it. It was expected, after all. I'd have to do it some time, and I was so freaking turned on I thought I'd explode.

"Louise's head broke the surface of the water and she watched me. Her face was this weird mix of hurt and come-and-get-me. I pushed Bobby away and she smiled."

Eden pictured Brandi smiling at her over her boyfriend's shoulder. When Brandi pushed him away, did his hand leave a hot, slick trail on her stomach? Did he beg? "Come on, baby. You know you want it."

"He was so desperate and I hated him for being so clueless."

The teenage Brandi in Eden's mind didn't care when Bobby called her a teasing bitch. She didn't notice when he tore out, scattering gravel, leaving her to find her way home without him. She simply straightened her clothes, zipped her shorts, and waited for Louise to come to her.

"God, she was beautiful. Water dripped off her. She looked like a damn centerfold. And she said, 'Looks like your ride left you.' I nodded. That girl seriously affected my vocal cords. And my brain. I just couldn't think with her around."

Had Brandi, flooded with her first real case of teenage lust, been as lush and ripe as she was yesterday when Eden kissed her? Eden pictured her, eyes dark and wanting, skin flushed, unable to speak. That woman was just insufferably sexy. Even if she refused to play with Eden.

Eden could see the town growing on the horizon. She wanted Brandi to slow down. Hell, she wanted her to stop, to finish her story pulled to the side of the road, naked, with lots of demonstrations to make her meaning clear.

"That's when she kissed me. She tasted like mint gum, and I held on to that kiss for dear life."

Brandi stopped in front of a battered building. A sign over the front door, worn and barely hanging on by one corner, indicated they'd arrived at Roger's Repair Shop. Brandi cut the engine.

"Aren't you going to finish?"

Brandi gave Eden's thigh one last squeeze, then a pat. "Story time is over."

Eden searched Brandi's face. How far would she go? How

far would she let Eden go? Would Eden find herself, hand down Brandi's pants, up against the proverbial tree, only to be told, "No, this fire's not for you."

Brandi's mouth curved into a half-smile and she climbed out of the truck. "Come on. I have work to do."

Eden climbed the dust gray steps leading into Roger's, little puffs of dirt scattering beneath her boots. Brandi paused at the end of the street and waved as she entered an office building.

A bell tinkled over Eden's head as she stepped into the repair shop. She tried to mentally shake off Brandi's effect. Brandi was right, there was work to be done. But maybe Brandi would finish her story on the way home.

Eden carved out the letters B-R-A-N-D-I in the thick layer of dust on the counter while she waited for Roger to check on her part. The smell of old grease and oil choked the air as Eden watched the single remaining blade on the box fan in the corner wobble around its axis. Roger coughed, a deep, lung-rattling cough that rumbled through the room like a freight train. Eden brushed away the letters when Roger ambled in from the back room.

"Well…" Roger added an extra *p* to the end of *well* so it sounded more like *welp*. "I found it."

"Awesome." Eden couldn't believe her luck. She thought sure she'd have to wait for the part.

"But it's not available in the U.S."

Fuck. Of course not. Next time Eden would listen to her inner voice when it screamed at her to buy a Honda, for the love of God. Parts would be easier to find. She'd squelched the protest as she signed the bill of sale for the Ducati, sure she didn't have a reason to give in to her grandmotherly impulse of better-safe-than-sorry.

"Okay." She pushed out a sigh. "Tell me what my options are."

Roger spat a quarter-sized wad of chewing tobacco across the room, and it landed in the metal trash can with a zing. "Well," he scratched his forehead, making his ball cap ride up, "I can order it, but it'll take a couple of weeks to come in."

Double fuck.

"That's my only choice?"

Roger smoothed his hair flat and snugged his grease-stained John Deere cap into position. "I know a guy in Portland. He might be able to pull a used one off a bike in his yard." Roger's face said success was doubtful at best with that option.

Eden smoothed her hands over her eyes. A used part out of somebody's yard—somebody in Portland, the land of rain, no less—or two weeks from Europe. Maybe she should just fly to Europe and pick it up herself. It'd be quicker.

She nodded. "Let's order it."

The brass bell sounded behind her and Roger smiled—a tortured half-grimace that said he wasn't really happy but smiling was his best plan of attack. "One second." He held up a finger to Eden and greeted the newcomer. "I'm still working on it, Frankie. Damn thing is giving me fits."

"Now don't talk about her like that. She's a sweetheart and you know it."

Roger's face softened, genuine fondness playing in his eyes. "Sweet or not, she's still not ready." He shook his head, including Eden with the gesture. "What is it with you young folk and your foreign bikes?"

Eden smiled for lack of a better response. With the exception of Harley and Indian, every motorcycle in the U.S. was foreign. "What do you have?" she asked the man—Frankie.

"A Norton. She's a beauty. Bought her at an estate auction in Star a year back. Roger's had her ever since."

Roger grunted. "She's fickle."

"Oh, it's all right. I still claim visiting rights. And I don't believe those rumors about Roger riding it around town after midnight when everyone else is supposedly asleep."

Eden looked at the calendar on the wall, sure she had stepped back in time to Mayfield in the fifties. Sheriff Andy and little Opie would walk through the door any moment.

Frankie grinned like a little boy with his first model car. "Want to see her?" he asked Eden.

Roger flipped a ring of keys to Frankie. "You know the way. I'll stay here and see to ordering her part."

The Norton was flawless—polished and sparkling and not a speck of dust or grime on it. Eden wanted to go for a ride. After midnight when the rest of the town was asleep would be absolutely fine by her.

"Does it run?"

Roger turned the key to the on position and kicked the starter. Perfect. No hesitation, no rough idle. Just the beautiful purr of a well-tuned engine.

"What's left to fix?"

Frankie revved the motor. "Not a damn thing."

"I don't get it."

"My wife hates it. When I bought it she threatened to change the locks while I was at work the next day. I brought it to Roger and never mentioned it to her again. When I got home that night, she had the doorknobs disassembled, new ones still in the box waiting to go up."

Eden couldn't imagine loving someone enough to give up her Ducati. Even now with it lying in pieces in Brandi's barn, she wouldn't give it up.

"By the way, I'm Eden." After sharing a story like Frankie's, she figured he deserved to know her name.

He gave her an aw-shucks look and shook her hand. "I know. You're staying at Maple Hearth with Jaylynn and her girl, Brandi."

"How'd you—?"

"Hell, everybody knows." He shrugged. "That's the way it works 'round here."

She thought Luther's network of spies was impressive, but they had nothing on this one-horse town.

They spent a few more minutes admiring the showroom-ready Norton before going their separate ways. Frankie headed back to work and Eden returned to the office part of Roger's Repair Shop.

Roger was deep in conversation with someone, a thick parts manual open on the counter.

"Nope, that's it. Just the one. All right? Send me the invoice." He ended the call and closed the book. "Done."

"That's it? One phone call?" Eden was impressed. Not many repair shops would dial direct overseas to order a part.

"Yep. When his son comes by later today, or maybe tomorrow, he'll place the order on his computer." The way Roger emphasized the word *computer* indicated that he likened the bit of technology to a venereal disease or an unpleasant medical procedure involving a latex glove and Vaseline.

"You don't have a computer?"

Roger spat.

"I guess not." Eden was at a loss. To her knowledge, she'd never known a person who didn't own a computer. "Should I pay you now? Or…?"

"Just wait until the invoice comes in, that'll be fine."

Roger narrowed his eyes, focused on the dust-covered window, his brow furrowed. Eden turned to see what had caught his attention. Two men were walking on the sidewalk across the street, close, but not touching. Their heads were tipped together, their smiles soft and intimate.

Surely Idaho wasn't so backward that the sight of two men, obvious lovers, was enough to upset Roger.

"It's not right." Roger clenched his jaw.

Eden waited in silence. Blatant homophobia made her stomach ache.

Roger turned toward the back room without further comment. Their conversation was clearly over.

"Right, well, thank y…" Eden called to his retreating back.

Such an odd place, Idaho. But at least the two-week delay had one bright side—more time to spend with Brandi. Eden left the repair shop, eager for a little lunch and an opportunity to share the news. They had two weeks, at a minimum, to get to know each other. How well depended entirely on Brandi.

CHAPTER SIX

Brandi buttoned her shirt up to the collar—too late to keep Bobby from peeking at her cleavage—took a deep breath, and stepped inside Daniel Leightner's office.

"Brandi." Daniel wrapped her in a bear hug, lifting her off the ground.

"Good to see you, Dan." Brandi patted his back and allowed his enthusiasm to calm her. No matter how many years went by, Daniel Lieghtner would always be the immovable rock whose protective veil encompassed all those around him. This was a man she could trust with her home. Or so she hoped.

Daniel rolled his sleeves up to his elbows and gestured for Brandi to sit. "Damn air-conditioning is on the fritz. Repair guy won't be out until Monday." Beads of sweat clung to Daniel's upper lip, and his bald scalp shone with perspiration. He pulled a bottle of water from the refreshment cooler behind the door. "You want some water or something?" He lingered in the open door of the fridge, reaching for a second bottle of Aquafina, a hopeful smile on his face.

"No, thanks. You go ahead." As much as Brandi liked Daniel, she didn't want to prolong their meeting.

Daniel settled behind his desk, the wooden desk chair creaking under his weight. "Bobby mentioned you might come see me. How can I help?"

Help? Brandi choked down her immediate response. It was not helpful to have her friends waiting to pick her bones clean while she struggled to stay financially afloat. Still, she reminded herself, Bobby and Daniel were not to blame for her father's poor judgment.

"I might need to sell some land." Brandi gripped the seat of her chair, but she hoped her voice sounded deceptively calm. "Can you tell me what that process would be like?"

Daniel described in excruciating detail about zoning laws and how to split lots. Brandi's brain swelled like a saturated sponge. The government, it seemed, was in favor of splitting up large land holdings like hers. She stood to make a a great deal of money.

"I don't want to sell it all, Daniel. Just enough to clear my debt."

"Of course." The phone on Daniel's desk rang. "Excuse me a moment, Brandi. My receptionist is at lunch." He answered the phone like a man with money on his mind, the carefully cultivated, completely false interest of a salesman.

Brandi let her gaze wander. Framed pictures covered the walls of Daniel's office. Daniel and Bobby at seventeen in their football uniforms. The whole team, baby-faced and fierce. Him with his high school friends, including Brandi in her too-small, itchy cheerleader uniform. Daniel and Bobby, suntanned and smiling, on the deck of a boat, a large fish between them. Daniel and Bobby cutting the ribbon on the new strip mall, built on what used to be Ron Plimb's land.

Realization settled in her heart. History or not, Daniel wasn't looking to help her. Unless she wanted a similar development for her new neighbor, she couldn't sell her land.

"No, she's still here." Daniel smiled at her and mouthed the word *sorry*. "We haven't discussed the details yet." Daniel struck up a muffled cadence with his thumb against the desk. "No." Pause. "Not yet." Another pause. "I can't answer that."

Brandi had heard enough. She stood and said, "I've made up my mind, Dan. I won't be selling."

Daniel's hand sagged, holding the phone midway between the desk and his ear. Brandi could hear Bobby's voice asking what was wrong. She closed the door as Daniel rose to his feet, a confused, open-mouthed expression on his face.

❖

Every table at Brenda's House of Pie was occupied save one in the corner. Brandi wanted to sit by the window and look out over Main Street, to show Eden her world over a piece of strawberry-rhubarb with cream. Still, sidewalk or cracked plaster, it wouldn't change the fact that Brenda's served the best pie in town. Bar none.

Brandi grabbed a couple of menus from the jumbled stack next to the clanking cash register. Tina, Brenda's youngest daughter, zipped down the aisle in front of them, white nurses' shoes for comfort and short ass-hugging skirt for show. Eden tilted her head and grinned at Brandi. For her part, Brandi looked straight ahead, keeping her eyes focused well above the hypnotic sway of Tina's hips.

"You having the usual?" Tina, heir apparent to Brenda's pie empire, wore a T-shirt printed with the words "Wanna taste my cherry pie?" The logo was written over a screen-printed image of Brenda herself. The question never failed to elicit all manner of naughty thoughts from Brandi, but the image chased them away before they fully formed.

"Give us a few minutes, Tina." Brandi sat with her back to the door—her least favorite position—because Eden beat her to the seat facing the room. "Eden needs to check the menu."

"Holler when you're ready."

Eden looked over the menu, her body at attention. "Do they serve actual food here or just pie?"

"Pie is food, you know," Brandi teased.

The light didn't quite reach the corner, leaving Eden's face obscured in shadows. She pulled her bottom lip between her teeth, worrying it as she studied the menu. A few strands of carefully controlled hair had worked their way free from her braid.

"Do you always wear your hair back like that?"

"What?" Eden slid her thumb up the menu, marking the place where she left off. "My hair? Usually, yes. It gets in the way otherwise."

Brandi pictured it flowing loose over Eden's shoulders the night before. "What does it get in the way of?"

Eden met her gaze and held it. Quiet and serious she said, "A lot of things." Then she went back to reading the menu.

Brandi knew exactly what she would order. A turkey and cranberry sandwich followed by a piece of lemon meringue. Strawberry-rhubarb was flashier and drew a crowd, but Brandi's taste buds demanded lemon meringue every time.

After several moments, Eden laid the menu face down on the table and Tina, always observant, yelled from behind the split wall separating the dining room from the kitchen area. "What did you decide?"

Eden looked at Brandi, apparently waiting for her to take the lead.

"She knows what I'm having. What do you want?"

"Really? This is the way you order in Idaho?"

"It's the way you order at Brenda's if you want to get served."

Eden shook her head and turned in her seat to face Tina. "Roast beef on white rye with havarti."

Tina blinked twice, like she didn't understand.

"What's wrong?" Eden asked Brandi.

"You didn't order pie."

"I'm supposed to do that now?"

Brandi nodded and laughed.

"Surprise me?"

Tina tilted her head to the side and pursed her lips. Half a tick later, she said, "Key lime."

Brandi agreed. Eden, like the pie, had a little bite and left her wanting more.

"So, you going to tell me any more stories about the wonder years?"

"Maybe. If you're good."

"Good at what?"

Mercy. Brandi no longer wanted to share the stories, she wanted to demonstrate. Starting with that kiss by the pond. Only without Bobby.

Instead she opted to change the subject. "Did you get the part you need?"

"I think so."

Tina set their plates on the table, along with two tall glasses of iced tea.

"Swear to God, I've never drank so much tea in my life."

"Really? I thought tea was the new coffee for you big-city L.A. types."

"That's true." Eden swirled sugar into the liquid with her straw. "But not the iced kind. And only if it sounds pretentious, like mint–passion fruit infusion or something."

"Yuck." Brandi scrunched up her nose. Passion fruit she could understand. And mint made for some tasty gum. The two together seemed to violate nature. "So tell me what happened at Roger's."

"He called a guy who has a kid." She pulled a string of beef from the edge of her sandwich and nibbled on it. "And the kid, apparently, has a computer."

Brandi laughed. "You're lucky he didn't call the manufacturer while you were there. Listening to him curse an automated system is a real treat."

"Maybe so," Eden shrugged, "but I still don't know if I'll get my part."

"When did he say it would be here?" Brandi had conducted business with Roger enough times to know he didn't let Eden leave without an expectation about when the part would arrive.

Eden swallowed hard, her bite of sandwich obviously not chewed sufficiently. "Two weeks, at least."

"Two weeks." Brandi took a bite of turkey and chewed slowly. "You know you're welcome to stay with us."

Eden's smile lacked conviction.

Again she changed the subject, eager to release Eden from whatever emotional reaction she was having. "He has a computer, he's just afraid to use it."

"Tragic. Enough talk of parts. Tell me more about your pond."

"There's nothing else to tell. She kissed me. I melted. Then she gave me a ride home."

Eden looked nonplussed and took a savage bite of her sandwich, chewing as she asked, "And? What happened next? Did you have a passionate love affair? Did she break your heart? Where is she now?" With each question, Eden edged forward, her elbows inching across the table.

Eden's curiosity amused Brandi. Was she always like this? Or did blooming adolescent lesbianism bring it out in her?

"L.T. left for college that fall. We had a couple of other fumbling encounters that were…" Brandi paused, wanting the perfect word to illustrate how important those moments of discovery with Louise really were. "Enlightening. Life changing."

With lunch most of the way gone, Tina dropped off their pie. An extra dollop of whipped cream topped Eden's, and Brandi felt a surge of proprietary ownership. If Tina wanted somebody special to whip cream for, she could find her own stranded biker and leave Eden for Brandi.

"And, where is she now?"

"New York, last I heard." Brandi took a generous bite of lemon meringue. She'd work it off later taking down that burned-out cottonwood tree. "I don't really know for sure. How 'bout you? You know where your first kiss is?"

Eden stopped smiling and eased back in her chair. "L.A., where I left her."

The door on their conversation slid shut with a tangible thud as Tina eased the check onto the table.

"It's on me." Eden laid her hand over the bill, palm down, before Brandi had a chance to register that it was even there.

She said a mental prayer of thanks that people in Idaho didn't feel the need to move that quickly all the time. With the summer heat and no air-conditioning, Brandi felt like she was navigating through dry, yet somehow sticky, soup most days. She wouldn't be able to move that fast even if she wanted to.

Eden left a tip that was L.A. obvious in its generosity and exited Brenda's without finishing her pie. Brandi scooped the last bite of lemon into her mouth and hustled out the door behind her.

❖

A ragged-edged sheet of notebook paper with wobbly block letters was taped to the door at Roger's.

CHECK AROUND BACK

Eden tried the knob anyway. It was locked.

"He was here an hour ago." In L.A. businesses stayed open all day. They didn't close at one in the afternoon.

Brandi tapped the paper. "He's still here. Come on."

"Seriously?"

"Do you still want to talk to him or did you change your mind?"

"Fine, let's go."

As a general rule, Eden avoided unknown alleys. It was impossible to gauge ahead of time what would be waiting at the other end. And in her profession, or rather *ex*-profession, that spelled certain death. She placed a hand on Brandi's arm as they rounded the corner, keeping her close. "You sure this is a good idea?"

Brandi looked puzzled. "Why wouldn't it be?" She pulled Eden along the dirt path separating Roger's from the hardware store. The opening was wide enough for an economy car, but too narrow for the farm trucks that populated the town.

A muffled Skoal-laced grumbling grew louder with each step.

"Roger?" Brandi called. "You back here?"

A dull thump followed by a loud clanking noise confirmed that Roger was close by. "Yes, dammit."

They rounded the corner and found him shaking his hand, the thumb a swollen purplish color.

"What are you two doing, sneaking up on a man like that?"

Brandi walked past Roger and entered the shop through a rusty screen door that squeaked with neglect. "Roger, you're working on small engines. What are you doing taking a hammer after one of them?" She re-emerged with a bag of frozen vegetables, which she pressed gently to Roger's injured appendage. "Sure you want him working on your Ducati?"

Roger seemed to notice Eden for the first time. "Oh, hell." He held his hand like an injured paw. "I forgot you said you're staying with Brandi. If that don't just spell trouble."

"Now be nice. We want her to think people from 'round here are friendly."

"Why do we want her to think that?"

"Then maybe she'll stay." Brandi focused on Roger's thumb, almost like the words were intended for it alone, rather than Roger or Eden. Her voice was so soft, Eden wondered if she'd spoken at all.

Roger pulled his hand away from Brandi. "Stop your fussing." He held the makeshift ice pack in place. "Tell me what you're doing here."

"Eden's worried about her part."

Roger snorted. "I told her I ordered it."

Brandi patted his arm and winked at Eden. "No, you told her you made a phone call to have someone else order it. That makes city folks nervous."

"Well, it shouldn't. You know it'll get here."

"I know, but let's turn on your computer and make her feel better."

Roger looked skeptical.

"It's like a car, Roger. You have to let it run every once in a while or it forgets how."

Brandi held the door open and he shuffled through. Eden followed.

"Still don't see why we can't do it my way."

"You already have. Let's just check on it."

The computer—a sleek iMac with a twenty-four-inch screen—was buried behind a haphazard clump of papers and manuals. Roger slid them to the side and looked at Brandi expectantly. Brandi pushed the power button on the machine and it blinked to life.

"Are these all invoices?" Eden inspected the pile.

"I'll get to 'em." He moved the papers to the other counter, next to a disassembled carburetor.

While Brandi and Roger navigated through several Web sites looking for the right part, Eden sorted through the pile of invoices, separating the payable from the receivable. This was her home. Granted, the results of her attention to detail occasionally got bloody, like with the college boys in San Francisco, but her ability to track money, not pull a trigger, was what made her effective in her former profession. Being able to shut off her emotions when needed certainly didn't hurt, but her worth was in the details. She made it through a third of the stack before Brandi claimed her attention.

"Eden, we're good to go."

The computer screen showed an order confirmation from Ducati.

"I'd rather just call Junior and let him take care of this."

"Don't forget to tell him that you already did it. Eden doesn't need two."

Roger noticed the work Eden had done while he was preoccupied with the computer. "What's all this?"

Eden took her cue from Brandi and responded with a directive, rather than an actual answer to his question. "You leave that alone." She pointed at him, then the paperwork. "I'll be back to finish tomorrow."

"Now wait a minute." Roger's protest was halfhearted, even to Eden, who didn't know the man well.

"It can sit in three piles instead of one until I finish with them. All you have to do is continue to ignore them." Eden was halfway out the door by the time she finished the sentence. She didn't want to argue with him. She just wanted to help him get paid. It wasn't what she'd planned for her time in Idaho. Hell, she hadn't planned to *spend* time in Idaho. But since she was here, she had to find something to occupy her time besides dreaming up naughty things to do to Brandi.

CHAPTER SEVEN

The truck crawled down the highway at an excruciating fifteen miles per hour. Eden, after spending the majority of her driving time in Los Angeles traffic jams, fought the urge to reach over and announce her irritation with the horn.

"What the hell is that thing?" Eden asked, gesturing toward the slow-moving piece of farm equipment. With faded and scratched fire engine red paint and metal arms extended upward, it looked like a prop from a science fiction movie.

"An International Harvester," Brandi said, her voice tight and distant.

"Okay"—Eden had no idea what that meant—"but what *is* it? And why is it on the road?"

Brandi glanced at Eden, then expanded her explanation. "It's a piece of equipment used to harvest crops. It's on the road because it doesn't have four-wheel drive."

Eden let the subject drop. Apparently, Brandi wasn't in the mood to discuss slow-moving, sci-fi looking farm equipment. "How was your meeting?"

"Fine."

On second thought, maybe Brandi wasn't in the mood to talk at all. Eden watched field after field crawl by in silence. Why didn't they label the crops so she'd know what she was looking at? After a couple of miles and countless unidentifiable plants, the harvester turned into a field.

"Thank God," Eden said as they accelerated to highway speed. "How does that not make you crazy?"

"He's just doing his job." Brandi shrugged.

The silence irritated Eden. How was she supposed to flirt if she wasn't even allowed to talk? "You have any more stories to share about Louise Taylor and your wayward adventures?" Eden prodded Brandi, hoping to draw her out.

"Plenty." Brandi offered a lazy, sexy smile and Eden's stomach dropped to her knees. "But first tell me something about you, your first kiss."

"First kiss? Or first time with a girl?"

"Whichever one meant more."

"My first kiss was with a boy named Peter in his backyard." Eden remembered her excitement, the way she'd held her breath as Peter slanted his head to kiss her. And then she waited for the thrill she'd heard her friends talk about. She'd opened her mouth and let him push his tongue inside. "I felt nothing. Mostly I wanted him to stop."

"So tell me about the first kiss that made you feel something."

"Penny." Days after kissing Peter, she'd led a giggling Penny under cover of night to the same spot. The location, Eden had reasoned, was fine. The execution, however, left a lot to be desired. While Peter slept safely in his bed a few feet away, Eden pulled Penny close and nervous laughing tension replaced the easy fun that had inspired the midnight escapade and left a layer of bumps on her skin. "We were both scared and excited. And rather than holding my breath, I forgot to breathe."

"Big difference."

"Yeah. And her skin was so…soft." She had trailed her hands down Penny's arms, bumps—like the ones that covered Eden—were there, rising in the wake of Eden's touch. The moment with Peter had been perfunctory, something they were expected to do eventually, so why not do it with each other? With Penny the reasons for doing it dissipated into the crisp night air, chasing the reasons for not doing it and getting lost in the pale moonlight that glinted over Penny's eyes.

Her deep cocoa irises darkened to coffee as Eden stared, daring not to blink. The moment felt like it was carved out of fairy tales. It felt the way it was *supposed* to feel with Peter. "And her eyes got all big and round, like she couldn't believe what was happening."

"I remember that feeling. And you're praying that she won't run away." Brandi squeezed Eden's leg, then returned her hand to the steering wheel.

"I was freaked out, but couldn't stop myself." Eden remembered how she'd moved in, tilting her head to the side and easing forward slow enough for Penny to stop her, say no, step away, anything. A shiver had worked its way across Penny's skin as she held perfectly still, waiting. Her heart pounding loud enough to drown out an entire drum line, Eden had raised her hand, then rubbed her thumb along Penny's bottom lip. "I even asked if it was okay. My voice came out all squeaky." Eden hadn't recognized the half-choked whisper as she trembled under Penny's startled scrutiny. She'd hated to ask the question. What if Penny said no? What if Penny ran away? What if Penny told all their friends at school? What if Penny never talked to her again?

"But she said yes?" Brandi prompted.

"She didn't answer, actually. I think she got tired of waiting for me to grow some balls." Without a sound, Penny had closed the distance between them, the slow gentle brush of her lips followed by the impossibly soft stroke of her tongue as it slipped into Eden's mouth. Eden dissolved into her, clinging and desperate with the flush of excitement. "Before I knew it, she'd kissed me." That kiss, her first *real* kiss, hadn't been terribly different than the one she shared with Peter. It was still clumsy and unsure. But the tingling energy that raced through her and left her breathless was nothing at all like the way she felt after Peter kissed her. He left her mentally sticky, unsure, and confused. Penny stole her ability to think.

"It sounds nice."

"It was." Better than nice, in Eden's opinion. That moment had defined a large part of who she would become, and she'd shared it with her best friend.

"What happened after that?"

Brandi slowed and turned into the long drive leading up to Maple Hearth.

"Penny was a lot of firsts for me." Eden pointed toward the house. "But it looks like story time is over for now."

The dogs swarmed the truck when they reached the house.

"Wait," Brandi said as Eden reached for the door handle. "One more question?"

Eden nodded. She was willing to prolong their return to the real world. As long as they stayed in the cab of Brandi's truck, she could dwell on the heat strung between her and Brandi, the rising tide of passion, and plot her next attempted seduction. She didn't have to think about Luther, Penny, and the heavy weight of failing to keep her brother safe.

"You know my family. Tell me about yours."

Did she *know* Brandi's family? She'd met Jaylynn, a few ranch hands, her dogs, and Ranger. But what about her father? They'd both shared abbreviated versions of the other's life and Eden wasn't ready to make hers available to Brandi. The memories of Gabriel—sharp and dangerous like broken glass—were hers to protect, not expose. Not yet. Maybe never.

"Actually, I don't." She sidestepped. "Tell me about your dad?"

Heavy silence grew between them. Finally, Brandi sighed and massaged her temple. "I suppose I have to answer that since I'm the one who brought it up."

Eden didn't respond.

The dogs clamored for attention and Eden wondered if they could bounce through the open window.

"Cheyenne, settle." The command was soft, but Cheyenne immediately sat and the others followed her lead. "My father... Where to begin?"

"You don't have to tell me if you don't want to."

"It's not that. It's just so hard to do him justice. He was complicated."

"Start with something you loved."

"He was so *alive*. Does that make sense? He did everything full-on, no regrets. He was kind and generous. He was a man that people listened to. They came to him for help, for answers."

"Sounds like a good man."

Brandi nodded. "When I was little, he'd take me into town and throw me up on his shoulders. I was so proud. He was my daddy and he loved me." Brandi's voice grew softer with every word.

"But?"

"There's always a but, isn't there?" She drew her mouth together in a tight smile. "But he wasn't very good to my mom. He ran around when he should have been at home. And he was bad with money."

Given the men Eden grew up around, Brandi's dad sounded like a saint, flaws and all. "That's not so bad."

"No, it's just hard to remember the good when the bad had a longer-lasting effect. I was very angry when I first realized all the things he'd done to my mom."

Clearly there was more to that story than Brandi was sharing. Eden reached out for Brandi, stopping just shy of touching her. The constant rebuff almost made her retract her hand. She wasn't afraid to face down a room full of gun-wielding dealers, but an Idaho farm girl made her timid? Finally she rested her hand on Brandi's shoulder. She didn't pat or rub or make any of the other little gestures of uncomfortable consolation. She just held her hand there and hoped the weight and heat would make Brandi feel better.

"And I was just as mad at *her*. Why would she *let* him do those things?"

"It's not that simple." Eden understood that people often did things they didn't want for reasons others couldn't see or understand.

"It never is, is it?" Brandi regarded Eden, her eyes red-rimmed and shining.

"Where is he now?"

"He died a few years back."

"Oh." Eden didn't know what else to say. She had ended too many lives to count, but she only mourned the loss of one.

"Yeah, oh." Brandi wiped her eyes and grabbed her hat from the dash. "We should get inside. But don't think I'm letting you off the hook." Brandi hopped out of the truck and hugged her dogs, her boots kicking dust up into the cab.

How could Eden ever tell Brandi about her past? About Gabriel? Brandi lived in a world where right and wrong were clearly divided. And the line was drawn much higher than Eden could ever hope to rise. No, her past needed to stay safely buried. As much as she wanted to deny it, Brandi's judgment had the power to hurt Eden.

Eden followed Brandi into the house, her movements slow and deliberate as she thought of a suitable family history to offer next time Brandi asked the question.

❖

The smell of cooking bacon and fresh coffee filled the house. Eden stretched the sleep out of her body and sat up in bed. No one from L.A. would ever look for her here. Who would believe it? Eden Metcalf, ice princess of Luther Wade's drug empire, wearing off-the-shelf farm clothes, working in a falling-down repair shop, and sleeping in a twin-sized bed outfitted with homemade blankets. Hell, *she* didn't believe it. Yet here she was. And happy about it.

Eden slipped into a pair of baggy sweats and T-shirt that smelled of fresh air and Brandi's detergent, then made her way to the kitchen. She faltered when she heard Brandi and Jaylynn arguing.

Brandi's voice, tense and modulated, was almost too low to hear. "They want to chop it up and sell the bits and pieces. I'll never let that happen."

"You may not be able to stop it." Jaylynn sounded tired, her response little more than a resigned sigh.

"I'll think of something else."

"What, Brandi?" Jaylynn's voice grew fainter, like she'd moved to the other side of the room. "Where are you going to come up with ninety-six thousand?"

"I don't know."

"I have a date this afternoon."

It seemed a strange change of subject to Eden.

"Please, don't go." This time Brandi sounded tired.

"Brandi, we can't keep sitting on the tracks hoping the train won't reach us."

Eden pictured herself astride Ranger, riding up in the nick of time to free Brandi and her mom from the ropes tying them down. Brandi would throw her arms around Eden's neck and kiss her as the train roared past them.

"There has to be a better way."

"A better way for what?" Eden asked as she entered the kitchen.

"Nothing." Brandi scooped up the papers scattered across the table, then closed her laptop. "Ready for breakfast?" Her hands trembled slightly.

Jaylynn poured a steaming cup of coffee and handed it to Eden. "Here you go, honey." She didn't offer cream and sugar. Eden liked that she remembered how she took it.

The strong blend scorched her tongue on the fist sip. Eden blew gently over the surface. The rigid line of Brandi's body worried Eden. Stress radiated off her, filling the room with tension. Eden ignored the cautionary voice that warned her to stay out of it. "Listen," she said, "if you need money..."

Brandi walked out, leaving Eden alone with Jaylynn.

"Brandi's a little wound up this morning. Don't you worry about it." Jaylynn handed Eden a plate. "Eat your breakfast."

"But I could help."

"This is something Brandi needs to work out on her own." Jaylynn patted Eden on the shoulder on her way out of the kitchen.

Eden nodded and scooped up a forkful of scrambled eggs. The answer to her question was on the papers Brandi had left behind, stacked neatly on top of her Dell. Eden stared at the documents. After several long moments, she shook her head and looked away. The last thing she needed was to get dragged into Brandi's family drama.

❖

Eden read the notices on Roger's bulletin board. There was a flock of sheep for sale. Wait, do sheep come in a flock? Or a herd? Brandi would know. It was whelping time for the Dunson family. *Whelping time?* Eden sipped her coffee. She needed to learn a whole new language to understand the events in rural Idaho.

Roger rustled over to her. "Looking for a new ride?"

"No." Eden rested her weight against the board, legs crossed at the ankles, and drained her coffee cup. "Just taking a break."

"You know you don't have to do all that." Roger gestured vaguely toward the desk.

"I have to do something." Eden would rather be back at Maple Hearth with Brandi, but spending time with her was just too confusing. She drew Eden to her, only to push her away with her words.

"You could be helping Brandi and her mama." It was an undisguised indictment.

Eden shook her head. "They don't need anything from me."

Roger grunted. "Shows what you know."

"No, really, I offered." Eden was still smarting from Brandi's sharp refusal earlier that day.

"That girl has too much pride."

Eden didn't know what to do with that assertion so she changed the subject. "Don't you have kids, Roger?"

He snorted. "Yeah. Who do you think bought that damned computer you've been working on? Sure as hell wasn't me."

Eden had wondered about that. Technophobes like Roger didn't own iMacs. "How many?"

"Two boys." Roger packed his bottom lip with chew and pointed at a flyer with a meaty finger. "Brandi likes to dance."

Town fair in a few days. Games, food, rides, and dancing.

"Hmm." What the hell was she supposed to say to that? Was the old guy playing matchmaker for the local lesbian or did he just cast Eden in the role of wingman?

"What? You don't like to dance?"

Eden glanced at the flyer then headed to the sink. "I like to dance," she said as she rinsed out her mug. What would Brandi wear to a hometown fair? An image of Brandi in tight-fitting blue jeans, polished boots, and button-down Western-style shirt two-stepping around a hardwood floor morphed into a the dimly lit, teeth-melting thumpa-thumpa club scene in Los Angeles. Mentally she traded Brandi's practical farm wear for a fatal black dress, hair teased and sparkling—glitter covered everything in the black-light-filled dance clubs—and a come-hither sway that melted Eden's panties.

"Then what's the problem?" Roger's gruff voice interrupted her thoughts.

A warm breeze blew in through the rusty screen door, rustling the stack of invoices. Eden sat at the desk and placed one palm on top of the stack. Maybe if she just went back to work, Roger would forget the question and leave her alone.

Roger didn't move away from the bulletin board. "Well?" His sandpaper voice was softer than usual.

Eden lifted her gaze to meet his. She didn't know this town, this man. What would be the point of testing the homo-friendly waters, so to speak? Roger didn't lower his eyes and they looked at each other, evaluating, for several heartbeats.

Finally, she sighed. "I don't want to watch Brandi dance with a bunch of farm boys."

"You don't know Brandi at all if you think that's what she'd do."

Eden remembered Roger's reaction to the two men walking together on the day she first met him. The bigoted grumblings from that day didn't reconcile with his blatant attempts to play matchmaker between her and Brandi.

The bell signaled the arrival of a customer and Roger shook his head and shuffled to the front of the building.

Eden agreed. She didn't know Brandi at all. But she wanted to.

CHAPTER EIGHT

Common sense pleaded with Brandi to go back to Maple Hearth before she did something stupid. She paused at the mouth of the alley, the reusable shopping bag dangling in her hand.

"Why am I even here?" Christ, now she was talking to herself without Ranger around to hold up his end of the conversation. The list of chores she should have been doing was too long for comfort, yet here she was, chasing after something she could never have. Brandi squared her shoulders and walked down the alley. No point in turning around now.

Eden was sitting at the desk, fingers flying over the keyboard, a bright yellow pencil tucked behind her ear. Her long braid divided the surface of her back, and the tension in her shoulders called to Brandi. Eden carried herself with haunted strength, a purpose that Brandi might never understand. Even without knowing Brandi's struggles, Eden offered her help, sure she could find a solution. And Brandi was tempted, but she didn't want Eden to increase her burden by sharing Brandi's troubles. Still, she was drawn to Eden. She felt safer. Eden would catch her fall.

Until she left.

Brandi forced the reality of Eden's nomadic plans to the front of her mind. She couldn't afford to lose sight of that detail. Eden was just passing through on her way to nowhere.

"Are you going to come in?" Eden asked without slowing her rapid-fire typing.

Brandi stepped through the door. "How'd you know?"

Eden turned and regarded her. She tapped her nose. "You smell better than Roger."

Brandi sniffed her shirt. Laundry detergent and Ranger. "Eau de Horse." Her ears felt hot. Too bad she didn't own any nice cologne.

Eden crossed to Brandi, took her Stetson, and settled it on her own head. She toyed with the edges of Brandi's hair. "I like the way you smell."

Brandi's scalp tingled as Eden's touch grew bolder. She outlined Brandi's ear and cupped her cheek, then nuzzled the curve of her neck. The edge of Brandi's hat, now on Eden's head, scratched against Brandi's cheek, then fell to the ground as Eden brushed her lips against her collarbone. When Eden's hot breath surfed across her skin, cascading into the open collar of her shirt, Brandi's lungs arrested, caught between inhale and exhale.

"Fresh, scrubbed clean, mixed with tangy sweat." Eden licked the curve of Brandi's neck. "It's very sexy."

Blood roared through Brandi's ears. Her brain screeched out "run," but her legs were rooted to the floor. She swayed closer to Eden and curled her fingers around the bottom hem of Eden's shirt. Pinpricks of heat fanned out from her throat down through her chest as Eden sucked the sensitive skin below her ear. Her eyes drifted shut.

"Isn't this the part where you tell me to stop and explain in painful detail why this is a bad idea?" Eden's lips brushed against Brandi's ear.

"Umm." Brandi knew she should do exactly that, but the loss of Eden's lips reverberated deep inside her. Legs shaking, she stepped back and held out the bag. "I brought you lunch."

"Really?" Eden's smile transformed from seductive to surprised as she took the package. "What's on the menu?"

"Roast beef on white and soda." Leftovers from last night's dinner.

Eden laid the food and drinks on the table, the three servings set equal distance apart. Eden's careful precision warmed Brandi.

"I'll get Roger." Brandi headed toward the work area of Roger's shop.

She found him reading yesterday's paper in a faded leather recliner with silver duct tape covering the arms. Bits of white stuffing poofed out at the seams.

"Come eat lunch with us?"

Roger lowered the paper but remained seated. "Answer a question for me? What are you doing with that girl?"

Brandi hopped up on the high sales counter. "I have no idea."

"She's nice." Roger regarded her steadily. "But she's not long for this place."

"I know."

"She's sweet on you."

Brandi nodded. Roger was from a different generation. Perhaps "sweet on you" was the same as having a serious dose of lust. Eden definitely had a double-sized helping of raging hormones, but Brandi wasn't at all sure Eden felt anything more.

"What's your plan?"

"Plan?" Brandi's plan hadn't changed much since returning to Maple Hearth. Work hard, save the family farm. Her life had the essential ingredients of a tragedy in the making. "I think it's fairly obvious at this point that I have no idea what I'm doing with my life, let alone with Eden."

"She's good for you." Roger stood, his pants drooping low, held in place by overtaxed suspenders. "I haven't seen you smile this much since before your daddy died."

"I miss him." Brandi climbed down and hugged Roger.

"I miss him, too, Brandi. He was a good man."

Brandi bit her tongue. No reason to advertise her problems.

Roger put his arm around her shoulder. "He wasn't without faults, but he tried to do right by you."

"Come eat lunch." She led him to the back office. "I made sandwiches."

"You didn't need to do that."

Eden sat at the table, elbows on the table, chin propped in her palm. "Don't tell her that, or she might not do it again."

Odds were seriously against Brandi having the same lapse in judgment twice in two weeks, but she liked the way Eden smiled at her over the short expanse of table.

"Eat up." Brandi motioned toward the food, then twisted the top off her bottle of Pepsi.

Roger took a generous bite and spoke with his mouth full. "Eden, how long are you planning to stay?"

Eden studied her sandwich. "I'll leave as soon as my bike is road-ready."

It wasn't news to Brandi, but hearing Eden say it knocked the fun out of lunch.

"Idaho is a world apart from what I'm used to."

"It can't be that different." The summer between her freshman and sophomore years in college, Brandi had made a road trip to Los Angeles with some friends. They only stayed long enough for Brandi to hate the traffic and leave. But she couldn't imagine that people were really much different.

Roger took a long drink of soda. "Tell us, Eden."

"People here are…thoughtful. Polite." She tipped her bottle toward Brandi. "People here do nice things for no reason."

"You act like no one ever brought you lunch before."

Eden took another bite and chewed slowly. "No one did." Her voice was small, contemplative.

Brandi's heart pounded. "Oh."

Roger pushed his last bite into his mouth and stood. "I'll leave you girls to it." He swiped his bottle off the table, along with a second sandwich, and left the room.

By most standards, Brandi's childhood would be measured as adequate, ideal, even. She had two parents who loved her, who taught her right from wrong and made sure she understood the value of hard work. The guarded glimpses Eden unveiled about her own life stood out in stark comparison. Brandi finished her lunch in silence.

"I should get back to work." Eden didn't move. "You wouldn't believe the unfinished paperwork in this place."

Brandi tossed the evidence of their lunch into the trash can, saving the bottle for the recycle bin. She chose her words carefully. "His son used to do that part."

"Roger mentioned that he bought the Mac."

"He told you about Paul?"

"That's his name, Paul? No, he didn't tell me about him."

Brandi shrugged. "You're doing a good thing here."

Eden pushed away from the table, not meeting Brandi's eyes. "It seems to be contagious."

"Why do you do that?"

"What?" Eden jiggled the mouse, but still didn't look up.

"Act like the good things you do don't count?" No, that wasn't right, Brandi clarified mentally. Eden acted like the good things weren't enough. Like she was working off some sort of debt.

"This," Eden glanced at Brandi and gestured toward the desk, "is very small compared to some of the things I've done."

The space between them grew as Brandi watched Eden withdraw. It'd only been a few days since Eden arrived, but the cocky woman bent on Brandi's seduction was disappearing by degrees the longer Eden stayed at Maple Hearth. Brandi wondered when the real Eden would appear and why she cared so much. "You don't have to carry it alone, Eden. I'm right here."

Eden looked at her then, her gaze hard and searching, and slightly accusing. "We all have secrets, Brandi. Even you."

Brandi hesitated. She didn't have secrets. She had debts, but most everyone in town knew about that. All she had between her financial worries and Eden was her own stubborn pride.

❖

The sick-sweet smell of Roger's chewing tobacco greeted Eden as he peered at the computer screen over her shoulder. The scent reminded Eden that she hadn't smoked since leaving Los Angeles. It wasn't enough to make her want a cigarette. She'd tried, on more than one occasion, to quit smoking. Ironic that the urge faded with the smog that covered the city. The farther away she was, the less she thought about it.

"That's some setup you've got going there." He jabbed his finger at the columns of numbers.

"I'll teach you how to use it before I go. Once I'm caught up, it'll be pretty simple to maintain."

Roger righted himself and shuffled away from the desk. "I suppose."

It seemed a waste for Roger to have a nice computer system that he clearly never intended to use. Not to mention pointless for Eden to spend all this time reconciling accounts only to have them fall out of order as soon as she left town. "Or maybe you could hire somebody to keep them up. It would only take a few hours a week."

Roger spat into the trash. "It's late. You should be getting home."

Home? Eden had no idea where that was, but it warmed her that Roger referred to Brandi's place as her home.

"How well do you know them?"

"Brandi and Jaylynn?" Roger asked, a warning in his eyes.

Eden nodded.

"As well as anyone, I'd wager."

"What's their story?"

Roger gave her a sharp look. "What's your interest? Brandi's a good girl. She deserves someone who's in it for the long haul."

"What makes you think—"

Roger snorted and jerked the door open. "Think about what you're doing before you go messing about with that girl. She's special to some of us."

One minute he was pushing her toward Brandi and the next warning her away. Eden was more confused than ever. She watched Roger leave and blew out a sigh. Leave it to a man to take away all the fun in seducing a woman.

❖

Eden rolled down the window and rested her arm on the door. One hand on the wheel, she dialed Penny's number. The wind rustled through her hair and rattled the brown paper bag in the seat next to her.

"This is Penny." She answered the phone with clipped professionalism. Penny was always looking for the next sale and took her business seriously, even if her customers were addicts and social deviants.

"Pen...it's me." Eden didn't want to say her name.

"I'm so glad you called. I've got a great new special I want to tell you about." Several people were talking in the background. Clearly Penny wasn't alone.

"I wish you could talk. I miss you."

"I knew you'd say that. Can we meet for a demonstration?"

"This was a bad idea." Eden watched the landscape rolling by, the tableau for her life at the moment. She missed Penny. That much was true. But she'd take Idaho over Los Angeles any day of the week. "I just wanted to tell you that I'm okay."

"Really?" Penny's voice changed, the background noise quieted.

Eden thought about all the things she wanted to tell Penny. About the people here who helped each other. How they stored motorcycles to keep their friends from getting a divorce. How they fixed meals for everyone in a five-mile radius, just to make sure they had plenty to eat. How they spoke with consideration, their love for each other subtle and present in every word, every gesture. How they worried about each other's health, but still ate pie with their neighbors. How orders were yelled across the restaurant, but it wasn't rude. It was just two friends talking. How there were horses and dogs and chickens, and they were quieter than the projects at night. How everyone worked hard, but they still took the time to stop on the road and chat through the open windows of their farm trucks. How futuristic pieces of equipment crawled down the highway and nobody honked. How a stranger on a horse would stop and help when your motorcycle broke down on the side of the road.

But she couldn't say any of those things.

"I'm happy, Penny." The truth and power of the words struck Eden. "I'm actually happy."

Eden heard someone call for Penny in the background. She pictured her holding up one finger in a just-a-moment gesture. Then she said, "Okay, I'll see you then." Penny disconnected the call.

Penny sounded so distant, so far removed from Eden. She longed for their friendship. Penny didn't blame her, she knew. Still, Eden felt guilty for escaping without her best friend. She'd found a place that somehow quieted the ghosts of her past, but Penny was still there, in the thick of it, fighting her conscience every day just to survive.

Would Penny like Idaho? Would she like Brandi? Eden closed her phone with a soft click. How much of the happiness she confessed to Penny could be attributed to Brandi?

Too much.

What the hell?

When had Brandi become more than simply a potential conquest? A sweet fuck waiting to happen? Things were shifting far too quickly in the quiet moments of their lives, and she wasn't prepared for this slamming reality. She'd only known her a couple of days, not long enough for the far-too-serious bent her emotions had taken. All the excitement leaked out of seeing Brandi again. She couldn't tease and torment her with subtle, lingering touches. She couldn't probe for surrender in her eyes. To touch Brandi now would be to promise. And she couldn't do that.

CHAPTER NINE

Panic rushed up Eden's spine as she parked Brandi's truck. A black Lincoln—Luther's car of choice—was angled in front of Maple Hearth.

Eden took a deep breath, forcing her heart rate under control. She needed to think, not allow emotion to dictate her actions. Her guns, the only logic Luther understood, were tucked into her saddlebags in the barn. Unless Ranger was secretly a marksman, she needed to get there before anyone noticed she'd arrived. Then she'd be able to plan her next move.

Leaving her packages in the passenger seat, Eden slipped silently from the truck. She crouched behind the tall fender of the truck and surveyed the driveway. Gravel, no matter how lightly she stepped, shifted and made noise. Hell, he was probably watching her now, alerted by the sound of the truck tires crunching when she'd pulled in.

Think, dammit.

She hated being caught with her mental pants down, with Brandi and Jaylynn unknowingly in the crossfire.

The screen door squeaked open and she heard Jaylynn's voice. "Brandi, we've got to get going. I'll introduce Marcus to Eden another time."

Marcus? Eden scrolled through the list of people she'd been introduced to since Brandi rescued her a few days back. No Marcus. She peeked over the fender and caught a glimpse of Brandi pointing right at the truck.

"But she's around here somewhere, look."

She straightened out and looked past Brandi and Jaylynn to the polished man waiting at the bottom of the steps. Not Luther. Her muscles released their ready-to-fight tension and she offered her most charming smile.

"I told you she was here." Brandi waved her over. "Come meet my mama's date before they run away for the night."

The emphasis Brandi placed on the words *mama* and *night* sent Eden back to high alert. She obviously didn't approve of Jaylynn's dinner companion and was stalling until Eden returned to Maple Hearth. What Eden was supposed to do was a mystery.

She circled the truck and approached the man. He was tall and slick, his tan the product of a tanning bed or possibly a bottle. Definitely not the same rich brown that came from being outdoors all day that she'd seen on the working people she'd met so far. His shoes glinted in the waning sunlight, battling with his perfectly uniform teeth for the "most shiny" award. Eden extended her hand as the cool veneer of her recently escaped life slipped over her. Brandi's voice as she made the introductions barely registered. She gripped Marcus's hand just a little too tight and held his gaze, letting him know that Jaylynn's well-being was of concern to her. If Brandi didn't like this man, that was enough for her. She would gladly hang him off the tallest building by the tiny buckles on his shoes if Brandi wanted her to.

"Bring her home safe," she cautioned, staring hard into his eyes. He tipped his head slightly. Good enough for Eden. She released her grip and brushed a light kiss over Jaylynn's cheek. "Have fun tonight."

"I plan to." Jaylynn laughed and moved toward the car. "You two play nice while I'm gone."

Brandi stared at her while Jaylynn and Marcus drove away.

"What?" Eden shifted uncomfortably.

"That's my question." Brandi continued to stare. "What was that?"

"What?"

"What, what?" Brandi asked, her voice annoyed and impressed at once. "That display of machismo, that's what."

"Oh, that." Eden escaped Brandi's scrutiny by returning to the truck for her packages. She held out the bundle of deep yellow tulips and bottle of shiraz—chosen for the playful monkey on the label. "These are for you."

Brandi eyed the packages suspiciously. "Don't try to change the subject."

"You don't like red wine?" Eden asked. "I thought about getting a zinfandel, but…" She shrugged.

"Answer my question, then we can talk about how sweet the flowers and wine are." Brandi relented, but like a dog with a good bone, she didn't let go completely.

Eden sighed and walked past Brandi into the house. "You obviously don't like him. I just wanted to make sure he knew that she is…that he needs to treat her with respect." Eden set the bottle on the table and searched the cupboards for a vase.

Brandi laid a hand Eden's shoulder. "Look in here." She reached across Eden to open the one cupboard Eden hadn't searched and pulled out a cut-crystal vase. Eden slid free of her touch and watched as Brandi filled the container with water. She unwrapped the tulips, submerged the stems, and trimmed the ends. Trailing one finger over the petals, she set the arrangement on the table. "Sweet."

❖

Brandi relaxed into the wooden rocker on her back deck, careful not to slosh the deep red liquid over the rim of her glass. Wine. Not her normal after-dinner drink. Truth be told, she'd rather Eden had brought home a six-pack of longneck Buds. But she wouldn't tell Eden that. She took a careful sip and settled into the cool evening air.

"Refill?" Eden tipped the near-empty bottle over her glass.

Brandi covered the opening with her hand. "I'm good."

Without missing a beat, Eden topped off her own glass. "I could get used to the quiet."

Brandi listened. Frogs, crickets, laughter from the men bunking down. Far from quiet. "What's it like where you grew up?"

Eden looked out over the field and took a long drink, but didn't answer. Maybe that was the quiet she was talking about.

Brandi set her rocker in motion, and the creak of old wood joined the symphony of sounds. "My grandpa made these." She ran her hands over the wood. The summer before he died, too old to work the farm, but too alive to do nothing, he'd worked with Brandi, showed her how to fit the wood together. Every piece had been shaped by hand, no power tools, then set with Elmer's wood glue and tiny nails that disappeared in his giant hands. He'd smiled at her, nails jutting out from between his lips as he guided her movements, a slight tremor in his fingers. "He died two weeks later." He'd gone to bed and never woken up. Tears threatened as they always did when she thought of him.

"You're beautiful." Eden stared at her, head tilted to the side, eyes heavy with wine.

Brandi set her glass on the side table between their two chairs. "We need to talk."

The look on Eden's face shifted, the softness firming to her customary guarded expression. "I know."

"You have to stop." Brandi's voice was too soft, too unsure for her own liking.

"I know."

She lifted her gaze to meet Eden's. "You know?"

Eden nodded.

"I don't do casual well." Especially when casual was living in her house, sleeping in the next room. It felt far from casual, the lines drifted and blurred, and it was too confusing to keep her emotions straight with reality.

Eden nodded again.

"You're leaving soon?" Brandi hated the question mark she inserted into what would otherwise have been a statement.

Eden looked at the rising moon then at Brandi, her face resolute. "I have to."

"Okay."

"You're still beautiful." Eden drained her glass.

With the window-filtered light from the kitchen wrapped

around Eden in a sixty-watt halo, Brandi pictured her in the future, hair more gray than brown, fine wrinkles framing her eyes. She blinked the image away before she got too comfortable with the idea of Eden sitting across from her for longer than the next week.

"You never did tell me about your family." Brandi couldn't stop herself from asking. Eden obviously wanted to avoid the subject and she'd been clear that she wouldn't be around long enough to fill in the details of her life. Still, Brandi wanted to know.

"What do you want to know?"

Everything.

"Who touched you most?" Brandi waited to hear the names Luther or Penny, the only two people she'd heard mentioned so far.

"Gabriel." Eden stood and stretched. "I need another drink. You?"

Brandi raised her still-full glass. "I'm still good."

She waited until Eden returned, brown bottle of beer dangled between two fingers.

"Who's Gabriel?"

Eden sank down, twisted the top off the Budweiser, and set the chair in motion. She took two long pulls of beer, sighed, then took another. Finally, she said, "My brother."

"You have a brother?"

"Had."

Eden's jaw flexed and she visibly tensed. She brought to mind the image of a rattlesnake coiled and ready to strike.

Brandi's chest ached, her body stretching across the ether to hold Eden and soothe old hurts. Whatever took Gabriel had claimed a large portion of Eden as well.

Chapter Ten

B reakfast at Maple Hearth was typically a warm, inviting experience, in startling contrast to Eden's grab-and-smash approach when she lived in Los Angeles. There she would cruise through the nearest espresso stand, order the biggest, most heart-palpitating drink on the menu, possibly indulge in biscotti, and gulp it down between traffic signals. One time she hit a large pothole at cruising speed and coffee flew out of the cup and laid claim to every surface inside her car. The detail service erased all signs of the incident from her upholstery, but she didn't have the same luck with her guns. She'd discarded them after several failed attempts to clean the dark liquid from all the crevices.

The seductive aroma of breakfast was decidedly absent Thursday morning when Eden awoke. A pang of disappointment hit her. Jaylynn's cooking was on her list of favorite things about Idaho, right behind the curve of Brandi's ass in her Levi's and the crooked, sexy smile on her face when she told Eden good night.

Brandi sat at the table, glaring at the bowl of cereal and milk in front of her.

"Good morning." Eden poured herself a cup of coffee and settled into the seat opposite Brandi.

"Cereal?" Brandi nudged the box toward Eden.

"No, thanks. I try not to indulge in foods that feature cartoon characters on the label." Eden kept her voice light, hoping Brandi would explain where Jaylynn was.

Brandi scowled and took an oversized bite of cereal. Milk dripped down her chin. She wiped it away with the back of her hand and kept chewing.

"You want me to cook something?" Eden offered.

"You can cook?" Brandi sounded skeptical.

"No, but you could teach me."

Each meal, Brandi and Jaylynn worked in tandem preparing it. Brandi's cooking, while not as good as Jaylynn's, was much better than a box of sugary cereal.

Brandi took another bite. The crunching grated on Eden's nerves and she looked out the back door.

"We need to feed the men." That was another part of the breakfast—and every other meal—ritual at Maple Hearth. The farm workers filed through the kitchen and filled their plates to overflowing.

"They can eat cereal."

"You have another five boxes?" No way would one small package satisfy their appetites.

Eden thought about heading out. Brandi obviously had other things on her mind. Playing hostess to Eden had to be getting old. Or better yet, she could help out instead of being a burden. She left her coffee on the table and went to the refrigerator. That was the appropriate place to search for breakfast-making food, wasn't it? The eggs at Maple Hearth were a light tan, rather than the white Eden was accustomed to. When Brandi explained that their eggs came from chickens on their property, rather than the market, Eden had been amazed. And a little reluctant to try them. "Is it safe?" she'd asked. Brandi had laughed and forked a mouthful between Eden's lips. Turned out they were safe and tasty. Eden set the flat of eggs on the counter.

"How many eggs?"

"How are you going to cook them?"

Good question.

Eden shifted her weight from side to side. Brandi sighed and pushed away from the table. She grabbed a large bowl out of the cupboard and set it on the counter in front of Eden. "Scrambled. That's easiest."

Brandi visibly relaxed as she settled into her morning routine. Except this morning Brandi took the lead with Eden trying to keep up. She showed Eden how to crack the eggs without dropping bits of shell in the bowl.

"You'll need twenty-four," Brandi said as she pulled a package of bacon from the refrigerator. Rather than laying the strips of meat in a neat line on the griddle as Eden had seen Jaylynn do every other morning, Brandi dropped them in a haphazard clump in a large frying pan. She added a lid and returned her attention to Eden. "You're doing good."

Eden tossed the last eggshell in the trash and wished for the checkered apron that Jaylynn wore. Brandi handed her a towel.

"Now what?" Eden asked.

Brandi indicated a whisk hanging with the other utensils below the cabinets. "Mix them up."

The whisk was foreign in Eden's hand, a tool intended to create rather than destroy. She stirred the eggs at a fraction of the speed Brandi would have, but she felt good doing it. When she finished, Brandi poured the mixture into a pan, then turned the bacon with a set of tongs.

"You want to make the toast?"

"Sure." Piece of cake. Eden had made toast before. She set about her task, watching Brandi move though the kitchen. The woman was comfortable everywhere, but she looked a little out of sync. "Where's your mom?" Eden asked the question carefully.

Brandi paused mid-step, then resumed walking. She pulled a stack of plates off the shelf and placed them on the table. "Not home yet."

"Oh." Eden put four new slices of bread in the toaster. "Is that normal?"

"No." Brandi sat in the chair heavily. The sizzle of bacon cooking filled the room.

"And you don't like Marcus?" Eden was pushing too hard, she realized it. She just couldn't stop herself.

"It's not that." Brandi looked at Eden, her voice hesitant. "He's a decent enough guy. But he has an agenda. And so does my mom." She fidgeted with her collar. "She doesn't love him."

"And that's required?" Eden's chest tightened and she had to fight to keep her breathing even. Brandi's answer, whether she wanted it to be or not, was very important.

"Isn't it?" Brandi looked away, then stood abruptly and went to the stove. "Bacon's done."

She removed the bacon from the hot pan at the same time the farm hands clomped into the kitchen.

"Smells good."

Eden watched as Brandi laughed and served and tried to fill the void left in the room by Jaylynn's absence. They didn't talk again until the men, with smiles on their faces and food in their bellies, left the same way they entered—in a boisterous tide.

"Is it really such a bad thing if Jaylynn spends the night with her friend?"

"No. But they're not friends."

"Then why—"

"Do we really need to talk about this?" Brandi moved with jerky efficiency, clearing the evidence of their collaborative breakfast.

"No. You could tell me what you need ninety-six thousand dollars for."

"I don't." The words came out brittle and sharp.

"Your mom thinks you do." Eden wanted to stop. Brandi didn't owe her any explanations.

Brandi finished the dishes in silence, the easiness of cooking together sucked out of the room. She jerked her hat on and slammed out the back door, leaving Eden alone and bewildered.

Eden fumed. To think she'd actually wanted to help that infuriating woman. Brandi pushed her away at every turn. First physically, now emotionally. Brandi had made her point. She was off-limits to Eden.

Brandi's Dell sat on the desk tucked into the corner of the kitchen. She told herself to leave well enough alone. She needed to fix her Ducati and get the hell out of Idaho. Eden powered up the computer, cursing her lack of good sense. Brandi didn't want to talk to her? Fine. She'd find the answers her own way.

❖

Brandi's boots clunked on the front porch, her steps heavy and slow. Some days she felt so old. The weight of her responsibilities, the potential loss settled on her shoulders and aged her seventy years in moments. She tugged open the door. Jaylynn, still wearing yesterday's outfit, sat at the kitchen table.

"You're home." Brandi set her gloves on the counter and poured two glasses of iced tea. She placed one in front of her mother, then rested her hip against the cabinet and took a careful sip of hers.

Jaylynn sighed and smoothed the wrinkles out of her clothes. "Long night." She offered an unconvincing smile.

"He's not going to help us."

Jaylynn pushed away from the table, iced tea untouched. "No. He's not." She looked weary. "I'm going to bed."

Brandi kissed Jaylynn on the cheek. "I love you, Mama."

"I love you, too, baby." Jaylynn paused as she entered the hall. "Rich is looking for you, by the way."

"Did he say why?"

Jaylynn shook her head and continued down the hall.

Rich had worked at Maple Hearth longer than Brandi had been alive. Her grandfather had hired him when he was a young man trying to find a home for himself. He'd traveled from town to town on the rodeo circuit and, tired of broken bones and the road, he'd offered his services in exchange for a place to sleep, food to eat, and a little bit of money in his pocket.

If Rich was looking for her, it wasn't to discuss the weather. The news was either really good or really bad. Rich handled everything in between, saving the extremes for Brandi. Her stomach tightened. Eden was playing havoc with her emotional equilibrium. She didn't need anything else on her plate.

Halfway across the back yard, she saw Rich headed her way. He greeted her with his cap in his hands, sweat and grease covering his face.

"Bad news, I'm afraid."

He turned back the way he came and Brandi fell in step beside him. Rich's long stride had Brandi moving double-time. When she was little, she had to run three steps and walk one to stay abreast of him. With age, he'd slowed a bit and her legs had almost caught up with his. Still, she had to work to keep up. Stress did that to him.

"Tell me."

"The baler stopped working."

They'd made it through the two cuttings of hay but were still several days shy of the alfalfa being ready to harvest again. "How'd you find that out?"

"It was giving me fits last time. I checked it out to see what was going on."

The baler took up a large corner of the equipment barn. When it worked properly, it collected the hay into large, rectangular bundles and secured them with baling twine. Just like Rich, it had been on the ranch longer than Brandi. She'd known the time would come when she'd have to replace the outdated machine, but the timing couldn't have been worse. Still, maybe it could be salvaged.

"How bad is it?"

"I can't fix it." Rich tapped a Kool out of the pack and slipped it between his lips.

That didn't bode well. If Rich couldn't fix it, no one could.

Rich squeezed Brandi's shoulder. "I'm sorry, girl."

"It'll be okay." She stared at the faded paint and nodded. "I'll figure something out."

The gleaming black-and-chrome beauty of her Ducati didn't pull at Eden the same way it did when she saw it for the first time. Sitting on an elevated platform in the showroom, it had shined and sparkled, whispering the promise of adventures untold. With its traditional European design—center of gravity set high with a short chassis—it looked almost otherworldly lying disassembled against a backdrop of hay and farm equipment. The machine had lost its luster. Eden trailed her finger through the fine layer of dust, revealing the glossy paint beneath. The only sensible thing to do was repair the bike, just like she'd told Roger, and be on her way. So why was she so reluctant for that day to come?

Eden heard hoofbeats entering the barn hard and fast. She turned to see Brandi sliding from Ranger's back as he came to a skidding halt. A cloud of dust billowed around them.

"Hey." The line of Brandi's shoulders, the tension in her jaw told Eden that her mood hadn't improved since that morning.

Eden dusted off her hands and walked over to Brandi. "How was your day?" She folded her arms over her chest to keep from pulling Brandi into a hug.

Brandi passed her a brush and led Ranger to his stall. "I've had better."

Ranger's flanks quivered. Eden regarded Brandi over his back, unsure how to proceed with the conversation. She put the brush to work on Ranger's shoulder.

"I'm sorry." Those words always sounded disingenuous and inadequate to Eden.

Brandi slipped Ranger's feedbag over his nose. "Not your fault."

"Still," Eden grabbed Brandi's hand and forced her to look at her, "I want you to be okay." Eden struggled for the right words. How could she explain how much Brandi's happiness meant to her? It was irrational. They barely knew one another and, she reminded herself again, she would be gone soon enough. Brandi's smile warmed her insides. And Eden ached to fix her struggles and her pain. Only here she was fighting the bank, an enemy she wasn't supposed to know about. And the solution, while simple, was impossible. Brandi would never accept her money. Even if it meant saving everything she loved.

Brandi looked at their hands for several beats, her eyes shining, then laced her fingers with Eden's. "It's just so fucking hard."

"I really can help."

"I really can't let you." Brandi's voice cracked. "You're leaving."

Eden pulled Brandi into her embrace, her heart pounding.

Brandi trembled. For all her strength, Brandi felt small huddled against her chest. How could she, with so much death on her hands, offer comfort and hope? She held Brandi tight and kissed her hair. The spikes brushed against her cheeks and tickled her nose.

Brandi snaked her arms around Eden's waist, her touch cooling and burning Eden at once. She needed this woman, needed her to be safe, needed to stay her tears.

"Please, tell me."

Brandi snuffled and hugged Eden harder. She clung to Eden, her grasp crushing and desperate. Her shoulders shook and she sobbed, face buried in Eden's chest. "The baler is broken."

Baler? How in the hell could Eden fix it when she had no idea what it was? She made nonsensical shushing noises and smoothed her hands over Brandi's hair. Brandi finally trusted Eden enough to share her problem and Eden was unable to help. She relied on past experience. Money and violence fixed everything where she came from.

"I'll buy you a new one."

Brandi's sobs morphed into a half-sniffle, half-laugh. She drew her head back and said, "You don't even know what I'm talking about."

Eden's breath caught in her chest, her stomach dropped to her knees, and her heart roared off to parts unknown. Brandi—tear-streaked cheeks, red-rimmed eyes, and snotty nose—was beautiful.

Brandi stepped back and wiped her face with her shirt. "Well?"

"I have no idea." Eden shook her head. "But I'd buy you an island if you wanted it. A baler couldn't cost much more than that." How could she prove to Brandi that she was serious? Should she whip out her bank account and show Brandi the numbers? Would that convince her? Would she then want to know how Eden earned that money? Or maybe she should offer to kill whoever broke the baler. Would that convince Brandi how much Eden wanted to take care of her?

Brandi laughed and, just like that, the storm receded and the sun came out. Eden would gladly spend her life chasing Brandi's laughter, coaxing her mirth to the surface.

"Thank you. I needed a laugh today." Brandi kissed Eden lightly on the lips.

Eden reeled. Brandi's kiss was rain on the dry desert of her soul. She touched her fingertips to her mouth. Their first heated kiss didn't hold a candle to this one.

Eden smiled. Everything about this place just felt right. "So, what exactly is a baler?"

"I'll show you after we eat." Brandi led her out of the barn by the hand. "Come on. I'm sure Mom has dinner waiting."

CHAPTER ELEVEN

The hot spray of water prickled Brandi's skin, washing away sleep and the tension of financial uncertainty. Eden's offer to buy Brandi a new baler had been sweet, and Brandi was pretty sure she meant it even if she didn't realize what she was saying. A baler, even a used one, cost several thousand dollars. It wasn't like picking up the tab for lunch. Strangers just didn't give that much to others.

But Eden, in spite of the short time she'd known her, was *not* a stranger, which was the real issue in Brandi's mind. Brandi massaged shampoo into her hair and imagined Eden behind her, pressed up against her, the water sloughing off her body, and her hands—gentle and firm—working through her hair. But Eden was leaving. When the repairs to her Ducati were complete, she'd be gone.

Lust was a simple but inconvenient physical reaction. Eden's touch, hell, her gaze, ignited a fire low in Brandi's belly. That was something she could deal with, understand, and safely ignore. But what about the emotional connection? The desire to *know* Eden. Why, when she said she had a brother, emphasis on past tense, did Brandi ache to hold her?

And what about last night? Brandi couldn't remember the last time she'd cried in front of another person. No, that wasn't true. It had been at her father's funeral. She'd wept openly, her grief on display for all her neighbors to see. Two weeks later she'd stumbled across the financial records for the ranch and her heart dried up. The man she'd loved and trusted to take care of her and her mom had left behind a mess too big to clean up. God knew she'd tried, but she'd failed. Soon enough the bank would be knocking on her door demanding their due.

Yet she'd fallen into Eden's arms and just let go. She trusted Eden to hold her, keep her safe, and protect her emotions. It felt good to let someone else share her burden, even temporarily. She'd cried and Eden had looked at her like she was beautiful. She'd felt cherished. And she'd wiped her eyes and laughed and still Eden had held her. The love in her eyes hadn't faltered.

Brandi rinsed the suds from her hair and body and watched the water swirl down the drain. Having Eden in her home, but unable to accept her offer of intimacy, made Brandi tired. She stepped out of the shower, wrapped the oversized fluffy towel around her body, and slipped out of the steam-filled bathroom.

"Good morning." Eden relaxed against the wall, coffee mug in her hand, an amused smile teasing her lips.

Brandi clutched her towel, pulling it tight around her chest. It just reached the tops of her thighs. Eden was safely covered by faded blue jeans and sleeveless shirt with shiny pearl snaps.

"Hi." Brandi licked her lips.

Eden sipped her coffee, then asked, "Did you sleep okay?" She took a couple of steps toward Brandi.

"I did." Brandi swallowed. Eden's demanding gaze raked over her, scorching her skin. "And you?"

Eden nodded and took another step. "I was worried about you."

"I'm okay." Brandi edged toward her bedroom door.

"Yeah?"

Brandi forced a smile. "Sure."

"I did some research this morning. On the Internet. Balers aren't that expensive. I found one—"

"I know how much they cost." Brandi hated the brittleness in her voice.

Rather than retreat, Eden took another step, stopping a few

inches from Brandi. She smoothed her palm against Brandi's cheek. "Brandi, let me do this."

Brandi pressed into the caress, the gentle touch soothing and shaking her at the same time. She closed her eyes. "That's not a good idea." So many things about her relationship with Eden were not a good idea. This was just one more item on a long list.

"Why not?" Eden trailed her fingers over Eden's shoulder.

The baler would be there long after Eden had gone, after her touch faded from Brandi's skin, after her face faded in Brandi's memory. The piece of farm equipment would linger, reminding her of the loss. The words formed in her mind, a plea for Eden to stay, to make Maple Hearth her home, but she couldn't bring herself to ask. The look in Eden's eyes every time she spoke of moving on, the haunted resolve that seeped into her voice, her movements, kept Brandi from clinging to her, begging her to never leave.

"Why do you want to?"

Eden opened her mouth, but said nothing. Eventually she closed it without answering.

"That's what I thought." Brandi stepped away from Eden's warmth and escaped into her room, closing the door before Eden could follow her through.

"Brandi." Eden spoke softly though the door. "I…care about you. I want to help."

Brandi collapsed against the back of the door and slid to the floor.

"Dammit, Eden, just go. That's what you'll do eventually anyway." Brandi sounded like a petulant child and she didn't care. Tantrums were never logical.

"I'm sorry."

Tears rolled silently down Brandi's face. Crying felt so much better when Eden's arms were around her.

Brandi heard the front door open and close, then her truck started. She drew herself up and crossed to the window in time to see Eden drive away.

❖

Eden stared at the stack of paperwork Roger had just plopped on the desk. This had been their pattern for the last week. She'd be a few papers shy of finishing and he would produce another mountain for her to work through. Once she had it all under control, she'd teach him to use the accounting program to track his transactions.

"Where are you finding this stuff?" She nudged a crumpled invoice with the pink eraser tip of her number 2 pencil. A dark stain of questionable origin covered most of the page.

Roger tugged at his chin and offered a crooked smile. "They just keep popping up."

"Popping up?" Eden pictured Roger reaching into the fridge for a beer and pulling out business records instead of a cold can of Miller. "How do you get paid if you don't even know who owes you money?"

Roger shrugged and tapped his can of Skoal against his palm. "They pay me when they can."

Eden powered down the computer and set a cleaned piston in the middle of the pile to keep the bills from blowing away. She hadn't thought to do that the first night when she left and came back the next morning to find an ancient box fan bringing cool air in through the window. The papers had been scattered to hell and gone.

"I'm done for today. That," she pointed at the stack, "will have to wait for Monday."

Roger scuffed his feet against the worn linoleum and dragged a worn leather wallet from his back pocket. He produced several bills, soft with age and handling, and cleared his throat. "Hand." His voice was rough and callused.

Eden held out her right hand, palm up, and waited.

Two hundred and sixty-two dollars. Roger stacked the bills precisely as he counted softly, his brow furrowed in concentration. "Twenty, forty, sixty…"

What the hell?

"You want me to pick up supplies or something?" Eden asked. He'd never sent her on errands before, but if he needed something, she didn't mind helping out.

"Them's your wages."

Wallet safely tucked in his pocket, Roger grasped her hand, forcing her fingers to curl tight around the cash.

"Hold on to that and don't you lose it."

"Roger," Eden pushed back, trying to reverse his hold and return the money to his hands, "I don't need this. You keep it."

"No. You earned it." He didn't budge. "I know it ain't much, but it's been a long time since I've had someone looking after things. Wouldn't be right not to pay you."

Technically, it wasn't right that she just showed up and started working. He didn't ask for her help and he shouldn't have to pay for it. Besides, two-sixty-two wouldn't even cover a new pair of shoes.

The look in Roger's eyes stopped Eden from arguing the point any further. All week he'd been threatening to throw her over his knee and spank her, and he appeared close to making good on the promise. If any other man had made a similar statement to Eden, she would have called him a pervert and punctuated her point with a round from her Glock. But from Roger the threat felt fatherly. She pocketed the cash.

"You still planning to leave?" Roger asked.

"That's the plan." One that Eden had to stick to regardless of Brandi's tears. The longer she stayed in one place, the more likely Luther was to find her.

"You don't have to, you know." Roger met her gaze. "As you can see, I can't afford much. But I'd be proud to have you."

Eden blinked hard as the burn rose in her eyes. Why, when she was so far past redemption, was she being offered a life she didn't deserve? Life in Idaho was simple. Everything moved slower, people were easier. Roger, bless him. For the first time, a man wanted nothing more from her than to care for her. She wished her own father had been half the man Roger was.

Then there was Brandi. She pushed Eden, challenged her, drew her in. Eden knew she'd be safe in the shelter of Brandi's love, and she longed to provide the same. But she couldn't do that. Not with the threat of Luther looming over her.

Eden's heart begged her to tell Roger, "Yes, I'll stay and help you and live happily ever after on a ranch in Idaho with the most perfect woman in the history of women." Instead she mumbled, "I don't know…"

Roger squeezed her shoulder. "Don't you need to get home to Brandi?" He flipped off the light and walked out the back door.

Sadness radiated through Eden's chest and threatened to drown her in the tide. Home would never be with Brandi. She deserved so much more than Eden could ever provide. She deserved stability and purity. Someone whose past wasn't stained red with other people's blood. She deserved someone who knew right from wrong, who didn't default to violence as a solution. She deserved someone to hold her who wasn't looking over her shoulder, waiting for the fatal blow to fall.

Eden grabbed her keys and followed Roger. She needed to get out of Idaho, and fast.

CHAPTER TWELVE

Brandi squeezed the trigger, but rather than roaring to destructive life, the chain saw sputtered, coughed out a cloud of blue smoke, and died.

Ranger snickered.

"I don't know what you're laughing at." Brandi hauled the damned thing over to her makeshift workbench and unscrewed the gas cap. "We're not leaving till that whole tree is down."

Ranger looked away, apparently not impressed by her declaration.

The once-tall cottonwood tree was separated into various stages. She'd arranged the gnarled branches around the stump in preparation for a bonfire. The bulk of it was quartered and piled nearby, ready to be added once the fire took hold. The small amount that was usable for firewood, she'd chopped and stacked near the fence line, easy access for her to pick up with her truck later, after Eden came home.

Brandi topped off the fuel tank with the last of the premixed gas/oil blend she'd brought along and refilled the chain oil. She left the saw sitting on the thick round of cottonwood when she heard the rumble of her truck engine drawing nearer.

Eden.

The truck threw up a cloud of dust in its wake. Eden, wearing a full-faced smile with dark, Hollywood-big sunglasses covering her eyes, stopped even with Brandi and killed the engine.

"Your mom told me I'd find you here."

Eden exited the truck and was up and over the fence that separated them before Brandi could respond. She freed her windblown hair from its customary braid and shook her head. Her hair shone in the sunlight and the long strands bounced back into place in slow motion. Brandi was mesmerized.

Her brain said, "No, no, no!" where Eden was concerned, but her body was full-speed ahead, whimpering, moaning, "Yes, yes, oh, God, yes."

Eden stopped a few feet shy of Brandi and pulled her hair back, her fingers working it quickly into a braid. "Everything okay?" She stepped closer and placed the back of her hand against Brandi's forehead. "You look flushed. You're not too hot, are you?"

Brandi shook herself loose, Eden's touch scorching her far more than the southern Idaho sun. "I'm fine." Sweat trickled down her face.

"Okay." Eden placed her hands on her hips and looked around. "What are we working on?"

Brandi picked up the splitting maul, careful not to look at Eden's shirt stretched tight across her chest. "I'm almost done, actually." She pointed to the small stack of rounds that needed split, then to the few lone branches that needed to be cut into manageable lengths.

Ranger nudged Brandi. He was long past ready to head home.

Eden laughed and said, "Even so, it'll be quicker with two sets of hands. What can I do?"

Brandi had several suggestions for what Eden could do with her hands. Fast or slow, she didn't care which. "Have you ever chopped wood?"

Eden's smooth, callus-free palms already gave Brandi the answer to her question. Still, you never knew. Maybe she'd spent one summer with her grandfather in some mountain cabin in the woods with nothing to do but fish and split wood. Doubtful.

"No, but I can learn. I'm good with my hands." Eden's tone suggested she'd like to demonstrate her skills.

One short week, Brandi reminded herself, and Eden would be

gone. It didn't matter how good she was with her hands. Brandi would never find out. She needed more than a summer fling.

"This is a splitting maul." Brandi ignored the innuendo and launched into a lesson on firewood 101. She placed one of the logs on the oversized round she'd been using as a chopping block. "It's not sharp, but it's weighted." She swung the ax, her muscles doing the job without thought. It split the wood, sending the two halves flying, and embedded in the block with a heavy thunk. "The key is to let gravity do the work for you."

Eden collected the two pieces and set one on the chopping block. She dropped the other at her feet. With a crooked grin, she peered at Brandi over the top of her glasses and said, "Show me again?"

Brandi laughed and did as she was asked. They settled into a comfortable routine, Eden setting up logs and stacking the quartered rounds, Brandi swinging the maul and trying to ignore the distracting scent of designer cologne that clung to Eden.

"Last one." Eden positioned the piece of wood and Brandi split it with a satisfying crack.

Brandi rested the maul against the chopping block and wiped the sweat from her brow with an oversized blue paisley bandana she kept in her back pocket. "Thanks." She dropped her hat back on her head and retrieved the chain saw.

"Now what?" Eden asked.

Brandi motioned her head toward the remaining branches and pulled the cord on the saw. It came to life with a roar. "You want to try?" she asked Eden, sure the answer would be no.

"Yes." Eden's mouth was drawn tight with determination. "But not yet. I want to watch you first."

Brandi made quick work of the first limb and was almost through the second when she heard Eden yelling for her to stop. She engaged the brake and held the saw loosely in one hand, blade pointed safely away from her body. "What?"

"My turn." Eden held out her hand.

"Do you have gloves?"

Eden gave her a what-do-you-think look, but didn't respond.

Brandi set the saw on the ground and pulled off her own sweat-soaked ones. She held them out to Eden and said, "You can't use the saw without 'em."

"Okay." Eden slipped her hand inside the first one, her face drawn together in a serious yuck face. Brandi sympathized. It was never fun to put on someone else's sweat-soaked work gloves. With both of them in place, she reached for the saw.

Brandi handed it to her, but didn't release her grip. "Let me show you how." She pulled Eden into the curve of her body, one hand on the saw, the other on Eden's waist, holding her steady. "Use two hands, one on the trigger, the other on the support handle."

Eden moved into position. "Like this?" She sounded out of breath.

Brandi nodded. "Good."

This was a bad idea, Brandi realized. With the saw jutted out in front of them, Brandi breathed Eden in, the glove-free tips of her fingers searching out the thin stretch of skin between the bottom of Eden's fitted top and the top of her low-rise jeans. She stopped herself shy of resting her head against Eden's shoulder and cleared her throat.

"Okay, right." She mentally focused on the task before them. "This is the brake." She nudged the lever with her fingers, but didn't release her grip on the handle, her thumb flush against Eden's rough leather-clad hand. "You want to push against it until the chain engages."

"How will I know that happens?"

"When it starts moving."

Eden nodded, her movement firm and a little stilted. "Okay." She disengaged the brake and the saw whirled into action. "Now what?"

"Pull the trigger. It'll make the chain go faster."

The air around them grew still, perfectly quiet except for the demanding whine of the saw revving as Eden experimented with the trigger. Brandi tightened her grip on Eden's waist, just a quick squeeze, then released her and stepped away.

"Now you just hold it against the log and let the saw do the work." She backed farther away and gestured toward the limb.

Eden made short work of the log and held the saw in front of her, a triumphant smile on her face. "Now what?"

Brandi reclaimed the saw and switched it off. "Now we get cleaned up."

While Eden tossed the scattered lengths of wood onto the bonfire pile, Brandi collected her tools and loaded them into the back of the truck. No reason to make Ranger carry them.

"Back to the house?"

Eden stood close enough for Brandi to feel her breath against her neck. She shivered.

"I have a better idea." She turned and sidestepped Eden, giving herself some breathing room. Brandi was tired. Eden pulled at her like the moon drawing the ocean. It didn't matter if it was forever or one night. She couldn't fight the attraction any longer. "Come with me."

❖

Sweat rolled down Eden's back and pooled in the waistband of her jeans, partly from the heat and exertion, partly from nerves. She tightened her grip on Brandi's hips and hoped she wouldn't lose her concentration and fall off completely. Her legs spread over the horse's back, she bumped against Brandi's ass with each of Ranger's undulating strides.

"You okay back there?"

"Yes."

Eden was unsure if she should keep her body separated from Brandi or cling to her. The first option would put more pressure on her close-to-exploding clit. The second would bring their bodies together, extending the explosion to her entire body. She sat miserably stiff.

Brandi relaxed into her, eliminating the need for Eden to decide. Eden slid her arms around Brandi's waist to maintain her balance.

"God, you feel good," Eden breathed into Brandi's ear. She'd promised herself she wouldn't touch Brandi. The seduction wasn't worth the emotional toll of leaving afterward. She pulled Brandi closer.

Perspiration beaded on Brandi's throat, daring Eden to lick the salty tang of hard work from Brandi's skin.

"You ever ridden a horse?" Brandi asked, her voice thick like syrup.

"No."

In Los Angeles, horses were a roadside attraction. For twenty-five dollars you could ride a time-worn horse around a predetermined course for thirty minutes. That prospect didn't appeal to Eden. Earlier, however, as she watched Brandi loosen the buckles on Ranger's saddle, explaining that it'd be easier for the two of them to ride with just the blanket, Eden wished she'd had more experience—even the inadequate lesson of riding a spiritless nag alongside scolding mothers and crying children. Then Brandi had slung the saddle over the tailgate of her truck, climbed on Ranger's back, and reached out to Eden. All thought disappeared as she fitted her front to Brandi's back, her thighs stretched wide with Brandi's perfect, Levi-clad backside pressed against her crotch. She'd held on and prayed she wouldn't make a fool of herself.

"I've got you." Brandi rested one hand over Eden's and guided her lower, bringing Eden's palm to rest on her inner thigh. "See?"

The muscles were flexed hard and twitched beneath Eden's touch. Eden squeezed and released, massaging inward.

"Ah." Brandi clamped down on her fingers and pulled her hand up to rest on her stomach. "I'm only human, Eden."

"Sorry," Eden muttered, frustrated and unsure how far Brandi was asking her to go. Not that it mattered. She couldn't. She *knew* she couldn't. But, God, Brandi smelled so good and her body fit perfectly against her—soft, hard, and pliable all at once. Eden wrapped her arms around Brandi's waist and surrendered to the ride.

❖

The sun hung low in the sky, on the verge of dropping below the horizon, but the heat clung to the air.

"Your mom's going to kill us for missing dinner," Eden cautioned. The pond before her looked suspiciously like the one in Brandi's story, and after spending twenty minutes pressed front to back against Brandi on Ranger's rocking back, Eden felt her control was stretched to the point of breaking.

Brandi wore a button-down denim shirt with the sleeves cut off. She'd knotted the two sides together at the bottom, leaving the tight ripple of her abdomen exposed. At first Eden had tried to find a safe, non-skin zone to rest her hands. Finally she gave up and let her fingers have their way.

"My mom isn't home, so she won't know." Brandi unknotted the shirt and released the buttons. The front of her shirt fell open.

Eden clamped her mouth shut, grinding her back teeth together, and turned away. She'd promised Brandi she'd stop trying to seduce her, and now Brandi was trying to punish her for being good.

She felt the heat radiating off Brandi's body moments before she spoke. "Eden, look at me."

Eden turned slightly but kept her gaze averted. "I can't."

Brandi rested her palm against Eden's shoulder. Her touch, barely an imprint, spread through Eden like wildfire. "Please."

She lifted her head slightly and Brandi's smooth, bare leg came into view. She clamped her eyes shut, too late. "What do you want from me?" Eden asked, her voice pathetically weak.

Brandi tugged at the bottom of her shirt, curling her fingers around the hem. "I want," she jerked the fabric up and over Eden's head, "skin."

"Brandi, please, I can't—"

"Shh." Brandi pressed her fingers to Eden's mouth. "Just swim with me, okay?"

Swim. Eden could do that. As long as she didn't look at Brandi she'd be fine. "Okay." She let herself be undressed like an ingénue, unsure and trembling.

Brandi removed her clothes, her movements patient and gentle, then led Eden to the water's edge. "It'll be a little cold at first."

The sharp bite of water shocked Eden out of the honeyed fog she'd slipped into. As Brandi drew her deeper into the pond, Eden collected her thoughts and gathered Brandi to her, with water up to her chin, toes barely touching bottom.

"What are we doing here, Brandi?"

"Isn't it obvious?" Brandi ducked her head under the surface and came up smiling, rivulets of water clinging to her. "Swimming."

"No, it's not obvious at all." Eden fought her body's reaction to Brandi's naked flesh pressed against her. God, she wanted to give in, to loose her passion, consequences be damned. But Brandi wanted more than just a sweet, hot fuck. And Eden couldn't bear the reproach she knew she'd find in Brandi's eyes in the moments following release. Brandi deserved someone who could love her for a lifetime without looking over her shoulder. She deserved someone who could be there for her and keep her safe. Eden was not that person. "I can't give you what you're looking for, Brandi. You know that."

Brandi pressed a kiss to Eden's neck, the sensitive spot just below her ear, and worked her fingers into Eden's hair. The sharp tug as she combed the braid loose sent shivers tripping over Eden's scalp.

"Yes, you can."

Eden surrendered herself to a world of *yes*, lost in the sensation of Brandi's touch on her heated skin.

CHAPTER THIRTEEN

The return trip to the truck was painfully long. Eden shivered against Brandi's back, her skin wet from the pond.

Brandi reached down and stroked the outside of Eden's leg. "You can turn the heater to high as soon as you start the truck."

"What about you?"

"I'll ride fast. Bet I'll get back and have Ranger tucked in for the night before you even make it home."

Home. There was that word again. Funny how Eden had never thought about it before, convinced it was a mythical creature meant for others but not for her. Drug dealers built empires on blood and the ruthless pursuit of money. There was no room for life's simple pleasures in that formula.

Eden slid off Ranger's back. "You want his saddle?"

"Nope." Brandi bent down and leisurely kissed Eden, bringing every sated nerve ending in Eden's body to screaming attention.

"Wow." Eden slumped against the side of the truck. "I wish everyone said *no* like you."

Brandi laughed and said, "I'll race you back."

Before Eden could get the keys out of her pocket, Brandi nudged Ranger's flanks and took off with a "Heyah."

Eden drove back to Maple Hearth, her thoughts blessedly silent. Brandi wanted her, had touched her, and had offered herself in return. The rest of her worries were irrelevant in the face of such simple truth. She followed the road, the headlights cutting a dim path in the dark. She didn't know the road well enough to drive by memory, but she trusted her instincts and her heart to take her to Brandi.

❖

Brandi sat on the top step waiting for Eden. True to her word, she'd arrived first, settled Ranger for the night, and even had time to change out of her wet clothes. She reclined on her elbows and stared up at the night sky. The stars, brighter here than anywhere else she'd ever been, blinked at her.

"What are you doing?" asked the red one that wasn't really a star but rather a planet.

She closed her eyes and shook her head. "I have no idea." She didn't look at the stars again, content to rest her eyes and wait for Eden.

She'd ridden Ranger hard, faster than she should have in the dark. But it kept him from asking questions she didn't want to think about. Questions she didn't have answers to. As much as she tried to ignore the pressing weight of the unknown, pretend the uncertainty of her relationship with Eden didn't matter, it still gnawed at her. Ultimately, though, she pushed the questions away and let her subconscious swallow them for a while longer. Eden was here, if only for a few more days. And that's all that mattered. She'd deal with her leaving when it happened.

The sound of truck tires on the gravel drive brought a smile to Brandi's face.

Eden.

A few moments later, Eden settled on the porch next to her. Brandi cracked her eyes and examined Eden through her lashes. Eden stared at her, brows drawn together, lips curved upward in a soft smile. Brandi hooked her pinky around Eden's and closed her eyes.

"Do we need to talk about this?" Eden asked.

Brandi pushed herself up and brought Eden's hand to her mouth. She brushed her lips over each knuckle, then pressed a kiss to Eden's palm. "No. We need to go to bed."

"Are you sure?"

"Positive." She pulled Eden up and drew her inside.

What could she possibly say to Eden? After telling her *no*, over and over, she'd ambushed her at the pond. Not that Eden had been an unwilling or reluctant participant. She'd been ready and eager, enthusiastic even. Still, Eden had to be confused and looking for answers Brandi couldn't provide. Not yet. She just couldn't deny herself any longer. Giving in to her carnal urges with Eden was emotional suicide. Why talk about it and have Eden confirm what she already knew? Or, worse, deny it with a lie in her eyes. That would hurt far more. That left silence as the only suitable option.

Eden paused at the door to the guest room and Brandi tightened her grip on Eden's hand. "Sleep in my room tonight?" She could have left the question unasked and simply led Eden to her bed, but she wanted Eden to come willingly, to know she had a choice. They both had a choice.

"Yes."

Brandi left the overhead light off, allowing the moon to illuminate her room. She considered candles, soft music, a repeat seduction done storybook-right this time. Instead she pulled Eden's shirt off and kissed the smooth skin below her collarbone. Eden shivered.

"Do you want to take a warm shower?" Brandi asked as she unclasped Eden's bra and slid the straps off her shoulders. The lace and satin fluttered to the floor.

"I'm good." Eden removed her jeans and panties.

For the second time that night, Eden stood naked before her, and Brandi's head swam with the image. Brandi pressed her palms flat against Eden's abdomen and fanned her fingers wide, touching as much of Eden's quivering hot skin as possible. She held her hands there, prolonging the contact, then slid them up to Eden's shoulders.

Eden tipped her head to the side, lips slightly parted, eyes dark and heavy. Brandi traced the curve of her neck, from just below her ear to the rounded part of her shoulder. Bumps rose to the surface of Eden's skin. Brandi followed a reverse path with her mouth, starting at the shoulder and ending just below her ear. Soft and light, not pressing hard enough to even be a kiss.

Brandi held her mouth close to Eden's ear and breathed her in. The smell of summer sun and outdoor swimming blended with the remnants of Eden's cologne. She whispered a one-word benediction. "Beautiful."

A groan filled with desperation and impatience rumbled out of Eden. She turned her face and dug her fingers into the short hair on the back of Brandi's head. Eden's mouth was demanding and fiery as she pressed her lips hard against Brandi's. The time for tenderness ended with the possessive thrust of Eden's tongue.

Eden's skin was soft. Soft enough to warrant a lifetime of devoted worship. Brandi moved her hands down the smooth surface and splayed her fingers over the top swell of Eden's hips. She lingered there, immobilized by the probing insistence of Eden's kisses and the shiver beneath her fingertips.

Brandi moaned into Eden's mouth. She slid her hands to Eden's ass and pulled her closer. Grinding against Eden with slow determination, Brandi flashed on the image of Eden stretched out on the dock, her back arched above the sun-bleached wood, skin flushed with desire.

"Why are you still dressed?" Eden spoke into Brandi's mouth, not breaking the kiss. She pushed Brandi's loose pajama bottoms over her hips and they crumpled to the floor.

Cool air played against Brandi's skin, a reminder that she'd forgone panties when she'd changed earlier.

"Let's find out what else you're not wearing." Eden kneeled and kissed a hot trail up Brandi's abdomen, pushing her top higher as she went. Eden raked her fingers along the backs of Brandi's legs, then cupped her ass as she sucked Brandi's nipple between her lips. "God, I want you." Eden exhaled.

Brandi fumbled the shirt over her head. Her need for more slammed into high-tension-line awareness with the urgent tug of Eden's teeth. She gripped Eden's hair. "Bed," she growled, "now."

Brandi wrapped her body around Eden and shuffled back until

her legs hit the side of her queen-sized bed. Eden stopped her from pulling them both down onto the bed.

"Wait." The edge of urgency dropped off Eden's motions as she cupped Brandi's breasts lightly in her hands. She dipped her head and kissed the top of the neglected one, then sucked the nipple between her lips, grazing her teeth across the sensitive flesh. Lightning ripped through Brandi. She was lost to the electric current, all else forgotten, until Eden slid her hand down Brandi's body and eased one finger into her slick folds. Just a quick, exploratory dip.

"So wet…" She abandoned Brandi's breasts and reclaimed her mouth, easing her onto the bed.

The room swirled out of focus, then back again with a jarring thud. Eden knelt at her feet, pressed Brandi's legs open, and slid into her. The rush of being filled shook Brandi. She wanted to go slow, be sweet, show Eden how good she made her feel. Eden's pounding invasion left her breathless, panting, begging for more. The passion gathered in her like a storm cloud desperate for release. "Please…"

Eden pressed her tongue along Brandi's clit in long, languid strokes. Brandi clutched the sheets with one hand and Eden's head with the other. Eden coaxed Brandi's nerves to attention, her muscles stretched piano-wire tight, toes curled in anticipation. She silently begged for more. Eden rose with Brandi, her tongue now focused and demanding. Brandi rode the wave to a pounding crescendo, clinging to Eden as her orgasm powered through her. She collapsed, completely shattered.

Brandi lay gasping for breath, her hips settling back onto the bed, and waited for the room to come back into view. Slowly the pinpoints of light took form and she looked up to see Eden smiling down at her. "My God." She didn't know what else to say. She'd started out in control, trying to please Eden. Next thing she knew she was on her back with her legs spread wide, crying out for more. "Amazing."

Eden collapsed on top of Brandi. Her breathing was shallow and uneven, her eyes glazed over and half-lidded. Brandi felt a new surge of primal energy as she flipped Eden onto her back. She tried to go slow, to explore every part of Eden's body. Tried. Eden wrapped her fingers around Brandi's wrist and pushed her hand between her legs. The slick, wet heat engulfed Brandi as she slid two fingers easily inside Eden. She pulled out and added a third, desperate to fill her completely. Brandi moaned. Perfect.

Her gaze fixed on Eden's, Brandi settled over her. She ground her hips slowly against Eden, in time with her thrusts. She used her whole body to worship the woman beneath her. Eden wrapped her legs around Brandi's hips, forcing her closer still, urging her to go faster and deeper. The slap of sweat-slicked skin filled the room and Brandi thrust into Eden. She watched as Eden's face, illuminated only by the pale moonlight, contorted, her mouth frozen in a half-open *O*.

Eden's body tensed and she arched up to capture Brandi's lips in a pounding kiss. She clung to Brandi, her nails scratching deep into the skin on her neck and shoulders. Eden's shuddered breath, hot and ragged, against her neck brought life into perfect focus for Brandi. All that mattered was making Eden come hard and long, to feel Eden's muscles clench around her fingers as she drove her beyond reason. Brandi pushed her thumb against Eden's clit and curled her fingers, thrusting into Eden's g-spot. She couldn't speak, couldn't think beyond her need to give Eden perfect release.

Eden cried out, a strangled half-moan, half-gasp, but all Brandi's name. Her name on Eden's mouth like a benediction as she came was almost enough to take Brandi through another quaking climax with her. Eden fell back against the bed, glistening and spent.

Brandi gently removed her fingers and gathered Eden to her. They fit together, naked and glowing, like old lovers, comfortable in each other's arms. Brandi couldn't wait for morning when she'd get to hold Eden in the early light of dawn.

CHAPTER FOURTEEN

The bare lightbulb swung haphazardly on its chain, casting demonic shadows throughout the room. Gabriel sat on a straight-backed kitchen chair, head down, shoulders shaking. His hands—too small to properly grip Eden's signature Glock 9mm—shook with the weight of the gun he held between his knees.

"Gabriel, what did you do?" Eden's voice was unsteady, the scene before her too much to take in.

Luther stepped farther into the room, his breath hot and unforgiving against the side of her face. "He signed his own death warrant."

Eden held her arms tight against her side, fists clenched and aching for a target. Gabriel had gone too far this time. Even she couldn't protect him.

"Luther, please, let me deal with this." Eden leveled her voice, forcing out her words with the deadly calm of a seasoned assassin.

Of course Luther couldn't just defer to her to resolve the issue. It wasn't about the money this time. Gabriel had stolen both money and product, but worse than that, he'd laughed at Luther, claiming he was untouchable. The deadly Eden Metcalf was his sister. She would stand between him and Luther's wrath. His friends ran to Luther, eager to trade Gabriel's misplaced trust for Luther's favor.

"No, Eden, not this time." Luther took another step forward, closing the distance between him and Gabriel.

Eden's heart screamed for her to run to Gabriel, to carry him away from the pain and misery of his broken-down life. Her legs

JOVE BELLE

morphed to liquid lead—fluid enough to shake, but too heavy to move.

Gabriel lifted his head. His hair, once golden and beautiful, streaked down his forehead in greasy strings that obscured his face. He met Eden's gaze and held it. "I'm sorry." Tears spilled out of his eyes—yellow where they should have been white, and shot through with red—and carved a wet trail down his hollow cheeks. The pattern was eerily similar to the track marks on his arms.

Luther reached for the gun tucked into his belt. It was a gaudy .45 that would blast Gabriel's head into the neighbor's apartment.

The blood drained from Eden's face and she dropped to her knees. "Please, Luther, no. I'm begging you." It was barely a whisper.

Luther paused, his gun a silhouette at his side. "It's the way it has to be, Eden." That Luther was here at all, rather than another of his enforcers, told Eden exactly how impossible the situation was. Luther had stepped out of his comfortable role of lord on high to dirty his hands with Gabriel's execution. This single act would keep others walking the straight and narrow for years to come.

"Please." Eden cleared her throat and spoke again. "I'll do anything."

"No." Gabriel's shoulders shook harder.

With his gun leveled at Gabriel, Luther turned his face toward Eden. "Anything?"

Eden nodded and gulped back a sob. She would beg, but she wouldn't let Luther see her cry.

"The only way to keep me from killing him," Luther lowered his gun slightly, "is to kill him yourself."

Blood surged through Eden's ears, her heart pumping like a freight train. Gabriel's road to destruction led to death. By whose hand was up to Eden. "No."

A flash of light on gunmetal drew Eden's attention to Gabriel. He smiled weakly. "I fucked up." Rain streaked the window behind him—a deluge from heaven with no redemption for sale on this side of the glass.

"Looks like." Eden rose from to the floor. She commanded

her unwilling hand to draw her gun from her holster, but it remained immobile on her thigh. *Kill Luther.* A small voice teased her subconscious. But she couldn't. No more than she could kill Gabriel. For the first time since Luther handed her a loaded weapon and told her to pull the trigger, Eden was too much the coward to follow through. She couldn't draw against her brother. Worse, she couldn't draw in defense of him. Eden regarded Gabriel, the drug-torn battlefield of his body, and said, "I love you." They were the only words left between them.

"I love you, too."

And then he raised his gun. Eliminating the choice for Eden and stealing the victory from Luther, Gabriel pointed the barrel at his temple and pulled the trigger.

"No!" Eden's screaming sob was drowned in the 9mm explosion.

Luther tucked his gun into his waist as Gabriel's body slumped to the floor. The pool of blood reached across the threadbare carpet to comfort Eden in its warm embrace.

"Come on." Luther pried the gun from Gabriel's hand and dragged Eden sobbing and boneless from the apartment.

In that moment, with tears covering her face and the blood of her brother rapidly spreading over the floor, the voice pleading with her to run, to escape the evil that touched every part of her life, was born. She realized, even in her half-dazed state, that it was only a matter of time until she made her move.

❖

"Gabriel, no, please, no," Eden moaned over and over. The plea was filled with desperation.

Brandi rubbed the sleep from her eyes in an attempt to clear her head. Two fifty-six in the morning. Who was Eden talking to? "Eden?" She reached out a tentative hand and stopped just short of contacting Eden's shoulder. It wasn't a good idea to wake people during nightmares. Or was that while sleepwalking?

Eden cried out, "Please, stop."

To hell with it.

"Eden." Brandi laid her hand on Eden's shoulder. "Baby, wake up."

Eden jerked away from Brandi's touch, her skin sweat slicked and dead cold.

Brandi shook Eden. "It's a dream. Wake up. It's okay."

Eden stopped thrashing and grasped Brandi. "I can't stop him."

"Shh." Brandi held Eden gently, like a fragile child. "I've got you. It's okay."

Several minutes passed as Brandi comforted Eden with nonsensical reassurances, promises that she'd make everything all right. Brandi felt the tension drain from Eden's body—vibrating tight muscles relaxed to ragdoll limp—and still Eden clung to her.

"You want a drink of water or something?" Brandi smoothed Eden's hair and kissed her head.

Eden shook her head and tightened her grip. "Just...don't go."

"Okay, you want to talk about it?"

Eden paused so long that Brandi thought she wouldn't answer. Finally, she drew a shuddering breath. "It was about Gabriel."

Moonlight lit the room, giving Brandi a shadowed view of Eden's face. For the apparent terror of the dream, her face was ashen, but tear free.

"Your brother?"

Eden nodded. "It's never quiet in the city. Even in the middle of the night."

Again the mention of quiet. Where Eden heard nothing, Brandi heard the symphony of her childhood. The soft whisper of wind through the trees. The rustling of the dogs shifting in their sleep. The curious owl flying low on the hunt. The persistent chirp of crickets near the water.

"Tell me what you heard."

Eden wrinkled her nose. "The neighbors above us always fought. Three o'clock in the morning and they'd be up there screaming and throwing things. The next day, they'd both be covered in bruises.

Black eyes. One time he had a big bandage on his face. When it came off, he had a thin scar from his temple to his chin."

Holy crap.

"Wow. How often did that happen?"

"Just about every night."

"Why didn't you call the police?" Brandi knew it was the wrong question before she completely formed it.

Eden shook her head and looked at Brandi like she was a particularly slow learner. "That doesn't work in the real world, Brandi."

"Okay." What exactly did Eden mean by that? Brandi's world of hard work and sweat wasn't real? She counted to ten before answering. Being baited into an argument wouldn't help the situation. "Tell me what would have happened if you called."

"Nothing." Eden's answer was automatic, her voice flat.

"Nothing?"

"The operator would have asked if we wanted to file a report. Then she would have told us to lock the doors."

"Where were your parents?"

Eden hesitated, her eyes fixed on the moon outside the window. "Not there."

"So that left you and Gabriel?"

Eden nodded.

Even with Eden huddled in her arms, Brandi had a hard time picturing her as afraid and helpless. But she must have felt that way. What child wouldn't with the sounds of neighbors trying to kill one another in the background?

"He would have liked it here." Eden smiled, her eyes distant, but not happy. "Gabriel loved the idea of farms and growing things."

Brandi kissed Eden's shoulder. She wanted to ask if Eden had any good memories from her childhood, but was afraid of the answer.

"What did you do without your parents there?" *How does a kid eat with nobody there to feed her?*

"We got by. There was this Italian family on the top floor. Mrs.

Abbiati made the best pasta. We ate better when my mom wasn't around."

"Well, that's good."

"When I left that neighborhood, I had trouble sleeping."

"Really?"

"After that, I lived in a building with a secure entrance. Doorman checking people in and out. I never thought I'd miss the sound of gunfire and sirens."

"When did you move?"

"The day I turned eighteen. I was old enough to sign a lease."

"What about Gabriel?"

Eden stared out the window and drew her knees up to her chest. "He stayed. I couldn't convince him to come with me."

"What about your parents?"

"My mom stopped coming home completely when I was sixteen."

Only her mom? No mention of her dad. How many more questions would Eden answer? Brandi was amazed she hadn't shut down yet. She could see her struggling with the memories, but as with watching any good tragedy, she couldn't force herself to look away. Her mouth kept asking questions in spite of her brain screaming at her to stop, leave it alone.

"Did Gabriel take care of you?"

"At nineteen, he couldn't even take care of himself."

If Gabriel didn't take care of her and she had no parents to speak of past the age of sixteen, what did she do? What kind of job could a sixteen-year-old hold that would enable her to move into an upscale building on her eighteenth birthday? Brandi shuddered. She wasn't sure she wanted to know.

"What did you do?"

Eden turned in the circle of Brandi's arms and regarded her. Her eyes were heavy and serious. "You sure you want to hear all this?"

No.

"Tell me."

"I worked for a man named Luther."

Luther. Now all the names Brandi had overheard were accounted for. Penny was her first girlfriend. Luther her ex-employer. Gabriel, her brother.

Brandi waited, letting Eden reveal the details at her own pace.

"I did some pretty terrible things."

Terrible things? Like cleaning the chicken coop in July? Or helping an impacted steer? Or worse? The more Eden talked, the more questions Brandi had.

"But the money was good and all my friends worked for him, too, so I thought it would be okay. And Gabriel needed me."

Brandi massaged Eden's shoulders. The tension had returned to her body the longer she talked about her past.

Eden shook her head. "Not that it matters. It's over now."

"What happened to Gabriel?"

Eden paused for a long time again. When she finally answered, the words were barely more than a whisper. "He killed himself."

"How?" The question was out before good manners and common sense could stop it.

For the second time since Brandi forced this little question-and-answer session, Eden looked away from the window. She met Brandi's gaze and held it. Up until that question—how?—Eden had been hesitant, but not completely closed off. Now her eyes were distant and hard, almost like she was guarding against the pain that accompanied the answer. Eden drew a long breath. "Brandi, you don't know what you're asking."

"I'm sorry." Brandi said it again, the words meaningless in the face of Eden's cold, dark reality. "I just want to help." She sounded lame.

The change in Eden's face was so slight that if Brandi hadn't spent every possible moment since she arrived studying her expressions, Brandi would have missed the slight softening. "This place would have been his happily-ever-after. And here I am instead."

For how long? It wasn't the right time—in the middle of the night, with Eden's nightmare fresh in her memory—to ask Eden to stay. But, God, she wanted to. Two weeks was not long enough to explore what was happening between them.

"I wish he could be here, too." Brandi kissed Eden gently on the lips.

"Thanks." Eden pulled one side of her mouth up in a crooked half smile and lay down. "What time do you have to get up?"

Eden's movements lacked her normal grace, but for once Brandi's brain engaged before her mouth. Rather than pressing further, Brandi snuggled into Eden's arms and sighed. "Too early."

"Are you going to be able to sleep?"

"Are you making a better offer?" Brandi nibbled Eden's neck. Her body was sand-heavy with the need to sleep, but the need to lighten Eden's mood, share her burden in even the smallest way, overrode her basic needs. And there was nothing like a middle-of-the-night orgasm to release tension.

"Not right now." Eden kissed Brandi. "Maybe in the morning."

Brandi drifted to sleep with the promise of Eden on her lips and the worry about her brother on her mind.

CHAPTER FIFTEEN

Breakfast was in full swing by the time Eden finished her shower and joined Brandi and Jaylynn in the kitchen. She filled her plate with bacon and a healthy portion of oatmeal. It seemed silly to escape the violence of L.A. only to surrender her health to fried pork products. She sat next to Brandi and braced herself for morning-after awkwardness.

Brandi lifted halfway out of her chair, draped her arm across Eden's shoulder, and kissed her. Eden was caught between the bliss of Brandi's lips on hers and the panic of having Brandi's mom as a witness.

"Don't look so shocked." Brandi smiled, self-satisfied. "She already knew. Apparently, I'm glowing."

Eden snapped a bite of bacon. Incredible. She was worried about awkward silence in the wake of what they'd shared last night. She was in no way prepared for Brandi's open acknowledgment that their relationship had progressed beyond longing gazes and inappropriate sexual banter. The fresh air must make people in the country crazy, and it was starting to affect her as well.

"Oh, honey, don't look so shocked." Jaylynn laughed. "I'm not that old."

Oatmeal. Perhaps there was sanity in oatmeal. Eden gulped down a spoonful.

"So, what did you girls do last night?" Jaylynn asked with a straight face.

Eden choked.

"Finally got to that tree. Enough wood for a nice bonfire." Brandi looked equally serious.

"Plant a new one." Jaylynn emphasized the statement by lifting her orange juice toward Brandi.

"Did that this spring."

"Plant another. Two new trees to replace what's lost."

Eden wondered if it was really that simple. Could she just plant a tree to make up for the lives she'd taken? Two trees per life, according to Jaylynn. Or would it be more for a person? She should start planting after breakfast. It would take a while to plot the orchard she needed.

"So, you ever going to tell me what you learned at the bank?" Jaylynn asked.

Brandi shot her mother an acid look. "I learned that I don't like bankers, even Bobby."

"Surely it wasn't that bad."

"It was about what I expected. He offered to cut me a special deal if I have sex with his wife while he watches."

Eden almost dropped her coffee cup. This Bobby character would obviously benefit from a friendly visit. Perhaps a heart-to-heart discussion about the appropriate way to treat Brandi, with the tip of Eden's gun pressed to his temple, would improve his manners.

Jaylynn frowned. "Well, that's not a suitable option."

"Clearly not."

The conversation stalled for a moment, the sound of Eden's spoon scraping the bottom of her bowl loud in the aftermath of Brandi's announcement.

"On the upside," Brandi said, "Danny doesn't have designs on my sexual favors."

"That's a relief." Jaylynn patted Brandi's hand.

"He just has visions of mini-malls and housing developments."

"The irrefutable signs of progress." Jaylynn sounded resigned.

"Don't sign up for the neighborhood association meeting yet. I still have that meeting at BSU."

"BSU?" It seemed wrong to jump into the middle of what was obviously a private conversation, but Eden rationalized her question. After all, they were talking openly with her in the room.

"Boise State University." Brandi pushed away from the table, but didn't stand. "I'm seeing the head of the agricultural department next Wednesday to talk about the possibility of growing some research crops here at Maple Hearth."

"Wow."

Brandi cleared the table and placed their dishes in the dishwasher. "Don't get too excited. You'll jinx me."

"Are you serious?"

"No," Brandi pinched Eden's arm playfully, "but it's not wise to tempt fate."

Jaylynn knocked on the table. "That's right."

"You must have something you do for luck?"

Eden shook her head.

"Good-luck charm?"

"Nope."

"Some ritual?"

Eden hesitated. She used to rub the back edge of her pistol grip for luck. When gunfire was your primary tool for negotiation, you could never be too careful. Or too lucky. Still, it wasn't the kind of thing she could tell Brandi. "No, nothing."

"Then we'll have to get you something." Brandi's smile was slow and sexy, inviting Eden into her world.

Jaylynn settled a Broncos cap on her head and pulled her ponytail through the gap in the back. "I'm off." She kissed Brandi on the cheek, then Eden. "I'll see you girls later."

"Have fun." Brandi held the door open.

It was those simple gestures, Eden realized, a kiss on the cheek, a door held open, clearing another person's dishes, those were all the signatures of love that she'd never experienced as a child. But Brandi and Jaylynn communicated in this secret language seamlessly and without effort.

Eden waved, her throat too tight to be trusted.

"What's on your agenda for the day?" Brandi snugged her arms around Eden and gave her a long, lingering kiss.

"Take you back to bed and not get up until New Year's?" Eden nibbled along Brandi's jaw to her earlobe.

Brandi's head lolled to the side and she sighed. "Tempting."

Eden worked her way down, following the line of Brandi's neck to her pulse point. She sucked the rhythm of Brandi's life between her lips and inhaled her scent. Clean, like fresh country air. Brandi didn't need the too-expensive perfume that Eden relied on to enhance her appeal.

Brandi moaned and pulled herself away. "That's a far better offer than what I have to do, but you know the old saying. No rest for the wicked."

"You're not wicked." Eden had met true evil. Brandi didn't qualify.

"That's where the rest of the adage comes in. The righteous don't need any. Either way, I've got work to do."

Before this, Eden didn't think of herself as clingy, but it took all of her willpower not to ask Brandi if she could come along. Besides, it was only a matter of time until Brandi pressed Eden for more information about the memory-cum-bad dream that kept them both up in the middle of the night. It was in her nature to question what she didn't understand, and Eden's childhood was so far removed from Brandi's own as to make it unbelievable. She would keep digging until she could place all the painful bits into nice tidy boxes.

Eden waved good-bye as Brandi pulled away from the house, then headed for the barn. She couldn't leave Idaho with her Ducati in pieces.

❖

Jacob Richter—ol' man Richter to anyone under the age of fifty—occupied the piece of land adjacent to Maple Hearth. He had the equipment Brandi needed to bring in her hay crop. He also had the disposition of a rattlesnake. Perfectly harmless until you pissed him off. Then he'd strike, causing a whole lot of pain and making a whole lot of noise while he did it.

"Mr. Richter." Brandi always remembered her manners around

him. One slip-up when she was in the seventh grade had left her scarred for life. She shook his hand—firm, but not too aggressive. "I'm in need of a favor."

Jacob didn't like it when others beat around the bush. He'd scolded her once for "hemming and hawing." That was enough for Brandi. Now she just got straight to the point.

"What can I do for you, girl?" He knew her name, but for some reason refused to use it. He shared this aversion with Cliff, who more often than not called her "girl" as well.

"My baler's busted."

Jacob fiddled with the jumbo safety pin that held up one side of his overalls. "Cliff may have mentioned something about that." He offered her a near-toothless grin. "How can I help?"

"I got to bring in that hay," Brandi said patiently. In the conversational dance she was expected to participate in, she'd say what she needed, bluntly. Then she'd keep nibbling on it until he offered. Jacob liked to help, but he didn't like to be asked.

"Yep, hay's got to come in." He shook his head slow, semi-remorseful. "Can't do that without a baler."

"Nope."

Jacob rocked back on the heels of his ropers and fished a treasure out of his gums. A remnant of chewing tobacco, maybe? "How's your mama?"

"Causing trouble, as usual. She said to tell you that she and Patsy both say hello."

"That woman." Jacob slapped his leg and barked a laugh. "She's something, ain't she?"

"She sure is." Not for the first time when talking to one of the older ranchers, Brandi wished she smoked or carried a pocket knife or *something*. It would keep her from just standing in her standard hands-stuffed-in-pockets pose that made her ass look wider from behind.

"Did I show you what Leonard made?"

Lord, this was going to take longer than Brandi expected. Anytime Jacob started talking about his boys, especially the oldest one, he'd go on for over an hour.

"It's right over here." Jacob led Brandi to the front of his house.

Brandi couldn't remember ever seeing Jacob's front porch. Friends and neighbors always used the side door.

"See here?" He pointed to a hand-carved wooden sign that said, Richter Family Ranch, est. 1947.

"Leo made that?"

The craftsmanship was meticulous. Brandi had a hard time picturing the pimple-faced little boy that followed her around as a kid creating such a high-quality piece of work.

"He did." Jacob's chest visibly swelled. "My boy finished it right quick, too. Made me real proud when he hung it up there."

"I can see why."

"He's starting up a business."

"I might need a sign." Of course, she didn't have any money and Jacob knew it. She wouldn't be here in the first place if she did.

"He might could make you one." Jacob scratched his chin. "You know he has them horses."

Leonard Richter didn't have horses. He had several 110-year-old nags that were well past their working prime.

"I know. He sure loves them."

"He does." Jacob nodded and shook his head at the same time. No doubt Leonard loved those horses. And no doubt Jacob didn't understand why. "Didn't plant a hay crop this year."

And there it was. Jacob's reason for dancing the dance.

"Well, I could help with that. Assuming, of course, I figure a way to get that hay baled."

"Hmm." Jacob smoothed his hair and settled his John Deere cap on his head. The white was stained brown from sweat and field work. "I'll expect Cliff by to pick up that baler in a few days."

"He'll be here." Brandi tried not to smile too big. Ranchers were supposed to be stoic and hardy. Smiling like a kid was no way to perpetuate the image.

"Good enough." Jacob started into his house. "And I'll tell Leonard you'll be by to talk about your sign."

Brandi thanked Jacob and made a hasty retreat while he was willing to let her. She could never extricate herself from men like Jacob. They were too much like her daddy, except twenty years older. It made it hard to do anything but say "yes, sir" and listen as long as they felt like talking.

She'd only been away from Eden for a few hours, but it felt more like a few days. Have mercy, she had it bad.

❖

Polished Ducati parts covered the table, laid out at precise intervals like a complex, incomplete three-dimensional puzzle. Eden brushed away an invisible bit of fluff, then gripped the edge of the workbench. Brandi had only been gone for a few hours, but it was long enough for Eden to miss her beyond reason.

A week, she reminded herself. *I've only known her for a week.* Another week, maybe two, and her bike would be reassembled and her excuse for staying would be gone. She didn't know how she would survive riding away. Leaving Annie in Salt Lake had been easy. Eden knew it wasn't the right place for her. She couldn't say the same for Maple Hearth.

Her whole life she'd survived on emotional scraps—the leftovers of love that were doled out sparingly and with a watchful eye on the returns. Her father? Well, who really knew? Her mother? Gone, possibly dead. And it was for the best because Eden had grown tired of coming in second to a bottle of ninety proof. Penny, her best friend, her first lover, and what did they really share in common? The same fucked-up neighborhood that neither of them had the sense to leave. Until now. Later, they went to work for the same man, Penny in sales, Eden in asset protection. Yet she'd been able to walk away and leave Penny to fend for herself. Luther, the king. He saved and damned her at the same time. When her mom disappeared and Gabriel climbed inside himself, he shook her out and gave her a job. A job that killed her soul, but provided a well-appointed life for her and her brother. Except Gabriel, the sweet lion guard of her youth, didn't want anything she could give him. All he wanted, all he craved, was one more dive into the murky depths of heroin haze.

God knew she tried, but her efforts weren't enough to pull him to shore. By nineteen—the same year Eden turned sixteen and went to work for Luther—he was in too deep. It was a miracle he lived as long as he did, and that was something for Eden to cling to. A tainted victory trophy. And then he'd pulled the trigger—twenty-seven and no longer able to cope. Without the silencer to dull the noise, the gunshot had been deafening. A roaring, destructive explosion that ripped him from Eden's life, leaving her adrift with a broken compass. Her reason for staying and fighting for Luther's empire was lowered slowly into the ground while a gospel choir sang hallelujah. Her brother's death left her taste for blood sated and her body bloated with the destruction of others. All she wanted was to be free.

And here she stood—her mechanical means of liberation broken and disassembled on the table before her—ready to forfeit the very freedom she fought for. But Brandi deserved so much more than Eden could ever offer. She deserved truth, untouched by greed and corruption. She deserved the safety of sharing her life—and her bed—with a woman who didn't have the ghosts of lives taken haunting her at night. She deserved someone who was…good.

CHAPTER SIXTEEN

Eden stood at the open back door, the gunmetal gray screen door blurring her view of Jaylynn. The Cornwell matriarch was full swing in the middle of lunch prep for the various men and women who took their midday meal at Maple Hearth. Eden inhaled deeply and stepped into the kitchen.

"Not sure what I can do, but I'd like to help."

Jaylynn paused. "With what?"

It was a fair question given what little Eden had learned about Brandi's financial situation.

"With lunch." Eden washed her hands in the oversized, white enamel sink. "What can I do?"

Jaylynn pointed toward makings for a salad. "Tear up that lettuce and put it in that bowl. Then dice those tomatoes."

Simple enough. Eden should be able to do that without much trouble.

"Tear the pieces small, but not too small. You want 'em big enough to hold some of the good stuff when it's on a fork."

"Like this?" Eden estimated the size Jaylynn wanted. It looked good to her, but salad, just like everything else, might be different in Idaho than it was in Los Angeles.

Jaylynn wiped her hands on her apron and patted Eden on the shoulder. "That's perfect, honey, do it just like that."

They worked in companionable silence. Eden didn't know what to say to Jaylynn. She wanted her to know that she had feelings for Brandi, that she *wanted* to do the right thing when it came to her daughter. If only she knew what the right thing was, or if her circumstance would afford her the time with Brandi to figure it out. These were things she wanted to say, if only she could find the words.

"You girls have plans this evening?"

"I don't know." Eden sliced through a tomato. "I'd like to take Brandi to the fair in town."

"Oh, that would be nice." Jaylynn's voice took on a wistful quality. "I remember when Brandi's daddy took me there for the first time. I fell in love with him that night."

"You think it would be okay?" Eden thought again of Roger's reaction to the two men.

"Why wouldn't it be?"

Eden slowed her knife. She didn't want to cut herself instead of the tomato while she decided how to explain her concerns to Jaylynn. "I'm not sure I could act like we're just friends. If people wouldn't react well to that, maybe it's best if we don't go." Eden hated closets and refused to pretend that her feelings for Brandi were platonic. Still, it wouldn't be fair to Brandi to make a spectacle of their relationship, especially since Eden didn't plan to be around long enough to feel the fallout.

"What do you mean, Eden?" Jaylynn dropped half a stick of butter into a large bowl of potatoes.

"The first day I met Roger he made a comment about two men walking together. They weren't even touching, but they were obviously in love. I don't want Brandi to feel like her neighbors are judging her because of me."

"Let me explain something." Jaylynn paused, her arm continuing the steady up/down motion as she mashed the potatoes. "Around here, folks have some pretty strong opinions of what is right and wrong. But when it comes to someone they love and claim as their own, all that black-and-white turns to hazy gray. Brandi's happiness is more important than some perceived sin."

In Los Angeles, Eden never took the time to consider right and wrong, sin and virtue. It was all a question of live or die, kill or be killed. Here she found herself surrounded by a whole new set of rules, dictated by a God she didn't know enough about to support or believe in. She was intrigued.

"Is that what you think? That it's a sin?"

"No." Jaylynn sounded shocked that Eden would even ask such a silly question.

"Why not?"

"Brandi is exactly the way the good Lord made her. To question his wisdom...well, *that* would be a sin. God doesn't make mistakes."

"Oh." Eden liked that answer a great deal. It wasn't a conflicted attempt to reconcile an ideal with reality. The others might be willing to excuse Brandi because they loved her, and that tentative acceptance transferred to Eden by association. For Jaylynn, however, there was no question. She loved God and she loved her daughter. The two stood in concert with each other, not at odds. "So, you want to go to the fair with us?"

"I'd like that." Jaylynn dropped one final pat of butter on the top of the mound of mashed potatoes.

Eden turned her attention back to dicing tomatoes. *Is this what normal looks like?*

❖

Brandi hopped out of her truck and patted Cheyenne. She scanned the yard, trying to decide if Eden was more likely to be in the barn or the house. Until a week ago, Brandi would arrive at the house after a day of work sweaty, tired, and ready for rest. As she finished her duties today, her body filled with rumbling excitement, a low-energy hum that made her feet dance. By the time her house came into sight, she was so wound up that her heart bounced to the ground, up to her neck, then back down again—a yo-yo racing the length of her body. And her stomach seemed to be three steps behind her.

House. Brandi needed a shower. Afterward she planned to get up close and personal with Eden. Again. Her heart galloped off completely at the thought of Eden's skin, slick with sweat, sliding against her own.

"You planning to stand there all day?" Eden pushed open the screen door, then rested her shoulder against the frame. She crossed her legs at the ankle and folded her arms across her chest.

Brandi drank in the view. Polished boots, crisp blue jeans, complete with creases, Western-cut shirt with one too many pearl snaps open at the top, and a new white Stetson tilted back on her head. Brandi took the stairs two at a time and pulled Eden into her arms. "You have a hot date tonight?"

"As a matter of fact, I do." Eden pressed her lips to Brandi's in a sweet, lingering kiss. "With you."

Brandi smiled without breaking the kiss. "Really?"

"Yes." Eden stepped away. "But you really should shower first."

"Care to join me?" Brandi eased through the door, drawing Eden with her.

"I'd love to, but we'd never leave if I did."

"And I want to get there sooner rather than later." Jaylynn sat at the kitchen table, dolled up and ready for a night on the town.

"You're going?" Brandi asked her mother before turning her attention back to Eden. "Where exactly are you taking us?"

Eden held up a flyer for the town fair and smiled.

"Seriously?" Brandi couldn't believe it. Jaylynn had been trying to get her to go to this event every year since she moved back home, but it was just a little too Mayberry for her. "I forgot that was this weekend."

"It is." Eden led her to the bathroom. "And we're going."

An outfit similar to Eden's was hanging in the bathroom. She didn't recognize the shirt, but assumed it was for her. "You picked out my clothes?"

"I hope you like them." Eden kissed her quickly on the cheek. "Now shower and get dressed." She closed the door on the sentence, removing all possibility of further protest from Brandi.

In record time Brandi was showered, dressed, and ready to go. She cinched her belt tight and scowled at her hair in the mirror. It refused to commit to one style or another. She'd have been happy if it'd all stood up in fun dykey spikes. Or if it'd all lain down, like a too-long-rancher-does-Caesar kind of thing. Instead, her hair did a combination of the two. It was not flattering. After a few unsuccessful attempts to wrangle it under control, Brandi gave up and dropped her dress hat on her head.

Eden sat at the kitchen table with Jaylynn discussing the finer points of an open beer garden. "I just can't picture it. Sometimes people would have block parties, but that was different. The city officials didn't supply the beer, and somebody always got shot."

"I'm ready to go," Brandi said. "But are you sure you know what you're getting yourself into?"

Eden stood and offered Brandi her elbow. "Yes. I want to dance with my best girl."

Best girl? Maybe the town fair wouldn't be so bad after all.

❖

Red and blue paper lanterns were threaded over the raised wooden dance floor. It was an extreme juxtaposition to the throbbing strobe lights Eden was accustomed to. It was nicer, she decided. More romantic.

"Can I dance with you here?" She rubbed her palms against her pant legs. In spite of Jaylynn's reassurances, here in the moment, surrounded by Brandi's friends and neighbors, Eden was inexplicably nervous.

"If you want." Brandi took her hand in hers. "But it'd be better on the dance floor."

"What?" Eden asked. She rubbed her thumb in a half-moon just below Brandi's wrist. Brandi's skin was warm, calming. She drew comfort from the touch.

Brandi pulled Eden to a stop and faced her. "It's okay." She gestured at their surroundings. "Us being here. No one will say anything."

"Are you sure?" Eden had never been worried about hiding her sexuality before. But that had been L.A. where she had been the baddest motherfucker on the block. Here she was an outsider poaching a local. She didn't have her reputation—or her guns—to protect her. And people were starting to stare.

"I'm positive." Brandi pulled Eden toward the table Jaylynn had claimed. "Decide quickly, do you want to dance first or make nice with the locals?"

"Make nice with the locals?" Eden swallowed. She wasn't at all sure that was the right choice, but followed dutifully behind Brandi.

"They're already lining up to meet you."

The crowd at Jaylynn's table had grown in the few moments Eden and Brandi had been talking. Eden had attributed it to Jaylynn's popularity.

Eden forced a polite, interested smile, the one she reserved for police officers and lawyers. She'd been told that it was charming. "Whatever you think is best."

"We'll start slow. Look, there's Roger."

Roger eased himself into a battered metal folding chair. It groaned with the weight, but held. A small, fluttering woman perched on the chair between him and Jaylynn. She used only the very edge of the seat, looking as though she was ready to take flight at any moment.

"Eden," Roger's tobacco-stained smile seemed genuine, "meet my wife, Fern."

Brandi sat opposite her mother and Eden remained standing at her side. She nodded politely to Fern. "Nice to meet you."

Fern clutched her black purse. "Likewise." Her smile reminded Eden of peanut brittle—sweet but easily broken.

"Eden's been helping with my books." Roger's voice was louder than normal. Either Fern was hard of hearing or Roger was informing the crowd.

"I figured."

"She's waiting on a part for that Ducati." Roger always said the Italian word wrong, placing emphasis on both the first and the last syllables, leaving the middle soft.

"And what will you do when the part arrives, dear?" asked a woman Eden hadn't been introduced to.

Brandi tensed beside her and Eden laid her hand on Brandi's shoulder. "Fix the motorcycle, of course."

Fern stared at her, no trace of a smile. "Then what?"

"I'm not really sure." *Shit.* Eden's head had no doubt what would happen. She'd get on her bike and ride away. Apparently her heart and body weren't interested in what her brain knew, because they answered without her permission.

Brandi relaxed and took over the introductions. Every person in town, it seemed, had an interest in meeting Eden and a stake in Brandi and Jaylynn's well-being. Understanding of Roger's earlier claim to her became clear in the endless parade of handshakes and how-do-you-dos. More than once she'd been told that if Roger thought she was good folk, then she must be okay.

"How you doing?" Brandi's warm breath tingled against Eden's skin, the low whisper evoking intimate memories of the night before.

"Piece of cake." It mattered to Eden, more than it should, that these people like her. That they find her worthy of Brandi's affection. Facing off against armed drug dealers was much simpler. They didn't need to like her because in the end she would kill them anyway.

"Ready for a little interruption?" Brandi's arm settled around her waist, her palm snugged flat against the inside curve.

Eden choked back a moan. "God, yes."

"Dance?"

They made their way hand in hand to the middle of the dance floor. Brandi's body melded into hers. She knew it would, but the perfection of the moment arrested Eden's thoughts. All she could do was cling to Brandi, swaying with her, the music and the crowd forgotten.

"This is nice." Brandi's lips moved against Eden's neck.

"Yes." Eden hooked her thumbs over the edge of Brandi's belt, the leather hard and biting against her skin, and fanned her fingers over the tight denim, tracing the ridge of Brandi's back pockets. "You sure this is okay?"

Brandi pulled back and looked at Eden. Her eyes were dark and heavy with desire. "Is it okay for us to dance? Yes. But if we keep going, the sheriff will arrest us for indecent exposure or lewd and lascivious behavior or something of the like."

Eden shifted her hands higher. "Then we shouldn't dance."

"No, we probably shouldn't." Brandi didn't release her hold.

"Maybe we could finish this later?" Eden stepped away from Brandi.

"Count on it."

Jaylynn intercepted them on the way back to the table. "Dance with me, Eden?"

Brandi patted her hip and kissed her cheek. "Go ahead. I'm going to say hi to Bobby and Erica."

Eden held Jaylynn at arm's length, unsure exactly how to dance with her lover's mother.

"Well, how you feeling?" Jaylynn asked eventually.

"About?"

"All of this." Jaylynn inclined her head to indicate the surroundings. "Your inspection."

"Awkward and nervous." Eden should have said fine, but Jaylynn inspired full emotional disclosure.

"It seems you passed." Jaylynn regarded her. "Even Fern thinks you're the decent sort."

Eden's heart slowed, then galloped off as Jaylynn's words settled in. Dazed, she asked, "Really?"

"But they don't have the same interest that I do." Jaylynn's gaze was hard and penetrating. "What are your intentions with my daughter?"

Eden swallowed, her steps faltered. "What do you mean?"

"Don't make her think you're going to stay if you're really planning to leave."

They danced for several moments, Eden looking at anything but Jaylynn. Finally she said, "I want to stay, but that would be unwise. Brandi deserves more." The softness of her voice surprised

Eden. *Timid* and *unsure* were not words she would use to describe herself, but in this moment, defending her future actions to Jaylynn, she felt no strength at all.

"Love isn't about deserving, Eden. It's about honoring your heart and cherishing the person you give it to. Anything less would be a disservice to both of you."

Love.

They finished the dance without further conversation. Eden led Jaylynn back to the table where Brandi was waiting. Her smile told Eden that Jaylynn was right. Brandi, whether she knew it or not, loved her. She shut down that line of thinking before her brain could turn the question inward. Love in her life was irrelevant. Survival was all that mattered, and staying here jeopardized that. Worse, it placed Brandi in danger, too.

The thought of leaving filled Eden with black, clinging sadness. How in the world would she ever get on her bike and ride away when the time came?

CHAPTER SEVENTEEN

Your part has been shipped. Eden blinked as the message took hold. Before the end of the week, Thursday at the latest, Ducati International promised, her part would arrive and she'd be out of an excuse to stay.

Eden closed the e-mail program and drummed her fingers over the dwindling stack of invoices. Roger's books were almost in order, her part was en route, and her good sense told her she should be relieved, anxious to go, even.

"You have fun at the fair this weekend?" Roger's question preceded him into the room. He opened the fridge and offered her an orange.

Eden shook her head at the fruit. She hated the film that covered her fingers when she pulled back the peel. "I did. Fern seems like a nice woman."

"Oh, my Fern is a real gem. Don't know how she puts up with a man like me." Roger's face softened.

"You're a good man, Roger."

Roger grunted as he dropped orange peels into the trash.

"Best man I've ever met," Eden assured him quietly.

"Now that's some sorry bit of news." Roger split his orange, the juice squirting up in an orange fog. He set half on the desk next to Eden's papers on his way to the workshop.

Eden ate a wedge, the citrus tang dancing over her taste buds. She flashed on an image of the sweet juice dripping down Brandi's chin, following the curve of her naked body. Eden shook the image loose as she wrapped fantasy lips around Brandi's tight nipple and licked it clean.

No matter where Brandi was working, she kept her cell phone with her just in case. Eden dialed the numbers from memory.

"Hi." Brandi was breathing hard when she answered, the roar of loud machinery in the background.

"Did I interrupt something?" She pictured Brandi, faded blue jeans clinging to her hips, sweat trailing into the cleavage peeking over her too-tight tank top, and her eyes daring Eden to do something about it.

"I'm throwing hay bales."

Eden had no idea what that meant, but it sounded sexy as hell when Brandi said it. "How 'bout I come home and throw you over a hay bale instead?"

Brandi groaned. "It's not nice to tease."

"That was an offer. Say the word and I'll be on the way."

"You have no idea how much I'd like that." Brandi sighed, a sort of strangled half-whimper. "But I have to get this done while I have Richter's baler."

"Oh, I meant to ask you if you found a new one." Eden felt like an ass. Even if she didn't understand what the machine did, it was obviously important to Brandi. She should have inquired about it before now.

"Jacob Richter loaned me his. Sort of a barter. They didn't plant hay this year, but they need some for their horses. Works well for everyone."

"What about next year?"

"I'll worry about that when I get there." Brandi sounded unsure.

"I have money. I wish you'd just let me buy you one."

"Maybe I will." Brandi paused. "Next year."

"Brandi..." Eden couldn't bring herself to say that she wouldn't be around next year to take care of it.

"I know." Brandi let her off the hook. "I have to get back to work. I'll see you tonight." Brandi disconnected the call.

Eden massaged her temples. Why couldn't they just enjoy the time they had together without placing expectations on the future?

❖

The red rooster strutted and bagocked at the entrance to the chicken coop, blocking Eden's path. Brandi waited to see how Eden would handle the opposition.

"Explain to me again what I'm supposed to do." Eden eyed the chicken uncertainly.

"Gather the eggs." Brandi tried not to laugh.

"And the chickens don't mind?"

"I never asked them."

"That one looks like it minds." Eden gestured toward the rooster.

"It's his job to protect their home."

"Great."

Brandi held out the bag of feed. "Here, use this to distract them."

Eden scooped out a handful and sniffed it. "What is it?"

"Chicken food." Brandi pulled some out and tossed it in a loose arc to the opposite corner of the pen. The chickens clucked and moved toward it. "Toss it over there."

"How much should I give them?" Eden asked as she spread the feed.

The rooster abandoned his post at the door and took up position on a fence post near the hens.

"That should be enough." Brandi traded a rake for the bag of feed. "Now just rake out the inside. After we spread new bedding, we'll gather the eggs."

Eden wrinkled her nose, but did as instructed, gathering the soiled straw in a pile at the entrance of the coop. Brandi forked it into the wheelbarrow as Eden laid down the new liner.

"I can't believe I came home early for this," Eden mumbled.

"You didn't." Brandi set her pitchfork and rake across the load, then kissed Eden. "You came home early for that."

"Mmm, and then some." Eden slapped Brandi lightly on the ass. "Let's finish this so I can finish that." She turned back toward the coop and stopped. The rooster was back in place. "Don't suppose we could just forget about the eggs?"

"You want breakfast tomorrow?"

Eden looked at Brandi, then at the rooster. "I could do without."

"I couldn't. Come here." Brandi walked to the back side of the coop and opened the hatch that gave her access to the roosts without going inside. "We'll get them from here."

"Nice." Eden pulled out a couple of eggs from the first nest and set them in the basket.

Brandi relaxed against the side of the building and watched. Eden looked so right in her world, Brandi couldn't believe she'd only been there a little over a week. "You're still going to leave, aren't you?"

Eden's hand wavered slightly, then she continued gathering eggs. "I have to." She didn't look at Brandi.

"Why?"

Eden's jaw clenched, but she didn't answer.

"Is it because of Penny?" Brandi knew so little about Eden's life, she snatched at one of the only names she had from Eden's past.

"No." Eden still wouldn't return Brandi's gaze.

"Luther?"

Eden stopped moving completely, her face frozen, eyes blank. Then she turned and advanced on Brandi. She stopped well inside Brandi's personal-space bubble, their toes touching, and said, "You need to forget that name." Her voice was dead calm and the statement felt more like a threat than advice.

"Why?" Brandi's voice shook and she fought the urge to smooth her hands over Eden's arms, to kiss the stress from her face, to hold her until the tension flowed from her body. Instead she held herself tight, her hands clenched at her sides.

Again, Eden didn't reply. She returned to gathering eggs.

"Eden, if this man is going to take you from me, I deserve to know why." God, she sounded like the women on daytime television fighting to keep their men. She hated those shows, and she hated herself for feeling so clinging and desperate. "Please."

"No, Brandi, you don't." Eden slammed the hatch closed and stomped across the yard, egg basket swinging wildly at her side. "No one deserves to know those kinds of things."

Brandi chased her. "I don't understand." She should let the subject drop, Brandi knew it, but she couldn't help herself. She wanted Eden to tell her who had her running like a bat out of hell. She caught up with her on the back porch and grabbed her arm. Eden swung around, her body coiled tight and ready to fight. Brandi gave in to the urge to reach out for Eden. She pulled her close and held on tight, ready to ride out the storm. "Tell me, please. I can't just let you go. I can't."

Eden deflated, all the anger bled out, and she collapsed into Brandi's embrace. "It's not that easy, Brandi."

"Nothing ever is."

"Tell me about the worst man you've ever known."

Brandi thought about it. All the people she knew, men and women alike, occasionally did things she didn't approve of, but none of them were bad people. "There was this guy in college who drugged a girl and had sex with her while she was out."

Eden looked expectant, then disgusted. "That's it? That's the worst person you know?"

"Yeah." Brandi suddenly felt very naïve.

"Okay, take that guy. Except instead of drugging her, he orders a hit on her. So his lackey hits the girl in the side of the head with his pistol butt, binds her wrists, and then tosses her in the trunk of his car. When he delivers her to the boss, the boss is pissed that she's still alive. He slaps her until she wakes up, rapes her, and slits her throat as he comes."

Brandi's stomach hurt. She didn't know which bothered her more. The image Eden evoked or the dispassionate tone she spoke with.

"Luther is like that?"

"No, Luther is worse."

"Oh."

"Yeah, oh." Eden sat heavily in one of the rocking chairs. "My being here places you in danger. And that's not okay."

"You worked for that guy?" Brandi's mind was spinning.

Eden dropped her head into her hands. "Yes."

"So all of this has been an act? From the moment I met you?" It couldn't be true, Brandi refused to believe it. Even if she didn't know the details of Eden's life, she knew her heart.

"Not an act." Eden shook her head. "Just me trying to—"

"What?"

"Find myself, I guess."

Brandi picked up the basket of eggs and checked them for cracks. It was easier to focus on the routines of farm life than to let Eden's revelations shatter her completely. Still, she couldn't help but ask, "What does that mean?"

"I've been out of Los Angeles for a couple of months, but it never really sank in. Yes, I knew it in my head, but until you stopped to help, I didn't realize that the people outside my old world really are different. And I just wanted to fit. It was surprisingly easy. The change began when I decided to leave, and it grew from there." Eden lifted her head, her eyes shining and clear. "I've been more like myself since I met you than I've ever been before."

Brandi settled into the chair next to Eden and covered her hand with her own. "Okay, but I still don't understand why you have to leave."

"Neither do I." Eden kissed Brandi's fingers.

"Then stay. At least long enough for us to figure this," Brandi kissed Eden for emphasis of what *this* she was talking about, "out."

Eden sighed. "You won't even tell me what you're worried about. The hushed conversations with your mom about money. The meetings with the banker and the real estate agent. Yet you want me to stay."

"You really want to know?" Brandi didn't like the turn this conversation was taking. She might be ready to face Eden's past, but that didn't make her ready to air her own dirty laundry.

"Yes."

"Okay. My dad took a loan against Maple Hearth. A balloon payment is coming due and I have no way to pay it. I think I'm going to have to sell part in order to save the whole, and that just sucks." Brandi rushed the words before she could change her mind.

"Brandi, I have money. I can fix this." The storm in Eden's eyes receded.

"I can't let you do that."

"Why not?"

All the reasons Brandi had were the same reasons that said it shouldn't matter if Eden rode out of her life tomorrow.

"You've been here a week."

"Long enough to place your life in mortal danger, but not long enough to give you money?" Eden stood abruptly. "That's crazy. It's just paper. A means to an end. Your life is worth far more than I have in the bank."

"I'm not saying it's not tempting. But it wouldn't be right."

"Of course not." Eden slipped through the back door. "I'm going to bed."

Brandi put the eggs away and headed to her room. She could hear Eden changing inside the guest room, but she didn't stop and try to change Eden's mind. She entered her room, collapsed on her bed, and waited for sleep. Wrung out and alone.

CHAPTER EIGHTEEN

The columns of numbers swam and converged into a jumble of number soup. Eden blinked and rubbed her eyes. She'd been staring at this screen for too long trying to explain how to reconcile the payables with the receivables to Roger. A quick glance confirmed that he was no longer tuned in to their conversation. His eyes were glazed over, his jaw slack. Not that he'd appeared much more interested when she'd initiated this impromptu training session, but at least then he hadn't looked like a zombie.

The bell rang, indicating someone had entered the main door of the shop.

"Let's take a break." Eden pushed away from the desk. In L.A., she'd been able to stare at accounting ledgers all night long, ferreting out the losses. And the entire time she'd been setting up Roger's bookkeeping, she'd been fine. But trying to explain the system to the obviously disinterested man made her tired. It'd be so much simpler to just stay and keep track of it all for him.

Roger stood and stretched. "'Bout time." He headed toward the front counter.

Eden filled a mug with the semi-warm coffee left in the bottom of the pot. It wouldn't taste good, but it might wake her up. She hadn't slept properly since she and Brandi had argued a few nights ago. Over money. Her long drink of coffee sludge went down hard, along with Brandi's refusal to let her help. She'd tried several times, but didn't know how to convince Brandi that she could give her what she needed.

In a few days, it'd be time to leave and she needed to square things with Roger, make sure he could carry on in her absence. But all she could think about was Brandi. She wanted to run to her, hold her, kiss her, explore her body again and again. There wasn't enough time to show Brandi everything she felt. Hell, she couldn't even define it for herself. Not really. She just knew that when she was with her, she couldn't get close enough, and when they were apart, she had to fight like a shark on the end of a fishing line. If she relaxed for even a moment, she'd give in to the relentless pull back to Brandi.

Eden rinsed out her cup and watched the thick black drink swirl down the drain.

Roger came back and dropped a package on the counter next to Eden. The return address said Ducati International. "That's that, then." He turned away.

"Roger, wait." Eden reached for his arm, but stopped short of touching him. "I—"

"Save it, kid." Roger kept walking. "We both knew this was coming. You should head home and fix that bike."

He was right.

Eden tucked the box under her arm, then surveyed the room one last time before pulling the door shut behind her—the computer still on, invoices entered but not explained.

❖

Brandi's heart quickened at the familiar sound of her old truck pulling into the yard. Eden was home early. Mentally, her body bolted for the door, but physically she forced herself to remain seated.

"How much are you planning to sell?" Jaylynn sipped her iced tea.

"As little as possible." Brandi tapped the yellow legal pad in front of her with the eraser end of a pencil.

"That's not a real answer."

"Danny and Bobby want ten acres." They'd finally revealed

their grand plan the last time she met with them. It didn't make her happy, but at least they were finally shooting straight. That was worth something.

"Housing development?" Jaylynn speculated.

"No, strip mall." Brandi would have preferred a housing development.

Jaylynn fished an ice cube out of her glass and popped it in her mouth.

"I'm pushing for seven." The plans called for seven acres of development and three as a natural sound barrier between the properties. A suburban barricade to keep the two worlds from encroaching on each other. Brandi preferred control of that barrier rather than trusting her relative privacy to others, even if they were old high-school friends.

"Could be worse, I suppose."

Brandi wasn't at all sure how, but she supposed Jaylynn was right. "I guess."

"It'll be enough?"

Brandi nodded. "And then some."

"And there's no other option?"

"None that I can see." Brandi closed her laptop. The meeting with the head of the agriculture program at BSU had been fruitful and the contract was being drafted. But the financial benefit was too little and far too late. The sale was the only possible way to satisfy the bank note.

"Then it's done. No use crying over it."

"Doesn't it make you angry?"

"Why would it?" Jaylynn looked at her levelly, her hands motionless against the table. Drops of condensation rolled down her glass.

"Because Daddy forced us to this." Brandi realized that she and Jaylynn had never discussed the reason they were in this predicament. Saying it aloud now felt like she was betraying her father. He'd been short-sighted, but not malicious.

"Brandi," Jaylynn sighed out the name, "your father…he tried.

I shouldn't have left so much to him. He had good intentions, grand visions, but he just couldn't quite pull it all off. But he loved us. He wouldn't have wanted this."

"If he'd just stopped to think even once." Brandi sounded spoiled.

"You're doing so well, so much like your grandfather. Neither of us, your father or I, had that built-in sense of self. You're solid. Your feet grow up out of this ground and you know exactly what to do to take care of it. Even when it hurts. You don't realize how lucky you are."

It was Brandi's turn not to answer.

Jaylynn went to the refrigerator and refilled her glass. "I'll sign whatever paperwork you need. Just let me know when and where."

"All right."

"Looks like Eden's not coming in. You should go see what brought her home so early."

Brandi didn't need to be told twice. She made short work of the distance between house and barn, stopped to wipe the sweat from her palms on her Levi's, then walked through the open overhead door in search of Eden. She found her working on her Ducati, black streaks of grease covering her arms, along with one long strip across her cheek. Brandi could hear her talking in a low voice to the parts, coaxing them into place as she worked.

"You got the part."

Eden looked up, her eyes sad and dark. "Yes." She lowered her gaze and continued working.

"That's good, I suppose."

"Is it?"

"Seems wrong for a beautiful bike like that to sit busted apart in a dusty Idaho barn, doesn't it?"

"When you put it that way, yes."

Brandi moved next to Eden, close enough to touch. "How would you put it?" She stroked Eden's hair, traced the outside edge of her ear.

Eden eased into the touch. "A reason to stay."

"Then don't fix it."

Eden's body stiffened and she moved to a new bolt, tightening it with an open-ended box wrench. "That's not really an option, is it?"

"It is for me."

Eden moved to the next bolt. "Hand me that part right there." Her finger shook as she pointed.

Brandi gave her the appropriate item, then kissed the hair at Eden's temple. It seemed that Eden was leaving and nothing Brandi said would stop that.

Eden tightened one last bolt, the muscles in her arms flexing and releasing as she worked. "Done." She wiped an invisible spot from the tailpipe.

"That's it, huh?" Brandi's eyes stung with the implications.

"That's it."

Brandi pulled Eden into her arms and pressed her lips to Eden's ear. "Please don't go."

Eden squeezed her tight. "Careful, I'm all dirty."

"I don't care."

"Why, Brandi?"

"What do you mean?" Brandi didn't loosen her grip.

"Why me?" Eden's voice wobbled.

"It's one of those things we don't get to choose." Brandi slid her hands under Eden's shirt. The feel of skin both grounded and confused her. She felt lightheaded and euphoric, powerful and weak. Eden was her aphrodisiac. "And, according to my mom, it's something we shouldn't question."

Eden followed Brandi's arms to her hands and pulled them away from her body, separating them. Brandi felt cold.

"I need to start it up. Listen to it run."

"Right now?"

Eden nodded and turned the key. With a tight, wry smile, she pushed the button. The engine roared to life and Ranger whinnied. Eden quickly killed it. "I'll roll it outside."

Brandi watched, not quite believing the Ducati was really

fixed. She needed to be able to deny it, if only for one more night, but Eden didn't seem inclined to grant her a reprieve. She stopped pushing as soon as she cleared the barn door and started the motorcycle again.

Eden inclined her head, listening as she revved the engine. She smiled, relaxed and happy, and said, "Want to go for a ride?"

Perhaps Brandi could put off the inevitable for a while longer. Maybe she could pretend that Eden would stay and they would take long, exploring rides through Brandi's countryside. She'd like that. Her front pressed to Eden's back, Eden's ass snug between her legs, the vibrating thunder of the Ducati pulsing through her as they leaned into a corner. Yes, she'd like that a lot.

She couldn't help but smile. "Yes."

CHAPTER NINETEEN

B randi stood in the doorway, one hand resting on the frame, watching as Eden pulled her riding chaps from the back of the closet where she'd deposited them the first day she arrived at Maple Hearth.

"You keep looking at me like that, we won't make it out to the motorcycle." Brandi smiled that confident, sexy smile that told Eden she knew exactly what Eden was thinking and she was open to the possibilities.

Eden forced herself to look away as she shook the dust off the black leather. She held the chaps in position and fumbled with the buckles. The way Brandi was staring at her, like she wanted to eat her alive, made Eden weak in the knees. A low, pulsing energy thrummed through her, starting between her legs.

"Let me help."

Brandi stepped far too close to Eden and rested her hands on Eden's waist. Eden stared at Brandi's mouth, the willing tease on her soft pink lips. She felt Brandi's hands moving around her, tugging at the leather, but she couldn't move. She was trapped in the wet invitation as Brandi sucked her bottom lip between her teeth.

"There." Brandi squeezed Eden's ass cheeks. "Now the zippers." She dropped to her knees and Eden forgot how to breathe.

"Okay," Eden said dumbly, and braced herself against the wall.

Brandi stared up at her, mouth level with Eden's button fly. She lowered her lashes and smoothed her hands down the outside of

Eden's legs, pulling the zippers as she went. Brandi rested her palms briefly against the bare skin of Eden's ankles—up under her pant leg and over the top of her boots—shocking Eden with the contact, before tracing Eden's inseam all the way to the apex.

The touch was fleeting, over before Eden really felt it, but the impression of Brandi's fingers—her palm flattened against her opening, her thumbs pressed directly over her clit—flamed through Eden, burning the memory into her skin. She cursed the thick denim separating her aching need from Brandi's willing touch.

"Sure you want to go?" Brandi hooked her fingers through Eden's belt loops and stood, pressing her body to the length of Eden's.

Eden tasted the sweet honey of Brandi's kiss, drank her in as their tongues glided together. She never wanted this dance to end. The thought jolted Eden. As much as she wanted to stay, she couldn't. And she wanted to take some part of Brandi with her. She wanted the memory of Brandi clutching her waist, body flush against her as the pavement raced by under her wheels. She ended the kiss, letting her lips linger over the contours of Brandi's mouth. With her eyes closed, she pressed her forehead to Brandi's.

"Yeah, I want to show you what it's like."

Brandi stepped back slowly. "Really?"

"Yeah, let's go." The thought of the Ducati between her legs and Brandi wrapped around her back inspired Eden to draw Brandi outside. Once they were on the road together, maybe they could just keep riding, away from Luther's relentless search, away from Idaho. Away from Maple Hearth.

No. Brandi would never leave. Like she said that first day, for better or worse, she was tied to this land.

"You look so sad." Brandi waited as Eden straddled the motorcycle, then started it.

"Really?"

"Sad," Brandi nodded, "and excited. And turned on. I don't know if I should hug you or kiss you."

Eden let the Ducati idle as she gathered Brandi close to her, her hands resting lightly on Brandi's hips. "How 'bout both?"

"I can manage that."

Brandi looked so sweet, so earnest. She cupped Eden's cheeks in her palms and traced the line of Eden's mouth with her thumbs. Before the pressure of the touch faded, she pressed her lips to Eden's. She slid one hand around Eden's head, her fingers fanned wide and threaded into Eden's hair, loosening her braid. Brandi's other hand drifted south, glancing over Eden's already charged breasts, then circled her waist. She flattened her palm against Eden's back and held her firm.

Eden opened to her, surrendering to the demand in Brandi's kiss. She heard—in the hot, probing invasion—the desire, Brandi's absolute need to possess. Without saying a word, Brandi claimed her.

Eden eased out of the kiss. "Is your mom home?"

"Yes." Brandi smiled, devilish and flirting. Her eyes sparkled with I-dare-you mischief. "Why?"

"It means no sex in the driveway."

Brandi laughed. "That would be bad."

"But very, very good." Eden licked the outside edge of Brandi's ear. God, she wanted this woman.

Brandi moaned and loosened her grip, and her hand slid out of Eden's hair.

"Ready to ride?" Eden asked as she seated herself astride the Ducati.

"Yes." Brandi climbed behind Eden and rested her hands lightly on Eden's waist. "I have something to show you."

Eden paused before accelerating. She loved riding without a helmet, the wind made her feel free. Idaho was one of the few states that still allowed a rider to choose how much protection to wear. But Brandi might want one. "Helmet?"

"How fast are you going?"

"How fast do you want me to?"

Brandi nuzzled the back of her neck. "I want to relax and enjoy the ride."

"Put these on." Eden slipped her sunglasses in place and offered Brandi a pair. The wind in her hair felt liberating. But protecting her eyes was required. Even a gentle breeze would sting and make her tear up. Hard to ride while blinking nonstop. "Where to?"

"Remember where we took down that cottonwood tree?"

Eden accelerated, the tires slipping in the loose dirt and gravel. She wasn't excited about riding the dirt trail along the fence line to the tree. "You sure that's where you want to go?"

Brandi laughed. "You telling me this thing can't go somewhere Ranger can?" The words sounded faint to Eden's ears as the forward motion of the bike left them somewhere in the dust behind them.

As they reached the blacktop, Eden increased speed through the corner and Brandi tightened her grip, but didn't snuggle into her. Perhaps her promise to go slow had been a bad idea. When she reached an easy twenty miles per hour, she reached back with her clutch hand and stroked Brandi's leg. The curve of her ass in soft denim made Eden's fingers tingle. They ached to find home inside Brandi. As she smoothed her hand in long, sweeping circles, Brandi finally embraced her, pressing her body dancing close to Eden's back. She worked her fingers under Eden's shirt and flattened her palms against Eden's stomach. Her world narrowed to the press of Brandi's hands against her skin and the black stripe of highway directly in front of her.

"Careful," Brandi breathed, "you'll miss the turn."

Eden regretfully moved her grip back to the handlebars and downshifted through the corner. She kept both hands in place and forced her attention to the uncertain terrain under her wheels. Brandi would not find her sexy at all if she dumped her motorcycle, complete with Brandi on the back. The jumble of bonfire wood came into view as her focus wavered, tempted by the delicious dance of Brandi's fingers as the traced the sculpted lines of Eden's abdomen. Her muscles twitched under Brandi's careful exploration.

"Thank God, we're here." She stopped. They could walk the rest of the way.

Brandi tweaked Eden's nipples. "I love your motorcycle."

Eden arched as the trail of fire between her throbbing clit and Brandi's touch threatened to engulf her. She climbed off the bike and offered her hand to Brandi. "What did you want to show me?"

Brandi didn't release Eden's hand after she slid her leg over the gas tank and stepped to the ground. She laced their fingers together and led Eden toward a new tree that hadn't been there when Eden and Brandi worked there before. Apparently, Brandi followed Jaylynn's directives when it came to planting trees. "Showing you how much your body needs mine isn't enough?"

"Trust me, it's more than enough. But you're the one who wanted to come here."

They stopped short of the little tree. It was only about six feet tall but had several apples growing from it. Eden was amazed that a tree so small could produce fruit. Of course, she knew nothing about apple trees, but in the movies they were always bigger. Before she could ask about it, Brandi plucked one from the branches. She polished it against her shirt, took a bite, and offered it to Eden. Juice ran down Brandi's chin. "You like apples?"

Eden took a bite. The perfect cross between inviting-sweet and biting-tart. Eden nodded as she chewed. She wanted to lick the juice from Brandi's face, but before she could, Brandi wiped it away with the back of her sleeve.

Brandi stepped to the side and pointed to a short pedestal sign. A tribute to her brother Gabriel was carved into the light-colored wood. Eden dropped to her knees.

GABRIEL

MAY YOU FIND PEACE

Eden traced the words with her fingers, the wood hard and unyielding. A tear slid down her face, and she watched it splatter and soak into the *G*. "I can't believe you did this." She couldn't look at Brandi. She was on the verge of coming undone.

"He deserves a home." Brandi stroked Eden's back, the warm circling touch comforting. "So do you."

"I can't believe you did this." Eden's brain simply couldn't come up with another sentence. She shook her head and more tears fell, splotching the wood. Her hands shook and she gripped the edge of the sign.

"Apples seemed appropriate. The fruit of life."

Memories of her brother, the sweet lion of her childhood, converged with the burned-out shell he was when he died. Eden's shoulders shook. "The last thing he said was that he loved me."

Brandi wrapped herself around Eden and she sank into the embrace. For the first time in what seemed like forever, she felt safe. Protected. "I don't want to leave you."

"Then stay."

Stay and lead Luther to Brandi? Impossible. Eden would die first. "I can't." Those two words just about killed her. She clung to Brandi, let her rock her and comfort her like a child.

They remained like that as the sun sank low on the horizon. Eden knew she could never survive outside the circle of light Brandi cast upon her. A seed began to flower in the back of her mind. There was a way to stay with Brandi and keep her safe. Eden hardened as she wrapped her heart and mind over what she had to do.

Eliminate Luther, the threat he posed. That was the only way.

CHAPTER TWENTY

The other side of the bed—Eden's side—was empty and cold. Brandi wiped the sleep from her eyes and glanced at the clock. Five forty-five. Surely Eden wasn't in this big of a hurry to leave, was she? She wouldn't go without saying good-bye. Brandi's confidence faltered. She didn't know Eden well enough to even guess at the answer. Her leaving ensured she never would.

Brandi rushed through her shower, scrambled into her clothes, and stuffed her feet into her boots. She slowed her pace as she drew near the kitchen. What if Eden really had gone without saying good-bye? What difference did it make? She was leaving one way or another. Nothing Brandi said would change her mind. What would one little word change?

Everything.

The realization brought Brandi to a halt. She craved Eden's touch and her affection. She didn't want her to go. Moreover, she couldn't bear the thought that leaving would be easy for Eden. If she was still here, what would it take to get her to stay? What if Brandi begged? Would that be enough?

Brandi forced her feet to move, one after the other, down the hall toward the kitchen. The work at Maple Hearth didn't stop for one broken heart. As she drew near the kitchen she heard the familiar sounds of Jaylynn preparing breakfast. She asked a question, the tone light and cheerful just as it was every morning for breakfast, but the words were indiscernible.

Eden answered.

Relief, like a cool rain after a heat wave, washed over Brandi. Eden stood at the stove, shoulder to shoulder with Jaylynn, heads close together, laughing easily.

"Morning, you two." Brandi slid one arm around her mom, the other around Eden, then kissed them one after the other on the cheek. "What's so funny about breakfast?"

"Omelets aren't easy." Eden poked the lump of eggs in the pan.

"That's an omelet?" Brandi retreated to the table before Jaylynn could reach her.

"Mind your manners, young lady." Jaylynn waved the spatula at Brandi. "And you're not only going to eat it, you're going to like it."

Eden looked over her shoulder and smiled. "Your mom's a good teacher. I'm just not a great student." She scooped the would-be omelet onto a plate and set it in front of Brandi. "Enjoy."

Brandi pulled Eden into her lap. "Don't you want to share it with me?" She forked a bite into Eden's mouth.

Eden chewed, her expression thoughtful, then delighted. "Not bad."

Brandi took a bite and agreed. "You're a good student. Just need to work on the presentation."

Jaylynn tasted a bit of egg. "Since when do you pick form over function?"

That was a good point. When given a choice between beauty and performance, she chose performance every time. But she also appreciated the beauty in the little things, like seeing Eden standing at the stove with her mom.

"I don't." She took another bite, then asked Eden, "How'd you sleep?"

Eden moved to her own chair. "Great. And you?"

"Amazingly well."

"Did Brandi tell you what she did for me?"

Jaylynn raised an eyebrow. "There are some things I don't want to know about your relationship."

Eden blushed. "No, that's not what I meant." She gave Brandi a save-me-here look.

"The apple tree, Mom."

"You showed her?"

"Yesterday."

Jaylynn covered Eden's hand with her own. "Did you like it?"

"It's amazing." Eden's eyes were instantly shiny. "No one has ever done anything like that for me."

"Sometimes it takes a while to find home."

"Yeah." Eden wiped her eyes as she stood. "I need to get going."

"What's on the agenda?" Brandi choked out the question, not wanting to know the answer.

Eden met Brandi's gaze. "Same as always. Roger's, then back here."

"Yeah?"

"Yeah." Eden rinsed Brandi's plate and put it in the dishwasher.

"I'll see you then."

Brandi kissed Eden good-bye at the door and watched as she mounted her motorcycle and rode away.

"What am I going to do without her?"

Jaylynn joined Brandi at the door. "She's not going anywhere."

"I don't know, Mama. She says she has to."

"She tell you why?"

"No, not really. Just a bad business deal or something." Brandi wanted to know more about Eden's past. What called her away from Maple Hearth? But the look on Eden's face, the absolute dead-calm lack of emotion, stopped Brandi from pressing too hard.

"She knows this is where she belongs."

Brandi nodded, afraid that if she agreed aloud, she'd jinx the possibility. Besides, she wasn't at all sure what Eden knew.

❖

The highway stretched out before Eden, long and inviting. The road didn't hold the same appeal when she was trapped inside a car. The isolation she felt when encased in steel and glass evaporated when she zipped on her leathers. On her motorcycle, life rushed by, the pavement hard and unforgiving, waiting for her to make a mistake. The thrill kept her focused. Sharp. The only question she needed to answer now was how far would she follow the road this time?

Smart money told her it was time to leave. But her heart refused to hear that message. The easiest solution was Luther's death, but she didn't think she had one more execution in her. Not even for a soulless bastard like Luther Wade. What was a professional killer who lost her taste for death to do in that situation?

Could she kill him if he posed a direct threat to her? Maybe. To Brandi? Definitely. Eden couldn't let it get to that point. Brandi wouldn't want her if violence continued to be her instant reaction. Of that much, Eden was certain.

If her life was a movie, she'd call up the U.S. attorney, work a deal, and live happily ever after. Real life, no matter how idyllic it felt during the past two weeks, didn't work like a fairy tale. Luther was a big enough fish to get the federal government's attention, that was certain. Then again, so was Eden. There was no guarantee that making contact wouldn't result in her own arrest and incarceration.

But maybe, just maybe, they would listen to her, take her testimony, and lock Luther away for good. Would it be enough to keep her safe with Brandi? Probably not. But if she did the right thing, the lawful thing, Brandi would believe her when she said her heart wanted peace. With Brandi.

Still, it would be naïve to think that Luther's wrath wouldn't extend beyond prison bars to touch her life. She'd betrayed him once by stealing his money and running away. More than that, she'd made him look a fool. She was his trusted right arm. For her to deceive him like that made him look weak to his associates. That was unforgivable, punishable by death.

If she were to turn to the authorities, she would increase the betrayal tenfold.

Eden's cell phone rang as she slanted her bike against the curb in front of Roger's. She didn't recognize the number, but since she was a on a disposable prepaid phone and she'd only given two people the number—Brandi and Penny—Eden answered.

"Hello?"

"Eden, I've missed you. It's time for you to come on home now." Luther's voice shot shards of ice through Eden's veins. The word *home* became a threat wrapped in his evil.

"Hello, Luther." She made herself sound surprisingly calm, not betraying the acrobatic stunts her insides were doing. "How can I help you?"

Eden could hear muffled crying in the background when Luther answered. "I just told you. Come home."

"I can't do that."

"That's really too bad." Luther paused. "Perhaps Penny can persuade you."

Eden reclined against the Ducati, legs crossed at the ankles. Roger waved at her through the window, a surprised smile on his face. The muffled cries grew louder until Penny's screams came through the phone sharp enough to cut glass.

"E, why the fuck did you do this? He's going to kill me. You know he's going to kill me," Penny screeched, panicked out of her normal calm. "You have to come back. You have to—"

"Put Luther back on the phone." He would kill her. Nothing Eden could do would change it. Her stomach rioted.

Penny sobbed. "Eden, please."

"Luther," Eden insisted.

After a moment, Luther spoke to her. "See you soon."

"No."

"What?"

Eden shivered in the heat, but refused to give in. Penny's already dead, she reminded herself over and over. What she did next wouldn't change a thing. "No."

"You disappoint me, Eden."

Penny screamed, followed by a gunshot. Then silence.

CHAPTER TWENTY-ONE

Cool evening air breezed through the window above the kitchen sink as Eden cleared away the evidence of the evening meal. The song of Maple Hearth—leaves rustling in the trees, crickets chirping, and the dogs wrestling in the yard—played in the waning sunlight. Eden thought about the apple tree Brandi had planted for Gabriel. Would she plant another for Eden after she left?

"You're quiet tonight." Brandi wrapped her arms around Eden from behind and hugged her. "Everything okay?"

Absolutely nothing was okay. Luther knew she was alive. Penny was dead—another in a long line of deaths that could be attributed to Eden. And she had to leave the only place that had ever felt like home. And Brandi.

"I'm fine." Eden turned and kissed Brandi on the cheek.

"You sure?" Brandi didn't look convinced.

Eden didn't trust her voice, so she simply nodded. Brandi obviously didn't believe her, but she let it go after squeezing Eden just a little tighter.

"What do you two have planned for tonight?" Jaylynn sipped her after-dinner coffee at the table.

Brandi inclined her head at Eden, her brow arched in question.

Eden dried her hands on the kitchen towel and took a deep breath. "I need to pack."

The shocked hurt on Brandi's face almost broke Eden's heart.

She had to leave, she reminded herself. Anything else would be foolhardy and dangerous.

"Oh." Brandi turned her back to Eden, her shoulders stiff and straight as she stared out the window.

Jaylynn set her cup carefully on the table. "Eden, you know you are welcome to stay."

"I know." Eden watched Brandi, looking for an opening to reach out for her, knowing that to touch Brandi would crumble her resolve.

"Where will you go?"

Should she answer that question? The attorney she'd spoken to that afternoon advised against it. And if Luther ever found Brandi and Jaylynn, if he felt they were withholding information from him… That's why she had to go. She couldn't let him find them. But how much could she tell them before she left?

Everything, she decided.

"I have a meeting tomorrow in Boise." She sat at the table across from Jaylynn, her attention roving between the two women. "After that, I don't know for sure."

"Then you'll come back here." Jaylynn nodded once, firm in her declaration.

"I don't think that will be possible."

Brandi turned around, her face stricken but her voice calm. "Why not?"

"Luther called me today. He had Penny." Eden mentally pleaded with Brandi to not make her share the details.

"Wait, who's Luther?" Jaylynn asked.

Eden picked up Jaylynn's empty coffee cup. "That question calls for a refill." She collected her thoughts as she poured the dark, aromatic brew, considering the right way to answer. How could she tell them what they needed to know if she kept them innocent of her corrupt history? "Brandi, do you want a cup?"

Without answering, Brandi sat next to her mom. She didn't meet Eden's gaze.

Eden returned to her seat and slid Jaylynn's coffee across the table to her. "Where do I start?" She pinched the bridge of her nose, hoping to find a begining to disclosing her sordid life. "Luther." Maybe coffee wasn't the right drink for the occasion. A shot of Jack would certainly be a better choice. "I went to work for Luther when I was sixteen. My mom disappeared and the other choices were far less appealing."

"Other choices?"

"Foster care for a few months or prostitution." Eden swallowed the helplessness she'd felt at that time. Her mom hadn't done much parenting, but she'd paid the rent. Most of the girls Eden knew were already turning tricks at that point. Even Penny. It was about survival, not sex.

To Jaylynn's credit, her expression remained impassive. "Go on."

"Luther controls the entire West Coast now, but then he wasn't as big, coming up in the neighborhood, expanding his power through L.A."

"What does that mean, controls the West Coast?"

"Drugs." Eden hated the answer. Hated that Jaylynn needed her to say it so explicitly.

"So you were a drug dealer?" Still no judgment from Jaylynn.

"Not exactly." Eden fought the urge to squirm in her chair. She reached her foot out under the table and touched Brandi. Even through their shoes, she felt instantly grounded. "I did other things for Luther."

Jaylynn sipped her coffee, waiting. Brandi finally looked at her and asked, "What other things?"

Eden regarded Brandi. The familiar wall slid into place, protecting her emotions, keeping her safe from those who would harm her. The part of her personality that allowed her to function, no, *excel* in Luther's world rose to the surface and hardened her in preparation for what she had to say next. "I was an enforcer."

She watched surprise, disbelief, and fear battle across Brandi's face. The answer was out there, everything she was running from was on the table. She'd never felt more vulnerable. Still, she wouldn't change the answer. The obtuse answer she gave strangers in the past—asset protection, acquisitions, contract negotiations—

any one of them would have been less shocking for Brandi to hear, but Jaylynn would have torn it down with her relentless stream of questions. Eden couldn't escape the truth.

"Enforcer?" Jaylynn's calm cracked. "Explain."

"I made sure people did what they agreed to."

"Through legal negotiations, right?" Jaylynn asked.

"No."

A tear slid down Brandi's face.

"You hurt people?" Jaylynn's voice seemed very far away.

Eden wanted to pull Brandi to her and promise everything would be okay. Instead she held herself rigid, not even chasing Brandi's touch when she pulled her foot away.

"Yes."

"Did you kill them?"

Eden closed her eyes and Luther's wall of dead soldiers stared at her. In her vision, however, the frames held the faces of the men and women she'd killed. Her sacrifices on the altar of drugs and money.

"Yes."

Silence—as sharp and cutting as the moments after Penny's scream ended with a gunshot—engulfed the kitchen. Eden wondered how long she should sit there. Neither Brandi nor Jaylynn was asking questions after that little bomb, but it was just a matter of time before they demanded that she leave.

Finally Jaylynn said, "Tell me about your meeting tomorrow."

"After I talked to Luther today, I called the U.S. attorney's office. I'm meeting with them tomorrow." She still couldn't believe she'd made that phone call. Contacting law enforcement was either incredibly brave or incredibly stupid. Possibly both. "I'm planning to testify against Luther."

"Will they put you in jail?" Brandi regarded her with red-rimmed eyes. Her voice shook slightly.

"It's possible."

"For how long?"

"I don't know."

Eden waited several minutes for Brandi to speak again. She didn't. Eden pushed away from the table. "I'm going to pack now."

Neither woman tried to talk her out of it as she left the kitchen and headed toward her room. And just like that, the feeling of home was gone.

❖

The soft glow of moonlight through the window left most of Brandi's face in shadow, hidden from Eden's view. Her jaw was slack, her lips slightly parted, and Eden longed to kiss her one last time before leaving. She turned away, knowing it would be an unwanted gesture.

Eden surveyed the kitchen, the tableau of her personal evolution at Maple Hearth. When she arrived, she'd known nothing of herself other than the killer a ruthless man had carefully crafted. Here she'd learned how to cook, how to laugh through hard work, and how to care gently, without the harsh edge of violence underlying every interaction. In Los Angeles loyalty was compelled through threats and deadly follow-through. Here it grew organic and free with every movement, every touch, every shared moment. Out of necessity and fear, she'd killed to protect Luther. Out of love, she would die to protect Brandi.

Hopefully things wouldn't reach that point.

Eden set a letter for Brandi in the middle of the table, checked the buckles on her black leather chaps, and stepped out into the night.

CHAPTER TWENTY-TWO

S he's gone." Brandi sat at the kitchen table, suddenly too tired to remain standing.

"Looks like." Jaylynn went about making breakfast. "She left you something."

A white envelope with Brandi's name written on it in bold, sweeping script rested in the middle of the table. Brandi picked it up and inspected it, one side then the other, looking first at the front, then the back, over and over. There had to be some clue, some indication of how to proceed written in the fine cotton fibers.

"Can't read it unless you open it." Jaylynn didn't look up from cracking eggs into a large bowl.

"I don't know if I want to." Brandi returned it to the table.

"Is it a question of want?"

Brandi pushed her hands through her hair. Jaylynn had hit the nail on the head. She had no idea what Eden was going through, what led her to make the choices she had. Understanding wasn't a want; it was a need. Brandi slid a finger under the sealed flap and tore open the envelope.

Brandi,

> *For the first time in my life, I found a place that feels like home. With you. Leaving here—leaving you—is the hardest thing I've ever done.*
> *When I left Los Angeles I knew my past would*

eventually catch up with me. I planned to run like hell until Luther caught me. I've always pictured my life ending at the angry end of his temper, and at least the fear and violence would be over. But I can't let that happen to you and your family.

I transferred the money you need into your checking account. I know you said not to. I doubt you'll actually use it, but it was the one positive thing I could leave you with.

I'm sorry I can't be the person you deserve. God knows I want to be.

I love you.

Eden

Brandi read the letter twice, the words growing blurrier with each passing moment. She set it carefully on the table and wiped her eyes.

Jaylynn dried her hands on the white broadcloth apron around her waist and retrieved the letter. "Can I read it?"

"I guess."

Bacon sizzled on the stove, coffee bubbled in the pot. Everything appeared normal, but the color had bled out of the morning. Eden was irrevocably gone.

"She loves you."

"I know." Even though Eden hadn't said the words when they were together, seeing them on paper didn't surprise Brandi. She'd looked into Eden's eyes and seen the love. Three words didn't change the strength of the emotion.

"And how do you feel about her?"

"Does it matter?"

"Doesn't it?"

Brandi poured a cup of coffee. She took a long sip, then said,

"I don't see why it would. She's gone. Besides, she's not the person I thought she was."

"You sure about that?"

Brandi didn't answer. She wasn't sure about anything right now.

❖

The open road before her was a curse rather than an invitation. Normally Eden faced life head-on, looking forward, never back. Now she could only think about what she was leaving behind.

She was so wrapped up in her thoughts, she almost missed the black Lincoln parked in front of Brenda's. Eden slowed to a crawl and watched as Peter Fuentes emerged from the driver's side door, pulled his sunglasses down to the tip of his nose, and surveyed the town. He pushed the glasses back into place, his judgment completed in less than thirty seconds. Less than worthy. It was written, clear as day, on his face.

Luther Wade rolled down the back window. He had the same polished smooth face that Eden had tried to forget. His mouth moved, directions for Peter on how to proceed, no doubt. Peter bent at the waist until his face was level with Luther's. Eden remembered Luther's quiet voice, his commands low and modulated, just above a whisper. It was about control, she'd realized early on. He liked knowing that the other person was listening intently, that he had the power to make that person strain to hear.

Peter opened the door and Luther stepped out. Eden was important enough that Luther wanted to accompany him on even the smallest fact-finding mission. Or perhaps it was a lack of trust for Peter's skills that drove Luther to emerge from his air-conditioned backseat. One thing was certain: Luther had never ventured this far from home when Eden was the one who did his bidding.

Eden almost dumped the Ducati into the gutter as she turned the corner. She accelerated hard, relying on the power of the engine to right the motorcycle. The people in this town, bless them, wouldn't just tell Luther where Eden was staying. They'd likely draw him a map.

The comfortable cushion of time and space that had existed between Eden and Luther evaporated in the hot Idaho sun. He'd obviously been on his way to her when Penny had called last night. Without a second glance, Eden doubled back to the highway, riding the throttle hard in her panic to get to Brandi ahead of Luther.

❖

"You need to get out of here right now." Eden burst through the door, not sparing even a moment for a greeting. She'd arrived before Luther, but that didn't mean they had time to waste.

Brandi remained seated at the kitchen table, shock written on her face. Who could blame her? Eden had disappeared without a good-bye earlier that morning. She was certain Brandi had not expected her to come running into the house yelling directions.

Jaylynn walked in with a basket of laundry on her hip. She smiled when she saw Eden. "Hello, Eden, we thought you'd gone."

Eden ignored Jaylynn's greeting and repeated her earlier statement. "You both need to leave. Right now. Please." Why weren't they moving? What did she need to say to get these two women to move?

"Why? What's going on?" Brandi recovered her voice. She stood and met Eden's gaze.

"Luther's here." Everything Eden feared about staying too long at Maple Hearth was coming true. Luther was bringing the nightmare to the only place where Eden had ever found peace, bringing it to the woman who offered her hope and a home. She'd waited too long to leave and now nothing mattered but keeping Brandi safe.

"What?" Confusion and a good amount of fear filled Brandi's eyes. "How?"

"I don't know. Does it matter? You have to leave. Hide. Anywhere but here." Eden crossed the room and grabbed Brandi's hand. She pulled her toward the door. If Brandi wouldn't take the steps herself, Eden would damn well carry her if need be. "Please, Brandi, we don't have a lot of time here."

Brandi held firm, refusing to be forced out the door. Jaylynn picked up the phone.

Eden whirled around, fighting the urge to jerk the phone from Jaylynn's hands. She needed them to trust her. Panicking completely would not help that happen. "What are you doing? We need to go."

"Calling the police."

"What?" Eden's voice cracked. The police? What could the local sheriff do to stop Luther? He would just kill him, too. Without hesitation and without remorse. Why couldn't they see that? If they'd grown up in her world, they'd know to be scared. They'd know to run hard and fast and not look back. Instead they were standing here, wasting precious time. What did they want to do? Discuss their options?

Eden rubbed her thumb in circles against Brandi's wrist, willing herself to calm down. She stared into Brandi's eyes, searching for a way to convince her, to get her out the door.

"Eden, we're not going to run away."

Eden pulled harder on Brandi's arm, her heart pounded high into her throat. "You have to."

Jaylynn finished her conversation and hung up the phone. "No, Eden, this is our home." She headed toward the family room, laundry forgotten in the basket by the kitchen table.

"He doesn't care whose *home* it is. He will *kill* you." She stared at Brandi, pleading. "I can't let that happen. Please, Brandi, I need you to come with me."

Jaylynn reappeared with a shotgun and a box of shells in her hand. She fed them one by one into the chamber, then snapped it shut.

No, no, no. Eden shook her head. This would never work. They wanted to have a shootout? Like this was a romantic Western and they were at the O.K. Corral? A shotgun might be effective for scaring off pushy Jehovah's Witnesses when they came calling with their *Watchtower* magazines and their message of salvation. For

Luther? It would barely get his attention. Hell, he'd probably laugh at the sight of it.

"Please, you can't win like this." Luther had bigger guns and no soul. He wouldn't think twice about pulling the trigger. The moment of hesitation when Jaylynn realized she was aiming at a living, breathing human being would be the only opening Luther would need. "Brandi, you're willing to let your mom get killed?"

Brandi flinched and Eden almost felt guilty. It was a low blow, but she had to say something to get them to understand the danger that would soon arrive at their home.

Jaylynn chambered a round. "It's not her choice, Eden. I'm not willing to let this man bully my family." A pause. "That includes you."

Family. The word left Eden reeling. She didn't have room for that ideal in her head right now. She was willing to die to protect Brandi and Jaylynn, of that much she was certain. She didn't consider what that meant beyond the immediate situation. "Fine." If they wanted to have a grand standoff, that's what they'd do. What was wrong with these women? People in L.A. knew to get out of the way when someone came looking for blood.

Eden didn't want it to be like this. She didn't want Brandi to ever see her holding a gun, see how natural, how comfortable she looked with two Glocks in her hands. But if they insisted on staying, on seeing Luther in all his hateful glory, she refused to be unarmed in that situation. She turned away from Brandi and ran out the door.

"Eden, wait." Brandi's voice chased her. That was fine with Eden as long as Brandi's body stayed inside the house where it was marginally safer.

It wouldn't be long until Luther arrived. She needed to be quick. She pulled her guns from the bottom of her saddlebags and tucked one into the back of her jeans, another into the front. She filled her pockets with extra clips and returned to the house, holding two more guns loosely in her hands. Four pistols and a few extra bullets. Not nearly enough against the high-powered rifles, the semiautomatics illegally converted to fully automatic at Luther's disposal. They would have to do.

❖

The change in Eden's demeanor, the way she carried herself, was immediate. She always walked with confidence, her presence filling any room. But when she returned to the house, the sunlight at her back, guns in both hands, Brandi could feel the power radiating off her. She looked every bit a warrior preparing for battle.

She sat at the table, her face focused on her weapons. She checked the two in her hands first, listening to the slide and click as she chambered a round. Then she dropped out the clips, inspected them, pushing down on the top bullet. Satisfied, she returned them to their home, knocking them in place with a loud click. She rubbed the back of the handles with her thumbs.

Brandi watched, mesmerized as Eden pulled two more guns from the waistband of her pants and repeated the ritual. Her movements were precise, economical, and rhythmic.

"Do you know how to use this?" Eden held one out to Brandi, butt first, her hand wrapped around the barrel.

"I think so." Brandi had shot plenty of rifles and the occasional shotgun. A pistol couldn't be much different.

Eden didn't smile as she began her lesson. Her face and body language remained neutral, distant. "There's no safety, so don't put your finger on the trigger unless you want to pull it. It's very sensitive."

Brandi took the proffered weapon and held it gingerly between both hands. She hoped she didn't look as uncomfortable as she felt. Finally, she set it down on the table in front of Eden. "I best leave this to you. I'll get my rifle."

The short walk to family room to retrieve the rifle from the gun rack on the wall gave Brandi a few moments to collect herself. She hoped like hell that they were making the right choice. What if Eden was right? What if by staying she was condemning Jaylynn to death? Surely it wouldn't come to that. The sheriff would arrive before anything could happen. Besides, Jaylynn would never leave. Even if Brandi changed her mind and rode off with Eden, her mother would remain behind, shotgun at the ready. She really had no choice but to stay.

How did things get so far out of control? Should she have passed Eden by that first day? Instead of returning with her truck, should she have left her to push her motorcycle all the way to town? Would she give up love in order to keep her home safe? It was a fool's question and Brandi knew enough to know there was no answer.

CHAPTER TWENTY-THREE

The constant squeak of the wooden rocking chair on the front porch grated on Brandi's nerves. She wanted Jaylynn to sit still. Or better yet, pick that shotgun up from across her lap and retreat into the house. If there was going to be shooting, Brandi wanted as much wood and sheetrock between her mother and the bullets as she could get. Instead, Jaylynn rocked, an open target in front of their home.

A black Lincoln turned into the long drive, dust flying up in its wake. Eden tensed but didn't move from her position of practiced calm. She stood on the driveway side of the porch, her shoulders casually against the rails, two guns visible in the front waistband of her jeans, two more in the back. She took one last drag on her brown-papered cigarette, then flicked it onto the ground. It was the first time Brandi had seen her smoke.

"You two should go inside now," she said as the Lincoln pulled to a halt. "Please." Her voice was soft, all signs of her earlier panic gone.

Brandi wished Jaylynn would heed Eden's warning. Of course she did not.

"I'm comfortable here, thank you, Eden." Jaylynn patted the stock of her shotgun.

The driver's door opened and a compact, heavily muscled Hispanic man stepped out. He met Eden's hard stare and held it, his eyes revealing nothing. He did not speak. After a moment, he opened the back door and held it as a large black man climbed out.

For all of Eden's presence, she seemed to shrink next to this man. He didn't say a word, but Brandi knew he was Luther Wade. She could see the malice in his eyes. This man was the stuff Eden's nightmares were made of.

Luther took a few steps toward Eden. Jaylynn raised her shotgun to her shoulder and drew down on the large man. "That's plenty far enough."

Brandi took a deep breath. Leave it to Jaylynn to get the dance started with a bang. So far neither man had brandished a weapon, but according to Eden, they were there and the men would wield them with deadly intent.

Luther ignored Jaylynn, keeping his eyes trained on Eden.

"Luther." Eden's spine was perfectly straight, shoulders squared.

"Eden." Luther tipped his head slightly. His voice was quieter than Brandi expected.

Silence followed the terse greeting. The two stared at each other, neither blinking. Eden's hand inched closer to her gun.

"You're supposed to be dead." Luther shook his head, looking every bit the disappointed father.

"I'm not."

"Imagine my surprise."

Luther spread his hands wide, drawing Brandi's attention with the movement. It did not work on Eden. Before Brandi realized it had happened, Eden and the driver had their guns out, leveled at one another. Eden's eyes, however, stayed focused on Luther. Brandi wondered how Eden was able to do that. It was like she was seeing both men separately, yet at the same time.

"Peter, put that away," Luther said.

Peter holstered his weapon at the quiet command from Luther. Eden did not.

"You killed Penny."

"What did you expect?"

"You're here to kill me." It wasn't an accusation, rather a simple statement. Eden's cool calm, her unwavering focus, unnerved Brandi. This was not the same woman she had come to know.

"Yes."

"You should have brought an army." Eden took a step, pulling a second gun with her left hand and aiming at Luther's head. Brandi imagined that Luther was rethinking his directive for Peter to lower his weapon.

Eden's comment registered with Brandi. *Should have brought an army.* Should have. Why didn't he? According to Eden, Luther was not a man to be underestimated, so why did he appear so ill-prepared in this situation? Not that Brandi wanted to look a gift horse in the mouth. She was almost ready to relax. Eden had both men under control and gunfire looked avoidable. Then again Jaylynn hadn't lowered her weapon yet.

"Eden, come with me. Spare your new friends"—he glanced briefly at Brandi—"the spectacle."

"Not going to happen."

"So be it." Luther gave a half shrug and dropped his hands to his side.

That's when the gunfire Brandi was so eager to avoid ripped through the late-morning quiet.

Like a slow-motion scene from a movie, Eden grabbed Peter. She twisted him around so that his back was to her front and held him tight against her chest with her right arm, her pistol crushed against his cheek. At the same moment two gun barrels poked out the open back door of the Lincoln. Before he could respond to the danger of his new position, the guns fired, hitting Peter over and over. His body jerked with the impact of each bullet.

Eden fired into the Lincoln, shattering the dark glass of the windows. Jaylynn redirected her aim toward the vehicle and pulled the trigger, the blast of the shotgun overwhelming compared to the pop-pop-pop of the other weapons. She chambered round after round, unloading all her shells into the now-silent Town Car. Brandi never even raised her rifle.

Smoke curled from Eden's gun, drawing Brandi's gaze up to Eden's face, her hard, vacant eyes. Luther had ruined her life, chased her across the West to kill her, yet Eden didn't show a hint of emotion. No fear. No anger. No remorse at having caused the death of the man still clutched to her chest and likely the person—or was it people?—in the Lincoln.

Blood was splattered across Eden's cheek and nose, like obscene, deadly freckles.

Eden released her hold on Peter and he slumped to the ground, his body sliding against hers, leaving a trail of crimson down her front. He lay in a heap on the gravel, blood spreading around Eden's feet. She didn't appear to notice as she dropped her spent weapon onto the ground next to him.

Jaylynn fed more shells into her shotgun as blood dripped out of the Lincoln and pooled on the ground below.

"Now, Eden." Luther took several shaky steps backward, away from Eden's steady approach. "Don't do anything hasty."

She didn't respond, just continued taking precise, measured steps toward Luther, her gun leveled at his head. Luther stopped backing away and took a deep breath. He squared his shoulders and stood his ground as Eden pressed the muzzle of her weapon to his forehead.

"On your knees." Eden was too calm, her voice smooth as glass.

Luther dropped to his knees, shaking.

Brandi snapped out of her stupor. Eden was going to kill him. Execution style.

"Eden, no!"

Eden tilted her head to the side, like a dog considering a command. She didn't lower her weapon, but she didn't pull the trigger either. Brandi considered that a victory.

"Please, Eden, don't do this." Brandi hoped that if she continued to talk she'd eventually get through to Eden, break through the perfect barrier she'd erected around her emotions.

"He'll never stop coming." Eden didn't look at Brandi as she spoke, the words almost too soft to hear. "This is the only way."

"No, let the police take care of him."

As if on cue, the sheriff's cruiser turned into the long drive, blue and red lights flashing, siren bellowing. He slid to a sideways stop—classic cop parking job—between the Lincoln and the barn.

With the siren still blaring, the sheriff stepped out of the car and unholstered his gun. "Drop your weapon." It was unclear who he was talking to.

The distraction provided Luther opportunity to make his move. He lowered his body to the side and pushed Eden away from him. Eden's gun fell to the ground, whether intentionally or by accident, Brandi couldn't tell. After seeing Eden wield those guns, Brandi didn't believe she was the type to simply lose track of her weapon.

Luther scrambled and scooped up Eden's handgun before Eden even recovered her balance. He turned the weapon on her with a malicious smile. The sheriff shot him through the chest as Eden pulled another gun from behind her back. Luther let out a surprised gulping whimper and fell to the ground. He struggled to return to his feet as a dark red stain blossomed on his chest. Blood gurgled out of his mouth and he collapsed, lifeless, on the gravel driveway.

Luther Wade was dead.

"Shit fire, there's going to be a lot of paperwork to go with this." The sheriff holstered his weapon and pulled out his handcuffs. "Jaylynn, put that shotgun away and call for the coroner."

The sheriff was a wiry little man with steel gray hair and a bushy mustache. He'd won his office in a battle against a much larger, and certainly more handsome, opponent. What he lacked in presentation, he made up for with his eloquent speech.

"Look at this mess. Dead bodies everywhere. Going to have to replace that gravel to get the stain out." He kept up a steady rant as he cuffed Eden, hands behind her back. She didn't struggle as he stuffed her into the back of his patrol car. He did not Mirandize her.

Against her better judgment, Brandi interrupted the tirade. "What are you doing with her? She didn't do anything wrong." While it wasn't entirely true, Brandi couldn't stomach the idea of Eden being hauled away in cuffs just for defending her life.

"She didn't do *anything?*" the sheriff squawked. "She had that man on his knees with a gun to his head. That's sure as shit *something.*"

"He was going to kill her."

"Looked the other way around to me, missy."

"That's because you got here too late."

"Too late?" The sheriff bristled. "Too *late?* Looks to me like I got here just in time." He stomped away from Brandi, still muttering under his breath.

Fear that he would take Eden and that Brandi would never see her again kept Brandi from arguing her point further. She needed him to be calm, not irrational and pissed off. She'd leave it to Jaylynn to explain the details. Until then, she just wanted to talk to Eden.

"Sheriff." Brandi tried her best to sound like a little girl in need of help. It wasn't a comfortable role for her, so she wasn't sure it worked. "Can I talk to her? Please."

"Talk to her?" The sheriff scratched his chin. "Well, I don't see why not."

Brandi could think of all sorts of reasons why not, but her knowledge of police procedure came from watching cop dramas on TV. Brandi thanked him and waited as he opened the back door of his cruiser. He removed the cuffs from Eden's wrists.

"You stay in there." He jabbed his finger at Eden before turning to Brandi. "And you stay out here."

The circumstances were less than ideal, but Brandi was grateful to be able to see Eden, speak to her, without the glass and steel separating them. She kneeled down in the opening.

"He's dead." Brandi didn't know what else to say.

Eden stared at her, her eyes wide, imploring. "I know."

Silence stretched long between them and Brandi shifted her weight from one side to the other, her hand on the seat for balance.

"You scared me."

Eden shrank with Brandi's simple statement and Brandi mentally kicked herself. Even though it was true, it was insensitive to say. Brandi wouldn't want to know if she'd genuinely scared Eden, and she guessed Eden felt the same about her.

After several more moments, Eden laid her hand atop Brandi's. "I love you."

Brandi stared hard at Eden as she said, "I love you, too."

They sat like that, without speaking, as the coroner removed the bodies and the sheriff drank iced tea on the porch with Jaylynn. With their hands barely touching, Brandi searched for some clue about what those words meant about their future.

When the last body was bagged and loaded, the sheriff gave up the comfortable rocker next to Jaylynn and returned to the car. "Time for me to go, girl."

Eden squeezed Brandi's hand and said, "It's not enough, is it?"

Brandi swallowed and answered without thinking. "I don't know."

Eden released her hold on Brandi and folded her hands in her lap. She turned her face toward the front of the car.

Brandi's heart broke as the sheriff drove away from Maple Hearth. Eden did not look back.

CHAPTER TWENTY-FOUR

Eden shifted in her seat and smoothed the front of her jacket. She smiled confidently—bordering on cocky—at the woman across the table.

"This would be easier if you would just talk to us." U.S. Attorney Jaime Simmons sighed. She'd been staring at Eden for over an hour, trying periodically to get Eden to talk.

After the local sheriff took her in to the station, he ran all the standard checks. She sat in his cell for two days waiting for the U.S. marshal who would transport her to the U.S. attorney's office.

"You contacted us, remember?"

Of course Eden remembered, but circumstances had changed. Luther was dead, and along with him went all her bargaining power. Still, she considered sharing every sordid detail about her life with Luther. What difference would it make? Whether she went to prison or not, Brandi no longer wanted her. She couldn't. She knew what kind of person Eden really was. No way could she overlook the magnitude of Eden's transgressions. Damn Luther Wade and his never-ending ability to fuck with her happy endings.

Self-preservation kicked in before she made a fatal error. If she talked to them now, she'd be signing her own death warrant. Deserved or not, Eden wanted to live. She didn't reply.

Jaime flipped open a manila folder. "Okay, since you won't talk, I'll recap what we already know. Luther Wade was a known drug trafficker, controlling the majority of the West Coast."

Eden fought the urge to smile. Luther was a malicious, evil

bastard. But he was also smart and careful. They might *know* that Luther was a major player in the drug underworld, but *proving* it was another thing entirely. Until she gave them something more to go on, she would remain safe.

"And you are Eden Metcalf. Luther's most trusted enforcer. His right hand. At least you were until two and a half months ago, when you fell off the radar completely. Presumed dead by Luther."

How could Jaime possible know what Luther presumed? Who had she been talking to?

"Then you resurfaced, very much alive in southern Idaho. Now Luther Wade and three of his associates are dead."

Eden raised one eyebrow, more on reflex than through intention. Three associates? Luther had come after her with only three men? Did he really think his influence over her was so great that he wouldn't need more firepower? He knew what kind of damage she was capable of inflicting.

"Still have nothing to say?"

Eden wondered how long it would take before they turned her back over to the local sheriff. He at least could charge her with assault. Not much of a consolation to the U.S. attorney, who had her sights set on a much bigger prize.

"You do realize that we can simply hold you until you recover your ability to speak."

"I want a lawyer."

Jaime set her mouth in a grim line. "That'll have to wait. We're transporting you back to Los Angeles."

Eden debated the merits of pushing for the lawyer. After all, this wasn't a television show; they couldn't just ignore her basic rights in favor of dramatic flair. On the other hand, the caliber of defense she wanted was available in L.A. As charming as the tractor-driving farmers of southern Idaho had proven to be, she didn't want her freedom dependent upon their legal knowledge.

Eden smiled at the U.S. attorney and reclined in her hard-backed plastic chair. She stretched her legs in front of her, crossed at the ankles, trying to look more comfortable than she felt.

It was going to be a long, silent return trip to her home city.

❖

Jaylynn slipped her arm around Brandi's waist and offered her an apple. "Don't tell me you're regretting your decision."

Brandi looked over the rapidly growing mini-mall that was barely visible on the horizon and took a bite of a juicy red delicious. "Of course I regret it," she said as she chewed. "But it was necessary." No doubt about it, Bobby and Daniel had the heavy machinery ready to move the moment they signed the closing papers. Before she was done mourning the loss of her property, ground had been broken and the building seemingly crawled out of the ground before their eyes.

"The view sucks, but the balance of our books is nice and healthy for a change."

Brandi nodded. The books looked doubly healthy. The sale of the seven acres put them far into the black. Three acres would have covered the debt, but she'd been unable to convince Bobby to scale back his plans. The remainder of the money went into some stable investment funds with plans for unforeseeable future speed bumps. The money from Eden remained untouched in Brandi's savings account. She wanted nothing more than to return it to her. If only Eden would contact her. Give some indication that she was all right. Surely she couldn't still be in custody. But if she wasn't, she would come back to Maple Hearth, right?

They watched the heavy machinery working in the distance, bulldozers and diggers molding the fertile soil to match their development plans. Brandi's heart ached with every swipe of the giant blade across what was until recently her land. "I hate this."

Jaylynn nodded. "Me, too."

The machines halted their slow steady movement, the exhaust blowing out one last final burst of dark gray smoke before the motors shuddered to a stop.

"I reckon they'll be back again tomorrow." Brandi turned away from the unsettling scene and started toward their house.

"Tomorrow's Saturday. Maybe they'll rest," said Jaylynn, the perpetual voice of reason.

"Maybe." Brandi sure as hell hoped so. She didn't know how much more of the noise her soul could take before it shattered completely.

"It was the right thing." Jaylynn squeezed Brandi's hand.

Brandi's answer caught in her throat. After a brief pause, she was able to say, "I know."

As they entered the back door, Jaylynn asked, "Have you heard from her?"

"No." Brandi ducked her mom's embrace. She couldn't cry for Eden again. She just couldn't. After months with no word, she shouldn't have any tears left, but the familiar burn settled just behind her eyes and she said, "I'll start dinner."

"You know she loves you."

"That's what her letter said." Brandi had heard Jaylynn's bold assertion time and again. And while it was nice to hear, it did nothing to warm her empty bed at night. It also did nothing to assuage her fears about Eden's whereabouts.

"It's okay to miss her."

Brandi shook her head once, hard and fierce. "You heard the things she said, the things she did." The memory made her miserable.

"Did I ever tell you about what your grandfather did in Korea?" Jaylynn peeled potatoes for dinner, removing the skins in long, thin slices. Her voice was conversational, but distant, her eyes focused wholly on the vegetable in her hands.

Brandi thought hard. She'd grown up with the case of medals to the left of the mantel in the living room. She'd even memorized their names. She frowned, realizing she had no idea what they meant or how he'd earned them. "Tell me."

"He was a sniper."

Blood rushed to Brandi's ears with Jaylynn's final word. *Sniper.* How could that be possible? The same man who'd taught her how to create beauty, to cherish the life they cultivated from the earth? How could he have done something so inherently brutal? "Are you sure?" Brandi's voice was small and very far away. What did Jaylynn want her to do with this information?

"I'm sure."

After a pause, Brandi asked, "Did he kill anyone?"

"He never said. But sometimes, I'd see him with his medals, rubbing them, worry lines creasing his brow. And when I asked him what was wrong, he'd just smile and say, 'It's an awful thing to be given a medal for the things I've done.'" Jaylynn quartered the potatoes into a pan of water, her hands never slowing at their task. "He cried a lot during that time."

Brandi caught the lone tear streaking down Jaylynn's face with her thumb. Her mother didn't cry often or easily, and it tore at Brandi to see her do it now. "He did what he had to do."

"As did Eden."

So that's where Jaylynn had been going with her emotion-laden trip down memory lane.

"That's different," Brandi insisted.

"How so?" Jaylynn faced her, her eyes dark and sad.

"Grandpa was at war."

"So was Eden. The life she lived was nothing but one prolonged battle. She's lucky she escaped at all."

"Oh." Brandi couldn't think of anything else to say. It would take a good long while for her brain to catch up with what her heart—and apparently her mom—already knew. Eden's past didn't matter. All she cared about was her future. Brandi could forgive every transgression so long as she had Eden. Without her, she was lost.

❖

Ten months passed without so much as a phone call, and finally Eden e-mailed. Brandi blinked, certain she was hallucinating. The constant ache in her chest had receded to an almost manageable level and *now* Eden popped back up. She stared at the screen, frozen.

Jaylynn set a basket of eggs on the table next to Brandi's laptop. "You look like you just saw a ghost."

Brandi deliberately looked at her mom, away from Eden's name on the screen. "Eden sent me an e-mail."

"Well." The beginning of Jaylynn's thoughts hung there, but she didn't elaborate.

"Right."

Brandi helped her mom transfer the eggs to cartons, carefully avoiding the computer. When they finished, Jaylynn said, "You should read it."

"I know."

"Are you going to?"

"Yes."

"Now?"

Brandi sighed. Whatever was in that e-mail would only hurt to read. Of that she was certain. "Okay."

"I'll be in the other room." Jaylynn pointed toward the family room. A few minutes later, Brandi heard the TV click on—Jaylynn's obvious show of giving her privacy.

Unable to avoid it any longer, Brandi clicked the message open and braced herself for impact.

Brandi,

It's been too long and I should just leave you alone. But I can't.

Things have happened that you should know about, but all I can think is how much I miss you and how good you felt lying in my arms at night. Maple Hearth felt like home and now that's all gone.

Has the tree grown? The one for Gabriel? How fast do trees grow? Did I thank you for doing that? For caring enough about me, about him, to give him a home with you, also.

I miss you more than I thought possible.

Yours,

Eden

Brandi read it three times, not stopping in between to let the words sink in. She'd savor them later, when the blood racing through her head returned to its normal speed. Without giving herself time to think, time to change her mind, she typed out her response.

I love you. Please come home to me.

They were the biggest eight words of her life, and her heart pounded in her ears as she hit Send. All she had to do now was wait.

CHAPTER TWENTY-FIVE

Ranger neighed when Eden pushed open the barn door. Brandi was not in the house, so the next logical place to check was the barn. Eden spoke soft nonsense words intended to comfort the horse, remind him who she was. He lowered his head and she placed her hand on the broad stretch of nose between his eyes.

"Where is Brandi?"

Ranger pawed the ground. Eden was not encouraged. She'd been gone too long and would be lucky if Brandi didn't kick her out before she could say hello.

The Ducati sat in the corner of the barn, keys dangling from the ignition. The high-gloss black paint was dulled by a layer of dust. Eden loved that bike. It had been her means to escape L.A. It had brought her to Brandi. She ran a cloth over the gas tank and seat, bringing out the shine, then pushed the bike out of the barn.

She'd spent months cursing herself for not being stronger, for not being able to forget Brandi and leave her to live her life in peace, to be with someone who deserved her fearless love. But she couldn't. She'd tried to find a way to peace in Los Angeles without running, struggled to feel at home in her hometown.

At a loss for how to live, she'd spent hours staring at Penny's headstone, talking to her old friend. Penny provided no answers.

All she really wanted was to return to Brandi, to the safety of her embrace, but she kept herself from reaching out. She'd been sure Brandi would reject her, disgusted and frightened by Eden's bloody past after witnessing its brutality. She'd been sure Brandi wouldn't respond to her message.

I love you. Please come home to me.

Brandi's words shook Eden out of her self-pitying stupor. Brandi wanted her and she'd wasted too much time. Almost exactly a year since she left L.A. the first time, she loaded her car and drove straight through. She needed sleep. More than that, she needed Brandi.

She gave in to the pull of the Ducati and fired the engine. Brandi would come home eventually. Until then, Eden wanted to visit Gabriel's tree.

❖

Flames leapt up in the night sky, engulfing the cottonwood stump Eden had helped Brandi cut and quarter. The bonfire Brandi had talked about. She couldn't believe they'd waited so long to actually light it. In the movies, bonfires always took place in the fall. Strange that Brandi would wait for spring.

People were everywhere. Some Eden recognized, but most she didn't. Eden tugged at her hair. It was shorter. And her tan had faded. And her clothes were different, simpler. She scraped one foot against the other. Would Brandi recognize her?

"You're here." Brandi found her before Eden had a chance to contemplate the question.

She'd yearned to see Brandi for so long. Now that the moment was here, it was like wading through mud. No matter how much she wanted to see Brandi, her body wouldn't respond properly to her commands. It took an eternity to turn to the right and lift her gaze to Brandi's face. Then time whipped into fast-forward and Brandi was in her arms.

"I was afraid you'd never come back." Brandi's tears soaked the front of Eden's shirt. "Don't ever leave me again."

Eden clutched Brandi, afraid Brandi would evaporate like a dream if she let her go for even a second. As she relaxed into

Brandi's embrace, the solid warmth of her arms, she knew Brandi would be strong enough to hold her. "Don't ever let me."

With Gabriel's apple tree to the left, the warm bonfire in front, and Brandi's love all around her, Eden was home.

About the Author

Jove Belle was born and raised against a backdrop of orchards and potato fields. The youngest of four children, she was raised in a conservative, Christian home and began asking *why* at a very young age, much to the consternation of her mother and grandmother. At the customary age of eighteen, she fled southern Idaho in pursuit of broader minds and fewer traffic jams involving the local livestock. The road didn't end in Portland, Oregon, but there were many confusing freeway interchanges that a girl from the sticks was ill prepared to deal with. As a result, she has lived in the Portland metro area for over fifteen years and still can't figure out how she manages to spend so much time in traffic when there's not a stray sheep or cow in sight.

She lives with her partner of fourteen years. Between them they share three children, two dogs, two cats, two mortgage payments, one sedan, and one requisite dyke pickup truck. One day she hopes to live in a house that doesn't generate a never-ending honey-do list.

Incidentally, she never stopped asking *why*, but did expand her arsenal of questions to include *who*, *what*, *when*, *where*, and, most important of all, *how*. In those questions, a story is born.

Her novels include *Edge of Darkness*, *Split the Aces*, and *Chaps*.

Books Available From Bold Strokes Books

Battle Scars by Meghan O'Brien. Returning Iraq war veteran Ray McKenna struggles with the battle scars that can only be healed by love. (978-1-60282-129-3)

Chaps by Jove Belle. Eden Metcalf wants nothing more than to flee from her troubled past and travel the open road—until she runs into rancher Brandi Cornwell. (978-1-60282-127-9)

Lightbearer by John Caruso. Lucifer dares to question the premise of creation itself and reveals that sin may be all that stands between us and living hell. (978-1-60282-130-9)

The Seeker by Ronica Black. FBI profiler Kennedy Scott battles ghosts from her past, deadly obsession, and the evil that haunts her. (978-1-60282-128-6)

Power Play by Julie Cannon. Businesswomen Tate Monroe and Victoria Sosa are at odds in the boardroom, but not in the bedroom. (978-1-60282-125-5)

The Remarkable Journey of Miss Tranby Quirke by Elizabeth Ridley. When love enters Tranby's life in the form of a beautiful nineteen-year-old student, Lysette McDonald, she embarks on the most remarkable journey of all. (978-1-60282-126-2)

Returning Tides by Radclyffe. Insurance investigator Ashley Walker faces more than a dangerous opponent when she returns to the town, and the woman, she left behind. (978-1-60282-123-1)

Veritas by Anne Laughlin. When the hallowed halls of academia become the stage for murder, newly appointed Dean Beth Ellis's search for the truth leads her to unexpected discoveries about her own heart. (978-1-60282-124-8)

The Pleasure Planner by Larkin Rose. Pleasure purveyor Bree Hendricks treats love like a commodity until Logan Delaney makes Bree the client in her own game. (978-1-60282-121-7)

everafter by Nell Stark and Trinity Tam. Valentine Darrow is bitten by a vampire on her way to propose to her lover Alexa Newland, and their lives and love are placed in mortal jeopardy. (978-1-60282-119-4)

Summer Winds by Andrews & Austin. When Maggie Turner hires a ranch hand to help work her thousand acres, she never expects to be attracted to the very young, very female Cash Tate. (978-1-60282-120-0)

Beggar of Love by Lee Lynch. Jefferson is the lover every woman wants to be—or to have. A revealing saga of lesbian sexuality. (978-1-60282-122-4)

The Seduction of Moxie by Colette Moody. When 1930s Broadway actress Violet London meets speakeasy singer Moxie Valette, she is instantly attracted and her Hollywood trip takes an unexpected turn. (978-1-60282-114-9)

Goldenseal by Gill McKnight. When Amy Fortune returns to her childhood home, she discovers something sinister in the air— but is former lover Leone Garoul stalking her or protecting her? (978-1-60282-115-6)

Romantic Interludes 2: Secrets edited by Radclyffe and Stacia Seaman. An anthology of sensual lesbian love stories: passion, surprises, and secret desires. (978-1-60282-116-3)

Femme Noir by Clara Nipper. Nora Delaney meets her match in Max Abbott, a sex-crazed dame who may or may not have the information Nora needs to solve a murder—but can she contain her lust for Max long enough to find out? (978-1-60282-117-0)

The Reluctant Daughter by Lesléa Newman. Heartwarming, heartbreaking, and ultimately triumphant—the story every daughter recognizes of the lifelong struggle for our mothers to really see us. (978-1-60282-118-7)

Erosistible by Gill McKnight. When Win Martin arrives at a luxurious Greek hotel for a much-anticipated week of sun and sex with her new girlfriend, she is stunned to find her ex-girlfriend, Benny, is the proprietor. Aeros Ebook. (978-1-60282-134-7)

Looking Glass Lives by Felice Picano. Cousins Roger and Alistair become lifelong friends and discover their sexuality amidst the backdrop of twentieth-century gay culture. (978-1-60282-089-0)

Breaking the Ice by Kim Baldwin. Nothing is easy about life above the Arctic Circle—except, perhaps, falling in love. At least that's what pilot Bryson Faulkner hopes when she meets Karla Edwards. (978-1-60282-087-6)

It Should Be a Crime by Carsen Taite. Two women fulfill their mutual desire with a night of passion, neither expecting more until law professor Morgan Bradley and student Parker Casey meet again…in the classroom. (978-1-60282-086-9)

Rough Trade edited by Todd Gregory. Top male erotica writers pen their own hot, sexy versions of the term "rough trade," producing some of the hottest, nastiest, and most dangerous fiction ever published. (978-1-60282-092-0)

The High Priest and the Idol by Jane Fletcher. Jemeryl and Tevi's relationship is put to the test when the Guardian sends Jemeryl on a mission that puts her not only in harm's way, but back into the sights of a previous lover. (978-1-60282-085-2)

Point of Ignition by Erin Dutton. Amid a blaze that threatens to consume them both, firefighter Kate Chambers and property owner Alexi Clark redefine love and trust. (978-1-60282-084-5)

Secrets in the Stone by Radclyffe. Reclusive sculptor Rooke Tyler suddenly finds herself the object of two very different women's affections, and choosing between them will change her life forever. (978-1-60282-083-8)

Dark Garden by Jennifer Fulton. Vienna Blake and Mason Cavender are sworn enemies—who can't resist each other. Something has to give. (978-1-60282-036-4)

Late in the Season by Felice Picano. Set on Fire Island, this is the story of an unlikely pair of friends—a gay composer in his late thirties and an eighteen-year-old schoolgirl. (978-1-60282-082-1)

Punishment with Kisses by Diane Anderson-Minshall. Will Megan find the answers she seeks about her sister Ashley's murder or will her growing relationship with one of Ash's exes blind her to the real truth? (978-1-60282-081-4)

September Canvas by Gun Brooke. When Deanna Moore meets TV personality Faythe she is reluctantly attracted to her, but will Faythe side with the people spreading rumors about Deanna? (978-1-60282-080-7)

No Leavin' Love by Larkin Rose. Beautiful, successful Mercedes Miller thinks she can resume her affair with ranch foreman Sydney Campbell, but the rules have changed. (978-1-60282-079-1)

Between the Lines by Bobbi Marolt. When romance writer Gail Prescott meets actress Tannen Albright, she develops feelings that she usually only experiences through her characters. (978-1-60282-078-4)

Blue Skies by Ali Vali. Commander Berkley Levine leads an elite group of pilots on missions ordered by her ex-lover Captain Aidan Sullivan and everything is on the line—including love. (978-1-60282-077-7)

The Lure by Felice Picano. When Noel Cummings is recruited by the police to go undercover to find a killer, his life will never be the same. (978-1-60282-076-0)

Death of a Dying Man by J.M. Redmann. Mickey Knight, Private Eye and partner of Dr. Cordelia James, doesn't need a drop-dead gorgeous assistant—not until nature steps in. (978-1-60282-075-3)

Justice for All by Radclyffe. Dell Mitchell goes undercover to expose a human traffic ring and ends up in the middle of an even deadlier conspiracy. (978-1-60282-074-6)

Sanctuary by I. Beacham. Cate Canton faces one major obstacle to her goal of crushing her business rival, Dita Newton—her uncontrollable attraction to Dita. (978-1-60282-055-5)

The Sublime and Spirited Voyage of Original Sin by Colette Moody. Pirate Gayle Malvern finds the presence of an abducted seamstress, Celia Pierce, a welcome distraction until the captive comes to mean more to her than is wise. (978-1-60282-054-8)